PRAISE FOR *BLA[...]*

"Dark, gritty, tense, atmospheric. I loved *Black River*."

—Candice Fox, #1 *New York Times* bestselling author

"Sharply plotted and relentlessly paced, it kept me guessing until the last page."

—Michael Robotham, *New York Times* bestselling author of *When You Are Mine*

"A meticulous thriller with a cast of stand-out characters and an intriguing setting. I could not stop reading it."

—Sarah Bailey, author of *The Dark Lake*

"Propulsive and intricate. A crime thriller that is absolutely not to be missed."

—Hayley Scrivenor, author of *Dirt Town*

"*Black River* hooked me and wouldn't let me go. You're going to want to read this one with all the lights on."

—Tim Ayliffe, author of *The Enemy Within*

BLACK RIVER

BLACK RIVER

MATTHEW SPENCER

THOMAS & MERCER

Published by Thomas & Mercer, Seattle

www.apub.com

Amazon, the Amazon logo, and Thomas & Mercer are trademarks of Amazon.com, Inc., or its affiliates.

ISBN-13: 9781662510069 (paperback)
ISBN-13: 9781662510076 (digital)

Cover design by Jarrod Taylor

Cover images: © olaser / Getty Images; © aiyoshi597 / Shutterstock

Printed in the United States of America

For Ritu

So I tom-peeped across the hedges of years,

into wan little windows.

—*Vladimir Nabokov,* Lolita

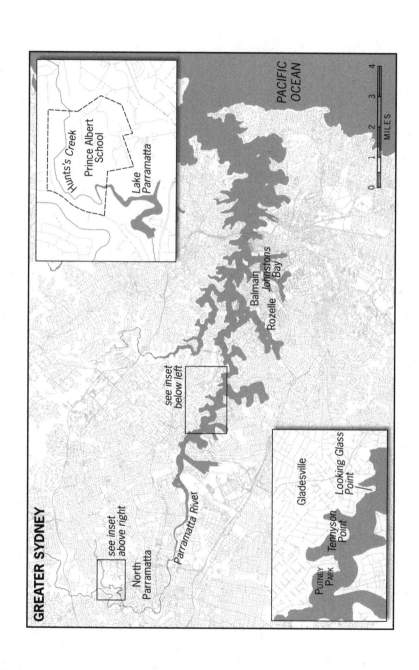

PROLOGUE

She drove into the school at the first gate and crossed the ridge above the oval. The stillness of the campus caught her again, a coiled presence in the lonely spaces. After parking out front, she got her house key ready before reaching for the bag from the trunk. She went down the path under the bunya tree and let herself in through the side door.

No Tatters to greet her, just the squeak of her sneakers on the worn polished jarrah wood. She missed him the most, his absence an ache like a phantom limb. With the dog gone, she knew staying at home on her own was a bad move, typically stubborn and stupid.

She placed the shopping on the bench and stood listening. Had she locked the door? She retraced her steps along the hall. Yes.

Back in the kitchen, she ran water into the kettle, put a tea bag in a mug, and leaned over the benchtop, arms folded. *Tired around the edges.* It was a phrase her mother used, and now she knew what it meant. Something had woken her at three, and she'd lain there for hours. She loved the grand house, but not now—not empty. The place needed to be filled with life or it creaked up on you and whispered its secrets.

Talk of Gladesville was everywhere: on her feeds, at work, at the shops, on the radio in the car.

She stared at the groceries on the bench and knew she shouldn't have bothered: she couldn't do another night alone. All her friends had scattered after finishing year twelve, so there was nothing else for it—she'd stay at Auntie Mel's. Her aunt was happy to have her.

The kettle clicked. She made the tea and headed for her room, glancing again at the side entry. Along the hall, her bedroom door was ajar. She stopped to stare at it. She thought she'd closed it . . . but going over it in her mind, she wasn't certain. She kneed it open, put the mug on the chest of drawers, and ran her hands through her hair to tie it back. As she reached for the wardrobe handle, she caught a flash of orange. Half stuffed under her pillow was her orange bra.

Dread burst. Fear had been behind her for days, but now it rose through her and held her. The bedspread was pushed too far one way—it wasn't how she'd left it. She sucked strangled air as the wardrobe door swung open.

He was standing inside, his face a foot from hers. For a steep moment they looked at each other and then she screamed. He moved lizard quick, whipping out and reaching down to her desk. His hand found her glass paperweight with the blues and greens swirled through it and she gulped for breath and smelled his sweat and tried to duck as his fist came up and smashed the glass dome into the side of her head.

1

Adam Bowman walked out of the newsroom to catch some air. Cabin fever on the late shift. It was after eight, the heat of the day still in the pavement and red dust blowing in like a veil on the fading summer light. He stood, the backs of his hands on his hips, reading the breeze. A bit of north in the westerly . . . It was worse out here than in the sick building.

Surry Hills, the end of December. The streets were dead, all the smug bars and cafés and restaurants shut for the holidays. Bowman didn't mind that he was out of step, that he worked nights and weekends. But when it got like this, when everyone cleared out and melancholy sloped in, he saw that life did exist—and that it was going on elsewhere without him.

He'd filed his story, a wrap of the bushfires, but he was on four to midnight, and it was too early to make himself scarce. He watched a couple of gray subeditors exit the building and torpedo downhill for the Aurora. The slot-machine pub sat across from Central, at Kippax and Elizabeth, a neon billabong of human flotsam. The Aurora never shut—not for the festive season, not even for the night.

His mobile rang. The news desk. *Fuck.* "Yeah."

"Have you heard? Brandy's going feral." Justine, hyperventilating. She was fresh out of university, armed with a doctorate and manning the phones. She was too smart to last long.

What Bowman heard was his night derailing. "Heard what?"

"BMK. Out west—at your old school?"

Bowman couldn't speak.

"He said to get your stuff and go. Plus take a camera. He'll call you in the car."

She hung up, and he stared at his mobile. He swiped for *The National* and saw they had the story breaking, two paragraphs from the wires under a banner headline: GIRL IN PLASTIC BMK'S THIRD VICTIM. He read it and then read the second paragraph again. "The body was found on the campus of Prince Albert, an independent boys' school at North Parramatta in Sydney's west."

The police reporter Benny Diamond came through the revolving door with a photographer in tow. Diamond had never acknowledged Bowman, and he wasn't about to start now. The photographer rolled her eyes as she passed and Bowman watched them cross the street and load into a company Prius with a driver. BMK was Diamond's story. They were going to the school.

Bowman went into the foyer and up the stairs. The news floor was denuded, ten years of redundancies and now silly-season empty. Through the glass wall of the editor's office, Brandy Alexander could be seen on his feet on a call. Bowman hesitated and then went and stood in the editor's doorway.

Alexander hung up and waved him in. "Beat-Up Benny's en route. He'll do the splash."

Bowman glanced out the window. "And what—you want me to go too?"

"Yeah." Alexander rippled with impatience. "Rumor has it you went to this school?"

Bowman didn't flash his private-school credentials—they were worthless in a newsroom. But word got around. "Long time ago."

Alexander scowled. "But you know the place—like, you could get in?"

"I lived there in the eighties," Bowman said. "My father was a history teacher."

"Right." The editor paused. "Well, fuck—that's gotta come in handy."

"But what about Diamond? He won't like me surfing in."

"Forget Diamond. He doesn't know you're going—and he'll be with the cops. The point is, if you sneak around, you might get something." Alexander shooed him. "Move. I'll call you in a sec."

Bowman went out. He took a camera from the picture desk, grabbed his bag, and headed downstairs and over the road to his Nissan in the car park. The driver in the Prius would take Diamond through Chinatown. Bowman went left on Elizabeth, down Cleveland onto Wattle. He could smell the fish market as he flogged the Nissan up the ramp onto the Anzac Bridge. The radio had ditched the evening quiz, and the announcer was cycling through the story, building as she went, a murder ballad on repeat.

Prince Albert—the name kept darting out at him, and he turned the volume down to think. BMK at Prince Albert? His head shook, he couldn't compute. There were things he could comprehend: he was forty-five, he was still kicking around on general news, Brandy didn't rate him.

It was not just any school. Bowman knew that as well as anybody. It was four hundred acres fenced off in the suburbs—patrician, blazered, and slap-bang in the center of the western sprawl.

The site had been a colonial estate, hacked from the great gums of the plain. The Church of England had come later, turning the land into a boarding school for the sons of the sunburned pastoralists: generations of indoctrination and conformity and bastardry had seeped into that earth. You conformed or it broke you—your spirit, your psyche, even your very bones. The school was a throwback: vast, gated, studded with sandstone buildings and hemmed by native bush. Bowman hadn't set foot in the place in three decades, but he knew every gully and trail.

He loosened his grip on the wheel, scratching a red flare of eczema up the inside of his left arm. Fraudulence was stressful—he wasn't cut out for this, for chasing the big stories. His mind linked to the school and other humiliations . . . Saturday sport, gangly under a high ball. He hadn't been cut out for that either.

Ahead he saw the Prius, and his loathing for Diamond evaporated. It took the pressure off, having the police reporter on the story—Bowman would play second fiddle while Diamond wrote the main piece and carried the can when they got beaten by their rivals.

The phone rang on the Bluetooth.

"It's just coming through on the wires," Alexander said. "The body was found at some place called the Hay Stand, up the back of the school."

Bowman pictured it, on its own above the playing fields. "Jesus."

"What is it?" Alexander said.

"Literally an old feed store for horses. It's ornamental now. Big sandstone columns, no walls. Like a rotunda, except square."

"Can you get near it? They've clamped the place down real tight. Media's corralled on an oval. No drones."

"There's lots of ways in."

"Good."

Bowman saw flashing lights in his mirrors. Unmarked police car at full tilt. It belted round him and hit the siren through a red light up the hill to Drummoyne. Heading west. Everything was heading west.

"The TVs have pooled, trying to get a chopper up," Alexander was saying. "The duty pilot's taken a dive—salmonella. If you get through, we should have it on our own."

"What have the cops said?"

"Not much . . . just he's used the black plastic again."

Bowman glanced in his blind spot, changed lanes. The moon was up, full, red-gold in the darkening sky.

"Listen," Alexander said, "Diamond and the snapper'll go in the front gate with the rest of the pack. You're on your own. We need pictures. We're pushing deadline back—you've got two hours."

The editor hung up as the Nissan climbed the bridge at Gladesville. Bowman craned his neck left as he crested the arch, but the height of the curb blocked the view of the riverfront real estate. BMK had killed twice here near the bridge, two nights a month apart. November first and then November thirtieth, under a big blue moon. A tabloid sub on *The Mirror* had cherry-picked the lunacy and christened him the Blue Moon Killer. BMK. Crisp—good for headlines.

Bowman was past Gladesville and into Ryde, still fifteen clicks from the school. Rows of redbrick houses stunted by traffic grime. He replayed the conversation with Alexander. The editor was aware Bowman had history at the school. How much did he know? There were things on the public record if he looked. Ferret-eyed Brandy was good at looking. Still, he was backing Bowman, trusting him to get through the police cordon and come back with a story. That made a change.

At Carlingford, he cut across to Kissing Point, turned right on Bettington Road and drove up past gauche commuter castles and the golf course at Oatlands. His heart beat fast. It was a long time since he'd been on these streets.

The two main gates to Prince Albert on Pennant Hills Road, two hundred meters apart, were both blocked by patrol cars with lights flashing. A television truck sat at the second entrance. Bowman didn't slow. Rounding a bend, he passed the stone gatehouse to the original estate and braked left onto a suburban street. He parked, grabbed his bag, and got out. He stood listening for a moment and then jogged across the road.

The old boom gate, hidden by foliage, sat over a dirt track leading into the property. He ducked under it and began to walk. He knew where he was going. It wasn't far.

2

Riley stood apart from the scene.

An hour ago, before the triple-zero call, she'd been dog-tired, ground down by the investigation and ready to call it a night. Now she was switched on, wired, good to go.

Wrapped in black plastic. With that, the general duties who'd responded had known enough to bypass the detectives at Parramatta and call it straight into the strike force at Gladesville. Riley had driven while O'Neil had worked the phone, locking the school down and sealing the site.

"Touch fucking nothing," O'Neil had said, and the uniforms had done well.

The victim lay on the raised hardwood floor of an old stone structure eight meters square and open to the elements like a bandstand. It had twelve columns, a pitched slate roof, a four-faced clock on top. Crime Scene had lit the body and got a tent around it.

It had gone eight, still some light in the sky. A hot wind over yellow grass. Riley hadn't eaten—now she was glad. This one felt different. Gladesville had been two houses, both waterfront, both girls wrapped and dumped in the river, nails through their right feet to hold them to mooring piles. Riley took a moment, did her breathing, and snapped on the gloves. Something in the process took her back to the river on the low tide.

She walked to the platform in her paper boots. O'Neil, on his phone, watched her go. A constable with the BMK strike force, code-named Satyr, logged her in, and she took the five stairs up to the rough timber floor, crossed to the lit blue tent, and squatted on her haunches inside to consider the black shroud. Builders' film. No prints in the light coating of red dust. She peered through a cut forensics had made in the plastic to reveal the head. The girl was young, maybe eighteen, lying on her back. Eyes open, glassy and blue green. A short laceration a couple of centimeters above and slightly forward of the left ear, blood dried around the wound. Blonde hair, shoulder length, loose, matted dark below the trauma. A red-purple coloration to the face, postmortem lividity. That was different. There'd been no hypostasis in Gladesville. He'd carved them up and bled them out. This girl had been killed and left on her front, then moved onto her back after several hours.

Riley's eyes went to the forehead. No calling card etched into the skin. No sign of tape on the face, no imprint of a gag—none of the savagery of Gladesville. Riley felt relief, yes, but there was something else, and she worried at it until she had it. Disappointment.

Satyr investigators had set up a command center fifty meters from the site. Riley came out of the tent and watched as the forensic psychiatrist, Wayne Farquhar, climbed from his Volvo and into a white Tyvek bunny suit. Homicide worked with forensic psychologists, but after the second attack at Gladesville, O'Neil had requested Farquhar. "Fuck the psychologists," O'Neil had said to the super. "I want a real doctor."

When they'd gotten to the scene, Riley and O'Neil had separated on instinct. O'Neil had gone straight to the victim while Riley had worked the edges, gleaning what she could from the teenager and adult male who had found the body and called it in.

Now, as Riley walked down the steps, O'Neil came up to her, lithe like a big cat.

"You reckon he did her here?" he said.

Riley bit her lip. "Bit out in the open."

"So he did her off-site, brought her in," O'Neil said. "Or there's a secondary crime scene at the school."

"We're looking. Place is big, lots of buildings."

"Lots of bush. I went to a bush school—wasn't like this."

"Yeah, not exactly Dubbo High." Riley flicked at her notebook. "Church moved the school here in the sixties. Wealthy city kids and country boarders, all boys."

"Fucking squattocracy." O'Neil's lips thinned.

Dusk gathered on the playing fields. Riley knew who the parents would be at a place like this. Bowral blowhards, bankers and born-to-rule barristers, airline executives who pocketed $20 million a year but couldn't fly a kite.

She'd have to keep her prejudice in check—prejudice didn't solve anything. But the wealth of the school was interesting. Money was the one theme in Gladesville. After a month of grunt work, the analysts were pretty much back where they had started. All they had to link the two victims was that they were both young white adult females, living at home with their parents, on different sides of the same street, on a peninsula that jutted into the river at Looking Glass Point. Neither family had been in the area long—the properties had been purchased from different real estate agencies in the past year. There was nothing else in the victimology: The girls didn't know each other and had no friends in common. There was an age difference of a couple of years. Different schools, different universities, different hairdressers, different gyms. Satyr detectives had dug everywhere and turned up nothing—no thread tying them together, no netball club, no dating app, no links between their acquaintances or families. Nothing in the electronic trails: credit cards, phones, red-light cameras, number plates, CCTVs. Nothing. Only the houses: both big, both waterfront. Rich people's houses.

Passion, grog, or money—the murder trinity. Any homicide veteran would tell you that this was where you looked for cause or motive, and this was where you always found them. Riley had added drugs to her list, a subclause between grog and money. She looked around. Talk about real estate—the school stank of money. Old money, new money, dirty money—big money. Money didn't drive Riley, but she understood the urge for it in others.

O'Neil was quiet beside her. She'd made detective sergeant under him, and they were easy in each other's silences. She rolled her neck to sneak a glance at his bald head. He had symmetrical scarring on both cheeks, which gave him a hint of spice, of danger—O'Neil would lop your head off with a scimitar if he had to. He was on full alert, everything heightened—he had another twenty-four hours in him, no question. He stood completely still, save for a throb in his neck above his white collar. The chase pumped in his veins. Another dead girl, wrapped and dumped on their watch. There was only one way to take it. You took it personally, you took it home.

"What do you think?" Riley said. "Changed his MO?"

"Still got the plastic." O'Neil paused and then jerked his head. "And a creek over there?"

"Tributary of the river."

"He's at the start of the river, but he doesn't use it?"

Riley looked toward the command center. A man in blue work clothes was sitting on a canvas chair outside the police gazebo, talking into his phone. "Kid found the body, and old mate over there called it in." She went back to her notebook. "Name's Craig Spratt. Calls himself the property manager. He's shaking the trees, getting us access to all the buildings, staff and student lists, data."

"How many staff?"

"About two hundred, when it's up and running. But it's mothballed for the holidays. Spratt says there's no one around, save a few stragglers."

"And who would they be?"

"Him and his wife, the headmaster, the family of the boy who found the body. A gardener. That's it, he reckons."

"They all live on-site?"

11

"Yeah, there's about thirty houses round the place. Most are empty, people away for the summer."

"CCTV?"

"All over the joint. Fifty-three cameras."

O'Neil looked up. "Where's the closest?"

"Couple of hundred meters either side."

"Make sure we get everything. From the company, not just what old mate wants us to see." O'Neil rubbed his scalp. "Let's have a chat to Wayne."

Riley handed him fresh gloves and booties. He pulled them on, and she followed suit and trailed him back up the steps. He moved like a boxer, light on his feet, a bit of swagger, a bit of bounce. He was battle hardened, with a density to him, but he carried it with ease.

The constable logged them back in. A forensic pathologist and six forensic investigators were working in and around the structure. Sketches, photos, video. Wayne Farquhar was hunched over the dead girl. The black plastic had been sliced open further, revealing her torso and limbs. She was dressed in only her underwear. Her bra, still fastened, had been hoicked up over her breasts, her undies pushed down halfway to her knees. Apart from the wound on her temple, her body was unmarked. No ligature marks at the wrists, and her feet were smooth and white.

Farquhar—stocky, sixty, gray bearded—straightened and moved to the door of the tent. "You can smell the spinifex in that breeze," he said.

"Jesus wept," O'Neil said. "It's Henry Lawson."

"There's the full moon again," Farquhar said.

"Are you for real?"

"I told you." Farquhar looked over his glasses. "Sadist on a lunar cycle."

"You're not here to parrot the media."

"I said it before they did."

O'Neil stared down at the dead girl. "You think this is our boy?"

"That's where my theory falls over."

"Go on."

"Gladesville—pure psychopathy with paraphilic disorders, really quite something. This . . ." The psychiatrist looked down.

Riley knew: it didn't compare.

"Nothing inflicted on her after death," Farquhar said. "We'll have to wait for the autopsy, but it's obvious. The pathologist says clocked on the temple with something solid and smooth. Extradural or subdural hemorrhage. Guessing extradural. Tore the middle meningeal artery. Lucid for a time, then good night Josephine."

"Could he be toying with us?" Riley said.

Farquhar went for his beard with a gloved hand and thought better of it. "No knife wounds. Plus look at the wrists, the mouth. She hasn't been bound, she hasn't been gagged. Those are big changes. Gladesville likes his cable ties." The psychiatrist met her eye. "And he likes his privacy."

"What about the plastic?" O'Neil said.

"The black plastic, the river—that's all you've released about Gladesville? That and the rapes?"

O'Neil blinked acknowledgment.

"I think he was aiming to put her in the creek," Farquhar said, "trying to mimic Gladesville and the river, but something spooked him. Whoever did this wants us to think it's Gladesville. He's had a fumble with the underwear, he's wrapped her in black plastic."

O'Neil sniffed. Riley waited.

"She's surprised someone, or annoyed them," the psychiatrist said. "They've lashed out and killed her. There are no defensive wounds. No staging, no calling card. Likely domestic, or at least someone who knows her."

O'Neil folded his arms, and Riley read the gesture: it was only a copycat in retrospect. The offender was seeking cover after he killed. The plastic was the only piece of physical evidence linking the scene to

Gladesville. There was the fact that this victim was another young white female, but after that, Farquhar was right: logically, it didn't connect with Gladesville. But there was no logic to Gladesville—and O'Neil had taught her not to impose logic on sick fucks. Start with it, but know it could be a trap—you had to be able to put it aside and think past it. Gladesville had killed twice, so his patterns were not yet dependable. It was easy to misinterpret a crime scene.

She left the tent. One detail had jumped out at the Gladesville sites: the offender had enjoyed it. He had taken a lot of time with the victims. He'd felt comfortable seeking his pleasure. It was possible the same thing had been happening here until circumstances changed. She looked back in at O'Neil.

"Maybe he was disturbed," she said.

3

The dirt road at the back of the school ran up to a homestead, gaunt and gabled at the top of the rise. Moss on the shingled roof drank in moonshine. The place wasn't as old as the sandstone buildings on the campus, but it was still long in the tooth for White Australia. A spectral, angular pile, a house with a name. Ghost Gum—the traditional residence of the school chaplain.

It'd been thirty years since he'd seen it. Bowman halted. As a child he'd had a friend who lived in there. Memory prickled, he felt it on his skin—innocence, come back to visit.

There was a turning circle in front of the house and a Mazda with red P plates parked on the gravel. A light on the porch illuminated the wide veranda, but the rest of the building was in darkness. He gave it a wide berth, crossed a lawn to the side, walked down a short slope, and emerged at a football field. At the other end, the land dropped to a second pitch, and at the end of that, on its hillock and lit like a monument, stood the Hay Stand. Police, vehicles everywhere, tents, floodlights. He snapped a quick picture on his phone and sent it to Alexander. I will get closer, he texted. No one else will have this.

He was out in the open in the moonlight and felt suddenly vulnerable, as if a long lens were trained back on him. Lugging the camera, he scuttled in a crouch along the southern end of the playing field and up its eastern flank, past the colonial stables and down the incline to the second field. A large, corroded green tin hut stood to his right. He skirted behind it and jogged along its length, stopping at the top corner. He was forty meters from the scene, the faces of forensic investigators clearly visible. Close enough. He took another pic with his phone, texted it through, and called the news desk.

"Got it." Alexander picked up before the first ring. "Sexy. Eight columns, page one. Use the camera."

"I can bash out thirty centimeters. What it looks like, where it is."

A pause. Alexander was talking to the night editor about time and space. He came back. "Forty centimeters, forty minutes."

"Done."

Bowman took the work Canon from its bag and fussed, fat-fingered, with the apparatus. There was nothing the picture desk hated more than reporters taking photographs. But point and shoot—what was all the fuss about? Bowman pointed and shot and peered at the frames on the LCD display. And there it was: photojournalism. He downloaded the images to his laptop and sent them. Then he sat with his back to the rusted tin of the hut and began to write.

He typed fast, two fingers pecking it out. It came easily. He didn't need to cover the news of the night, the context with Gladesville—Diamond would do all that in the main story. Alexander had sent Bowman looking for a point of difference, something fresh, and it had paid off. He finished typing, read it over, pressed "Send," and called Alexander again. There was silence as the editor skimmed the copy.

"You little fucking beauty," Alexander said and hung up.

Bowman stood. He could see the bald detective, Steve O'Neil. Books had been written about the top dog at Homicide, the alpha male. O'Neil had a reputation for blowing his stack—and for blowing cases open.

The Hay Stand and stables sat deep inside the grounds, a good two kilometers from the classroom blocks and administration offices at the front of the school. The creek, winding through the bush to Bowman's left, had been dammed in the 1850s, creating Lake Parramatta for water supply. The lake was still there, as was the long, arched dam wall, built out of rock quarried from the watercourse.

Bowman knew the cops were withholding details on the Gladesville slayings. Everyone knew that. The police had revealed three things that were common to both crimes—the victims had been raped, wrapped in black plastic, and placed in the Parramatta River—and then the shutters had come down. Bowman looked toward the creek. It had history, he knew, because his father had taught him. A First Fleet party had got out here to the headwaters of the river, eating lorikeets and crow soup with white cockatoo. Eating kangaroo. They had used the river, in April 1788, and now BMK was using it too. The river was what linked Gladesville to the school, the river that wound down from the creek.

He put his laptop into his bag and started back the way he had come, past Ghost Gum and out to his car. His brain was smoked by the freak evening, and he struggled to find the ignition. He put the windows down. The westerly had died with no correction from the south, leaving heat and dust and the tang of bushfire. He headed east, crossing the river at Gladesville and then again at Iron Cove. There was no one on Darling Street all the way down the gentrified peninsula, no one on the balcony at the London. He cruised past the bowling club and up into Balmain East.

It had gone midnight when he parked outside the Commercial and walked onto Datchett Street. *Street* was an embellishment, local government hyperbole—it was a lane, cobbled and narrow and steep. A greasy black rat the size of a possum bolted across his path.

Bowman opened the door to his cottage and flicked on the light, put his keys in the bowl and his bag on the couch. He thought about Scotch—medicinal, for his sizzled synapses—but went instead for a bottle of red from the rack. He cracked the screw cap and poured a heavy slug, a third of the bottle. He slammed it down fast, then freshened up the glass and raised it to himself in a mute toast.

Putting the drink down, he trod out of his shoes and went through to the bedroom, where he changed into his sarong and Shakespeare T-shirt. *And thus I clothe my naked villainy.* Retrieving the glass and the bottle, he went down the hall. In the kitchen, he put the wine on the sink drainer, washed his hands, and opened the fridge and the freezer. Bacon, eggs, Sweet Baby Ray's sauce, sliced white bread. He liked brunch for dinner. He pulled out the frypan and went back to the fridge and grabbed a beer. He'd jumped the gun on the red—he needed a cleanser.

He lit the gas, put oil in the pan, and made his meal. As he ate, he opened his laptop and pulled up *The National*. The run they'd given his photo, it was like he'd discovered a civilization out past the Milky Way. Silence settled around him as he stared at the screen. The image took him back to those last days at the school, so long ago. He saw his mother, wet hair plastered to her scalp, cradling Chick. He couldn't see Chick's face. But Bowman had learned all about life in an indifferent universe in that split-second look into his mother's face.

4

Strike Force Satyr officers had delayed taking a statement from the boy who'd found the body until they'd brought in a parent. The boy's mother and father had sat with their son on one side of a trestle table as he'd told his story to two detective constables. Now, the interview over, the family looked up as Riley and O'Neil came into the police gazebo.

Riley, who had spoken with the kid earlier, nodded to his parents and wrote down their names: Scott and Sarah Green. Scott Green was a science teacher, and they lived in a campus house not far from the scene. Sarah Green worked part time in an office in Epping. Tom was heading into year eleven at Prince Albert.

"Tom said you were home this evening?" Riley said.

Scott Green looked at her and then around at O'Neil, who was standing behind the table. Sarah answered. "Yes, watching TV."

"What'd you watch?"

Sarah told her. Riley hated musicals. She made a note and looked at the boy. Tom Green was awkward between his parents, in an Eels cap, shorts, sandals, T-shirt. He had acne around the chin, and his top lip needed a shave. Riley had put him at seventeen and been out by a mile. Fifteen. She had no children, and teenagers did not make her clucky. "You all right, Tom?" she said.

He mumbled and looked at the table. Riley turned to the detective constables. "Finished?"

They nodded. "Sarge," one of them said.

Scott and Sarah Green stood up. The husband was the same height as his wife. Brushed back, his thinning hair reached his collar, and he had a mustache. There was a diffidence to him that could have been shock, or affectation, or medication. His wife spoke again.

"Who is it?" Sarah's face creased with pain. "I mean—a man or a woman?"

"There's a process," Riley said. "We need to think about the next of kin."

"We have a daughter," she said.

Riley's eyes flicked to O'Neil's. "Where is she now?" Riley said.

"Heading home, I hope." Sarah was holding her phone. "From work. She never answers."

Riley kept her face blank. She didn't want a family stampede, but she needed to get an officer over to the Greens' house.

Scott Green took a step from the table and spoke for the first time. "I could look, if you like."

Riley thought he meant at his house, for his daughter, but he tossed his head toward the scene. "If you need to identify the body," he said.

Sarah Green's eyes lowered, and Tom was busy staring at a spot on the side of the gazebo. Scott was smiling at Riley. She let the moment spool, swung all her focus onto Scott Green. Before joining the force, Riley had studied occupational therapy and then speech pathology. She'd finished neither, but in Scott Green she caught the whisper of a treated childhood lisp. Solicitude on his face, a quiver below the surface. Expectation? Riley felt she was looking at a full-grown Boy Scout, for whom this was an adventure.

"It's time you got Tom home," she said. "Detective Constables Hatcher and McCormack will go with you. They'll need to talk to your daughter."

Riley watched the family exit the gazebo with the officers and then turned to O'Neil. He was scrolling on his phone, reading an electronic copy of the kid's statement. She had already heard how things had unfolded from both Tom and Craig Spratt. The boy had been out trying to fly a drone on the playing fields when the wind had picked up. He'd packed it in and was riding his bike home past the Hay Stand when he'd spotted the black shape on the wooden platform. He'd stopped to look just as Spratt was driving past.

"Drone footage?" O'Neil said.

"We've got the memory card. The boy's got a hard drive at the house—we're picking it up now."

"Good. Where's Spratt?"

Craig Spratt was still in a camp chair outside the gazebo. He stood as they approached. "This is Detective Chief Inspector O'Neil," Riley said. "New South Wales Homicide."

Spratt stuck out a hand.

Riley watched as O'Neil shook it. Spratt was fifty, weathered, still some copper in his cropped hair. No fat, at ease, practical. No jail. Maybe not the smartest chook in the coop.

"Not many people around at the moment," O'Neil said.

"Nah, she's dead quiet." Spratt pulled up and puckered at his faux pas.

"We'll need a list of who lives at the school normally, and who's here during the holidays," O'Neil said. "You got kids?"

"Yeah, two."

"Boys or girls?"

"Boys."

They needed a name for their victim, and it wasn't Spratt's child lying wrapped on the hard floor.

"I'm sorry to ask," O'Neil said, "but we're trying to identify the deceased. We were hoping you might be able to help."

It took Spratt a second, and then he nodded.

They gave him booties and went up the stairs in single file. In the blue tent, Spratt looked at the girl's face and sucked in air. He dropped his head and ran a hand down his scalp to the back of his neck. "Margy," he said.

It was hot under the lights. "Margy?" Riley said at last.

Spratt didn't respond. Riley touched him on the arm. "Mr. Spratt?"

He took a rag that smelled of diesel from a pocket and dabbed his eyes. "Sorry." He looked at Riley's hand.

"Can you tell us about Margy?" O'Neil said.

"Marguerite," Spratt said. "I call her Margy."

"And her last name?"

Spratt blinked. "Christ, sorry. Marguerite Dunlop. Her old man's the chaplain. They live in the big place up there." He nodded south.

Riley's eyes met O'Neil's. *Chaplain.* Strike Force Satyr had run hard on the religious aspects of the Gladesville crimes—the carvings on the foreheads, the nails through the feet. Investigations that had led nowhere.

"She was worried—about stayin' by herself," Spratt said.

He wanted to talk, so they listened. Marguerite was seventeen, maybe eighteen, had just finished at St. Anne's, a smaller girls' school adjoining the Prince Albert grounds. Her parents had a place at Noosa, where they went every year. She hadn't gone this year because she'd got a job. Spratt wasn't sure where. But she had been staying at home alone—he was sure about that.

"Any siblings?" O'Neil said.

There was an older brother, Robert. Spratt called him Bob. He was at university in the US—again, Spratt wasn't sure where.

"You said she was worried," O'Neil said. "About being on her own? She told you that?"

"No. Bruce said."

"Bruce?"

Bruce Dunlop was Marguerite's father. The chaplain. He had asked Spratt to install locks on some of the internal doors of the house, to create a secure group of rooms for his daughter while she was home alone.

◆ ◆ ◆

They came up to the house, Ghost Gum, from the rear on a dirt track—Riley at the wheel of the Calais, Spratt in the passenger seat pointing the way, O'Neil in the back with a uniformed constable from Parramatta.

It was close to midnight, eerie and still. The homestead was lonely on its hill, no neighbors in view. A tennis court to one side had a crumbling surface and weeds coming through. There was a windbreak of poplars before a group of outhouses, and lean-tos ran down a slope off the back lawn, then rusty gates and fences and a series of holding pens resembling sheep or cattle yards. The house itself was huge—a thousand square meters, Riley guessed, with a steep roof, four chimneys, two stories, and an attic. Tall trees stood sentinel, scattered and forlorn. There was a sense of sorrow, like the end of the road.

Spratt had a key to the back door.

"You got a key to all the houses, Mr. Spratt?" Riley said.

"Pretty much, yeah."

O'Neil and Riley pulled on fresh gloves and booties and took torches from the boot of the Calais. Spratt handed Riley the key and moved off to stand on the lawn with the constable.

They entered into a modern kitchen, tidy in the torch beams, and touched nothing, not even a light switch. Gladesville had been hyper-careful, cleaning up and leaving nothing of himself behind, just the smell of ammonia and the victim's blood on the floor. They couldn't afford the smallest error, transferring or mixing DNA. A second forensic team was on the way.

There was a jute bag on the bench, holding groceries—fruit, nuts, milk, yogurt, cereal, chocolate—and a receipt. Riley used a pen to unfurl the docket: Coles, North Rocks, 8:47 a.m., Wednesday, 28 December.

"Yesterday," she said.

The house was divided as Spratt had described. A cluster of five interconnecting rooms—kitchen, lounge, bath, hall, bedroom—had

23

been secured. It was simple but effective—any internal door from this suite that led elsewhere in the house was padlocked, cutting off the rest of the ground floor and access to the second story and the attic.

Riley and O'Neil went down the hallway to the bedroom, stood at the threshold, and played their lights around. They backed up. The side door was locked. There was no sign of forced entry, or of any struggle. Nothing was broken.

Spratt was still on the lawn. O'Neil clicked off his torch in the moonglow. "Has this place been on the market in, say, the last twelve months?"

"No way," Spratt said. "Never. School owns it."

Other vehicles were pulling up—forensics, Shoe and Tire, fingerprint techs. Officers were starting to tape off the house to establish a second crime scene.

Riley moved away to the back of the yard. If you didn't have a suspect, then all you had were the victims. First Lena Chatfield, then Jill Sheridan. And now Marguerite Dunlop. Lena had been twenty-three—two years older than Jill Sheridan. Marguerite was younger again. The killer had hit the Chatfield place, then gone round the bend in the river and hit the Sheridan house. In both cases, the parents had been away from home. That fit with what had happened here.

But the Gladesville houses had been nothing like this. Both were nondescript from the street—fenced-off, windowless facades that gave nothing away. Then, out back, they opened up, three-leveled glass cathedrals in worship to the gods of the river. Neither had blinds or curtains on the bottom two floors. They were completely open to the water views—and completely exposed. Farquhar was adamant that the killer was obsessed with reconnaissance and surveillance, that it was part of his pleasure, and Riley agreed. Gladesville was a prowler and a peeper. He watched for a long time, until he had the household pattern of life, and only then did he strike—an ambush predator coming out of the river.

Riley stared down the slope, away from the property. You couldn't see the creek from the house. Lake Parramatta was hidden too, a kilometer off as the crow flew. She turned and ran her eye over the hunkered rear of the homestead, a built-on extension that was all angles and shadows. The place seemed to drool into the earth. There was nothing open and inviting about it, no large windows or clear lines of sight. It wasn't a peeper's paradise.

Farquhar's black Volvo pulled up, the druid in his hybrid SUV. Riley was conditioned to work from a practical standpoint, common sense and training harnessed to experience and instinct. O'Neil had brought Farquhar in to extrapolate. The forensic psychiatrist looked at the scenes and stroked his beard and postulated his theories. Riley was happy to listen. But she didn't need Farquhar to tell her that Gladesville hadn't happened in a vacuum. Gladesville was an escalation. But from what? O'Neil thought rape and Riley agreed—they had the strike force looking for unsolved violent sexual assaults. Farquhar wasn't so sure. Gladesville was raping *after* he killed. It was controlled: no torn condoms and semen leaking out, no skin under the victims' fingernails from scratching. For Farquhar, the rape was an addition—it wasn't the motivation. The psychiatrist had Satyr looking for strange break-ins, peculiar ransacking, fetish burglaries where nothing of real value was taken. Being alone in other people's houses, looking, going through their underwear—that was where the killer had started to build his fantasy and find his stimulation.

The Volvo's headlights went out. Riley knew Farquhar would argue Marguerite Dunlop's killer wasn't their boy.

O'Neil came from the house through the back door and waved her over. She crossed the lawn.

"Point of entry," he said.

She walked with him to a tiny room off the kitchen, a butler's pantry, now home to boxes.

O'Neil pointed with a gloved finger to a small window, high on the wall. It had a lock on the inside, and the latch was open. "There's enough room to wriggle through," he said. "Every other window is latched shut."

There was a bench running the length of the pantry. Riley trod carefully to peer out the window. Everything locked down tight but one latch open? She didn't buy it—it didn't look right.

The points of entry at Gladesville had been identical: glass sliding doors between the open-plan kitchens and the gardens down to the river. The doors had been unlocked, and the killer had strolled right in. He knew how the families lived their lives and how they used their houses. Indoor-outdoor living was a thing. Wealthy people on the water, sashaying between the lawn and the patio and the kitchen, doors pushed back, bringing the outside in. They'd brought the outside in, all right. The question was, had the killer gathered his knowledge of the layouts from sitting and watching, or had he been inside the houses before he'd hit? Both the Sheridan and Chatfield properties had been on the market last year, sold to the families who had now lost their daughters. Coincidences did happen—they happened all the time—but Riley was wary of them. Strike force detectives had upended the real estate agencies that made the sales and almost arrested one broker, a suave prick in a duck-egg-blue Bentley and a $4,000 suit, but in the end they'd pulled back. The bloke was a cokehead from the Eastern Suburbs who trawled Tinder and bars and got a bit rough with women. That made him a real estate agent, but it didn't make him what Satyr was looking for.

The selling agents kept lists of everyone who had been through the properties on inspection—hundreds of names—and Satyr had looked at them all. There was plenty of overlap, with the houses being so close, and a couple of men had been elevated to persons of interest, but in the end—nothing: every last name rubbed out. Still, O'Neil couldn't shake the idea that the killer had spent time in the houses before the murders.

Maybe he'd slipped through at an inspection without leaving his name at the door. Maybe he could operate like that, out in the open, without anyone taking notice. Maybe.

They kept Satyr looking closer to home: movers, painters, locksmiths, plumbers, electricians. Telstra, NBN, meter readers, tree loppers, couriers, taxis, Ubers, appliance repairs, every dickhead on a scooter with a bowl of noodles. And then the canvass of the suburb itself: the street, the joggers, the dog walkers, the cafés. They'd gone to the phone towers—they knew every number that had been in the area on the nights.

O'Neil's mobile rang, and Riley watched as he listened and hung up. "The headmaster just turned up," he said. "He's over at the first scene."

"Where's he been?"

"Roseville, having dinner. They're taking a statement."

"He'll see we're here at the house," she said. "We don't want her name getting out."

"They won't confirm anything, and they'll tell him to keep his mouth shut."

Dawn was hours off. Marguerite Dunlop's parents had been woken in Noosa and would be on a plane from the Sunshine Coast at first light.

Riley looked again at the open window latch. Point of entry. It was easy to misinterpret a crime scene. Craig Spratt had spent time in the house. Craig Spratt had a fucking key.

5

Bowman woke at eight. Before sleep, he'd squeezed half a lemon into a tankard of water and left it by his bed. He sat up now and drank it down. He was not a morning person, but he felt pretty good, still a spring in his step from a job well done last night. There it was, a universal truth before breakfast: the deepest principle in human nature is the craving to be appreciated.

He sauntered to the bathroom in his sarong and T-shirt, then stepped into the lane to pick up his paper. In the kitchen, he made coffee and spread *The National* on the bench. It was the only broadsheet left in the country, and when they chose to unleash, they went big. They'd gone big today.

Bowman knew that in all the other outlets, the story would be generic, controlled by the cops. No name had been released—there'd be no images of the scene, no footage on the networks. So Bowman's picture was the only thing. They'd run it deep and wide across the whole front page, under the headline BMK STRIKES AT BOYS' SCHOOL. Broadsheets might be old media, but under full sail, when the wind was up, they looked magnificent.

Alexander called. Bowman was off the late shift: the editor wanted him back at the school right away. "Look for staff to interview, look for anything, just don't get shunted by the cops," Alexander said and hung up. Bowman turned on the radio and headed for the shower. Ablutions done, he stood back in the kitchen, listening to the news and checking the websites . . . Still no name from the cops.

In the Nissan, he put the windows down and made a U-turn on Darling. At the roundabout at the London, he turned right and followed the backstreets. Right again on Glassop and the river was laid out before him, Cockatoo Island sitting clean off his bow. Twenty-five years in Balmain, and every day it took his breath away. Water everywhere. People always looked east, to the harbor and the big bays and then the bluffs, the stratified promontory drama of the Heads. Bowman liked to look west, to look homeward. To the scars of industry and the way the light played, the shimmering scales of the serpent river.

The worker's cottage had come down to him through his mother's side, stretching back to the convict past. She'd never lived in it. After Chick, Bowman had watched his mother crumple, and then he'd turned away, unable to bear witness to her grief for her little boy. She'd died adrift from her living son and estranged from her husband. John Bowman had the gene: he dissolved himself in alcohol. Toward the end, he had come to stay on Datchett Street, and Bowman had watched his father drink himself to death. Drowned in drink in the drowned river valley.

He took the same route as the night before but this time crossed straight over Pennant Hills Road and down to a flat strip of shops adjacent to the school. Chemist, dentist, doctor, hairdresser, newsagent, deli, minimarket morphing into bottle shop. He parked and got out.

Prince Albert sat up to his left. A patrol car was moored at the top of a cul-de-sac where a path led into the campus. Head down, Bowman walked away from the police along a road parallel to the school's northern edge. After fifty meters, there was a gap in the suburban houses and a track veering off. He took it and dropped into scrub, then walked up a rocky rise, through a hole in a cyclone fence that rode the boundary, and onto the school grounds. The way was well worn, beaten down by generations of boys ducking out to visit the shops. Bowman had trod it hundreds of times.

Remnant forest, turpentine and ironbark, ringed the property. He continued until the track led him out into the belly of the place: the maintenance depot, laundry, loading dock, kitchens, dining hall—all shuttered for the holidays. The road he was standing on looped through the grounds in a long figure eight, connecting the outlying boarding-houses and playing fields to the communal center and the classrooms. There was a pocket of gums to his left, and he slipped into them for cover.

Movement caught his eye: a man in a pale-yellow shirt walking along the edge of the road. Cargo shorts, sneakers, white socks, a soft khaki hat pulled down to protect his face—if he was a cop, he was deep undercover, ready to infiltrate bird-watching trainspotters. He was about fifty meters away, something robotic in his gait as he headed down a short drive and disappeared behind the maintenance block.

Bowman rubbed at his nose. His best bet was to follow and try to get the man to talk. If he was a staff member, anything he said could be turned into a story. Moving out from the trees, Bowman was about to cross the road when he heard a vehicle. It rounded the bend and caught him stranded, one foot in the gutter. Calais, unmarked—definitely cop. The driver pulled up behind him, unbuckled, and got out, her movements fluid, nonchalant, assured.

Streaked blonde hair pulled back, supple in a T-shirt, a Glock on her hip. "Morning, sir." She pushed her sunglasses up. Hard emerald eyes—turn you to stone. "You live round here?"

"Working here."

She looked him over. "Teacher?"

He tried to stall. "My parents lived here."

She squared off, her own foot in the gutter, facing him. "Sir, I'm Detective Sergeant Riley, New South Wales Homicide. We're running a major investigation on these premises. Do you think I might see some ID?"

Bowman pulled out his wallet and gave her his driver's license. She studied it, handed it back.

"Like to tell me what you're doing here, Mr. Bowman?"

"I'm a reporter. With *The National.*"

She stared, blinked, and walked back to the vehicle. She opened the passenger door, pulled out the newspaper, and returned with it.

"Nice picture," she said.

"Thanks."

"Press were corralled on the oval. How'd you get it?"

"Came through a hole in the fence." He tossed his head. "I can show you, if you want?"

She looked at him, then nodded at the Calais. "Get in."

The aircon was blasting. She reached for the knob, turned the fan down, checked her wing mirror, and pulled out.

Bowman slid a side-eye. "What'd you say your name was?"

"Riley."

"Riley what?"

"Detective Sergeant Riley." They came to an intersection and stopped. "Which way?"

The front oval with the media pack was down to the right. Network vans, camera crews, tents, desks, cables, a mobile canteen, newspaper and radio reporters, photographers, *bloggers*. A police media tent stood in the middle, the big top at the circus. Bowman was on the high wire, looking down. To stay on the trapeze, he needed the cops.

"Left," he said, and she started up the hill. After several hundred meters, they came to a dirt driveway off the bitumen. "It's down there," he said. "There's a path through the bush to the local shops. I left my car there."

She edged along. "You came in the same way last night?"

"Yes." He lied like a sociopath. Tell them what they want to hear—that was his motto.

"So you drove and parked off-site." She watched ahead. "Last night you came through the fence there, walked all the way over to the scene, took the picture, and then walked out again?"

31

"It's not that far. Twenty minutes each way."

She picked up her notebook from the console. "You said your parents live here?"

"Lived here. Not anymore."

"Did you live here?"

"As a kid."

"And now you live in Balmain?"

His license. He nodded.

She bit the lid off a pen. "Can I grab your number?"

Bowman gave it. She asked for the make, color, and registration of his vehicle and wrote it all down.

"Can you tell me where you were on Wednesday night?"

He went still. Five seconds, six.

"Today's Friday?" he said.

She raised her eyebrows.

"I worked Wednesday night. Four till midnight."

"In the office?"

"Yeah."

"And after that?"

He'd had two beers at the Aurora and gone home.

"Did you drink with anyone?"

"Locals." He didn't know their names.

"Was anyone with you at home?"

"No."

She made a note. "As you know, media's restricted to the front oval. The school grounds are a crime scene. I don't want to see you wandering around again."

He opened the door, got out, and looked back in. "Thanks for the ride."

6

Shock had hit Bruce Dunlop hard, but he was functioning. In fact, he couldn't stay still. O'Neil had seen it before with loved ones and knew his detectives had to move fast: Marguerite's father wanted to help, but they needed to get everything out of him before they lost him to grief. The mother was a different story. Beverley Dunlop could barely stand up.

The Dunlops had landed at Mascot at 8:00 a.m. and been brought to the school. O'Neil wanted them to take a look at the house, but for now they were being interviewed in a classroom block nearby. It was Friday morning, and no one had slept since the body had been found.

They separated the parents in adjacent rooms. Their alibis were watertight. They'd left for Noosa by car on Boxing Day, Monday. They had made calls to their daughter and exchanged texts until things went quiet on Wednesday morning. They'd assumed she was busy, or just needed some space. About a month ago, Marguerite had got a job at a shop in the Westfield Parramatta mall. She was to have been there for the post-Christmas sales until the end of January, when she'd have left for Canberra and university. Philosophy and religion. According to her father, there had been no recent changes in her behavior. He and his wife didn't just think their daughter was a good kid—they knew it. She was positive, organized, civic minded, well meaning, kind. No drugs, no alcohol, no boyfriend. She hadn't gone to schoolies events after graduation because the party scene made her nervous. Bruce and Beverley had taken her to Fiji instead, a trip they had promised to mark the end of her schooling. The family had missionary friends on the islands.

O'Neil moved between the two classrooms, closing the doors behind him, as the parents gave their statements to separate pairs of Satyr detectives. Farquhar sat silently behind the father. O'Neil had no doubt the Dunlops were telling the truth, but there was no way it was the full picture. No parent knew everything about their seventeen-year-old child. Marguerite was a teenager from a closeted upbringing with sudden access to freedom. Had she been taking risks? Had her lifestyle got her into trouble? Toxicology would take a week. They had her phone, her laptop, her Opal transport card, her debit card, her driver's license, the registration for the Mazda.

Looking from room to room at the Dunlops, O'Neil wondered at their marriage. Would it survive? He felt a wave of fatigue . . . he didn't want to think about marriage. Beverley Dunlop appeared to be slipping further away, her face a hideous gray.

When the mother's statement was done, O'Neil led her from the classroom to the house. There was a spot on the carpet in Marguerite's room about the size of a fifty-cent piece. Someone had scrubbed at it, trying to clean it up. Crime Scene had run the lights over it and confirmed it was blood. O'Neil withheld that detail from the mother but wanted to know how long it had been there, and Beverley Dunlop, when she saw it, said it was new. O'Neil asked her to look around the room to see if anything had been stolen. Nothing had been taken, as far as she could tell.

In both the victims' rooms in Gladesville, things had gone missing: shoes, one earring from a pair, underwear, holiday snaps, Jill Sheridan's driver's license. It sounded like Hollywood bullshit, but Gladesville was taking trophies.

The house was now the primary focus of the investigation, and a second police gazebo had been set up on the front lawn. They were working on the hypothesis that Marguerite had been killed in her room, left on the floor on her front for a few hours, and then moved somewhere unknown to be washed and wrapped before being moved again to the dump site.

O'Neil's head throbbed. He left Beverley with a female constable and headed back to the classrooms. Bruce Dunlop was finishing his statement, and O'Neil pulled up a chair beside Farquhar to wait. He stared at the father from behind—the man looked like he couldn't knock the skin off a rice pudding. O'Neil snarled the thought away: looks could be deceiving. The school chaplain. What did he know about new religious movements, Satan worship, wizards in the suburbs? What did he know about Gladesville? O'Neil growled at himself again. He had to be careful in pushing for links that weren't there. He'd done that before and left ruined lives in his wake, innocent men he'd destroyed with his blind, righteous fury.

The Satyr detectives taking the statement left the room, and Farquhar stood and took a seat next to Dunlop, placing a piece of paper on the desk. O'Neil stayed put.

Farquhar had made a sketch on the paper: the figure that had been cut into the foreheads of the Gladesville victims—an askew *t* shape, an inch-long vertical line with a wavy crossbar.

"I need to know if this symbol means anything to you," Farquhar said. "Have you seen it anywhere?"

Dunlop sounded vacant. "What is it?"

"It appears to be a religious sign. Christian, or perhaps pagan."

"You mean witchcraft?" Dunlop spoke softly.

"Marguerite was to have studied religion. Is it something she was interested in, the transition from paganism to Christianity?"

Dunlop stared at the drawing. "She's interested in the history of religion, yes, but purely as a student. She's High Anglican. It's not possible she would veer into that."

The psychiatrist nodded. "Why isn't it possible, do you think?"

O'Neil moved down the side of the room and perched on a desk where he could see the father's face.

"Theology is what fires Marguerite," Dunlop said. "It's a philosophy for her. But she does also have faith. She's not a lost soul, searching for meaning. Nor is she evangelical."

"I see," Farquhar said. "She had no interest in the occult, no speaking in tongues?"

"No, nothing like that. She's very humanist in her thinking. Evolution, for example—she accommodates it with ease."

The psychiatrist gave a doleful smile. "Was your daughter's thinking something you accommodated?"

Dunlop considered for a moment and turned to O'Neil. "I hope this is not some witch hunt, the backward Anglicans and their odd customs. That's not Marguerite."

O'Neil pushed off the desk and went to him. "It's all right—that's enough. Your wife is waiting."

He took the chaplain by the elbow.

Farquhar stayed in his seat. O'Neil guided Dunlop out into the hall to a waiting constable and watched the chaplain shuffling away.

Back in the classroom, Farquhar didn't look at him. "This school is Sydney Diocese," the doctor said. "Have you come across them?"

O'Neil kept quiet.

"They're everything Marguerite was not. They're Low Anglicans, evangelical." Farquhar stood and walked to the door. "Fundamentalist. Let's just say they don't accommodate evolution with ease."

Bruce Dunlop had stopped under an exit sign at the end of the corridor. He couldn't have killed his daughter—he hadn't been here.

"He's the chaplain," Farquhar said. "The diocese would only hire in its image."

A father-daughter religious war? "Understood," O'Neil said. "But you need to consider his alibi. It's what we might call—"

"Omnipotent?"

"Yeah, that'll do."

They took Dunlop to his house. O'Neil felt the weight of the grief and wanted to help shoulder the load. It was impossible, but you had to try. A uniformed constable brought Beverley Dunlop from the gazebo, and the couple were packed solemnly into the back of a waiting patrol car, to be taken to Beverley's sister's home in Beecroft.

O'Neil needed Panadol, a shower, and a ten-minute kip. A combat nap, he called it, and Chrissie had always given her reply: a nanna nap. The repartee had been the first thing to dry up, then talking at all, and finally the whole marriage had been wrung out. That was the nub of it: he'd lost the ability to talk with his wife. He took his work home, but he didn't discuss it, and he didn't think to ask her about her day. The house was hers—she'd been paying it off before they'd met. O'Neil had considered moving in with his widowed father, but he wasn't there yet—a man had to have some pride. He'd found a flat in Redfern and taken a six-month lease. That had been five months ago. He still couldn't sleep properly in the empty bed.

Beverley Dunlop stared straight ahead as the car pulled away. The Dunlops' vehicle was in Noosa. The analysts would run the plates. Bruce Dunlop mightn't have killed his daughter, but they had to cross him out for Gladesville.

O'Neil looked at his watch: 10:30 a.m. Riley would be finished at the Spratts'. O'Neil texted her to pick him up and waited in the shade, running through lists in his head. There were divers in the creek, and more than a hundred officers walking the line across the terrain between the house and the dump site. The headmaster, Philip Preston, had given a statement to Satyr detectives at the Hay Stand last night and then been sent home. O'Neil read the statement on his phone. No sleep, no shower—not yet. They needed to see Preston.

7

Riley let the Calais idle and watched the journalist walk into the scrub. She called a Satyr analyst on Bluetooth. "Got some plates," she said. "Want to see if they ping with anything you're getting from the school. Or Gladesville."

She read out Bowman's license plate number and put the car into gear as O'Neil's text came in. She thanked the analyst and drove past blocks of classrooms, a gymnasium and swimming pool, the oval and pavilions, a sandstone chapel, and the turreted, stained-glass Victorian seat of the original estate. No one lived in the manor, Spratt had explained, and it was now a function center.

O'Neil was standing on the turning circle at the Dunlop house. Some men looked good completely bald. He got in, closed his eyes, and rested his head back. Riley put the car in park but left the engine running.

"Spratt profile in train?" he said.

"Mm," she grunted. It was one of O'Neil's paranoias: witnesses morphing into suspects. All his paranoias were running hot.

"What's he saying?"

"He's confirmed the head count. Reckons there's eight people on-site. Everyone else has bolted for the holidays."

"What about his wife?"

"She gave her statement this morning. Checks out with his. She's been working all week, a deckhand on the charter boats out of Darling Harbour. She's been on the day shift, home with him every night. Except last night. She was out with colleagues when he found the body."

An eye opened. "A deckhand?"

"Yeah. Does the ropes, pours the drinks. Spratt used to be a skipper on the harbor—that's how they met."

"Do they own a boat?"

"A Quintrex on a trailer, fifty horses on the back. It's in good order, down the side of their house."

O'Neil looked across at her, both eyes open now. There was a decision to be made—and it was O'Neil who had to make it. The question was whether to inherit the case, to bring the Dunlop girl into the Gladesville investigation. The alternative was to pull out now and shovel it elsewhere.

It wasn't clear cut. Really, all they had tying the cases together was black plastic and the full moon. But they had to move fast—because Gladesville was going to hit again. And if it turned out the cases weren't linked and Gladesville hit while O'Neil had Satyr focused on the private school, things would get shitstorm messy. Career-ending messy. O'Neil had plenty of enemies, buzzards in the trees looking down. They hated his ego and the way the media fawned over him. But ego, ambition, strength of character—Riley knew he needed all that to do what he did.

She felt him weighing it. She knew which way she was leaning, but leaning was easy. It was O'Neil who had to make the call. Riley's gut was telling her Marguerite Dunlop and Gladesville were linked. She had no idea how, but she knew to listen to her gut.

O'Neil counted on his fingers. "Spratt's got a key to the Dunlop house, an alibi from his wife, knowledge of the river, and a boat."

Riley didn't answer—he was just running through his lists aloud. She had a mouth ulcer starting, and her tongue kept finding it. Farquhar thought the Gladesville killer was local, working from a fixed point near the houses. O'Neil at first had him coming in by car, parking down the end of a road and jumping through backyards. But they'd got no footprints, no fiber off any fence. They'd looked hard at the river—the first thing they had done was look at the river. Then they'd looked again. They'd looked at the houses from different angles—both properties had good, secluded access by water, well screened from the neighbors. Standing in the shadows of the Sheridan yard one evening, Riley and O'Neil had come to the same realization: he was scoping by boat.

O'Neil straightened a leg under the glove box. "This school," he said. "They'll have a rowing shed?" The Satyr investigation had taught the detectives one thing—there were school and club rowing sheds all along the river, including three at Gladesville.

"Yeah," Riley said. "To go with the rifle range."

"Where is it?"

"Upstream of Gladesville, not in the radius." She picked up her notebook. "Putney. I'll ask Annie's boys to take a look."

O'Neil closed his eyes again and rubbed at his temples. "What are you hearing about the parents and the girl?"

"Quiet, religious, solid," Riley said. "They'd give you the shirts off their backs. No séances, no scuttlebutt."

"What else?"

"There's been a bit of buzz on the Satyr hotline," she said. It made sense. The use of black plastic had got out, and the media—and therefore the public—had no doubt BMK had killed Marguerite Dunlop. It had been reported as fact even before the picture in *The National* had placed O'Neil at the scene. Riley knew O'Neil would be happy to let it run. "A few calls about this headmaster, Preston."

"Who's been calling?" he said.

"A parent, some former staff."

"Saying?"

She turned pages in her lap. "He's suave but vicious. Bit of a show pony. He hits on the mothers. He's got the board in his pocket."

"You catching any whiff of kiddie fiddling?"

"Nup. Not with Preston, at least. Seems too far up his own arse to be interested in anyone else's."

O'Neil's mouth stretched, half a smile.

"For a church boarding school, it seems pretty clean." Riley looked over her shoulder and reversed. "Nothing out of the Royal Commission."

"You read the Preston statement?"

Riley nodded and put the car in drive. The hotline chatter was likely just hearsay, about as useful as pub talk. Spurned lovers, sacked teachers, petty politics. But in the statement, something had jagged out. Philip Preston had said he'd been at dinner in Roseville last night, and this had been verified by his hosts, and by the electronic trail he'd left on the M2 and the CCTV at the school gate. The autopsy wouldn't be done until tomorrow, but the pathologist was clear on one point: Marguerite Dunlop had been dead at least twenty-four hours when she was found early on Thursday evening, so Wednesday had come into focus. And what had Philip Preston been doing on Wednesday? Home alone, day and night.

The headmaster's house sat at the front of the school, to one side of the classroom blocks and administration buildings. A black Range Rover with purple vanity plates, PRINCE, was parked on the drive. Next to it sat a long-wheelbase Caprice with a red government Z plate.

They got out of the Calais. Riley shielded her eyes to peer through the blacked-out windows of the Caprice. Empty. It had to be federal— and someone high up.

"COMCAR," she said. "You think a judge?"

From here you could see the entry gates to the school on Pennant Hills Road, where the police roadblock was still in place. O'Neil scratched his neck. "Question is, how did they get in?"

The house was boxy and big, a 1960s two-story brick job. O'Neil rang the doorbell, waited awhile, and rang again. Riley felt better— fresh adrenaline was coursing.

There was muffled noise inside, and the door opened in a citrus blast of tangerine polo. The shirt drew the eye, blinking, to the hint of a belly. Philip Preston looked to be not long out of the shower, black hair slicked back. Dyed? He was six foot, late fifties, blandly handsome, corporate and smooth. The duke in his domain, he surveyed them: the naughty schoolchildren. They hadn't called ahead.

His demeanor shifted to an obsequious welcome, like a dog showing its belly. "You're the police?" The voice was high, slow, confected . . . striving for languid. The remains of an accent. American?

"Mr. Prest—" O'Neil said.

"Doctor."

O'Neil's face folded. *What the fuck?*

"I beg your pardon," Preston said. "It's *Dr.* Preston."

Riley was attuned to every register of male insecurity. "You're a medical doctor?"

Preston looked her down and up, an insolent second too long at her breasts. "I have a PhD—from Cambridge." He stepped back with sudden deference. "Please. I wasn't expecting you."

From the hall, the headmaster ushered them to an anteroom with a single chair and side table guarding a second door. A man in a shiny suit sat in the chair with *The Mirror* and a mug. He acknowledged them in silence, ex-cop written all over him. Preston ignored him and led them through the doorway.

They came into a long, formal room with a timber dining table for twenty and a cluster of green Chesterfields on the left. Heavy curtains, drawn back to let in the day, leatherbound books on shelves, scenes of pastoral life on the walls, cut pile on the floor. At a window halfway down the room, a man stood with his back to them, talking on his phone. An Akubra sat on a coffee table.

Preston gestured. "Please," he said again. "Sit."

They remained standing.

"Good," the man at the window said into the phone, ending the call. He wheeled and started toward them—a carpet stroller, used to working a room. Light-blue shirt, cuff links. Riley knew his face from TV.

"The Honorable Hugh Bishop," Preston said and squared his shoulders. "The minister for agriculture, the member for Yuranigh."

"Yeah, yeah," the man said and shook hands with O'Neil and then Riley. "I'll get out of your hair. I flew in this morning and heard the news. Poor girl. It's just . . . devastating. I wanted to check in on Philip."

Poor girl. Preston had gleaned Marguerite Dunlop's identity and coughed it up to his mate.

"You came through the main gate?" O'Neil said.

"Mmm." His pebble eyes were bagged in a ruddy face. Liked a shandy on a hot night. "My driver talks the talk."

A hospital quiet descended. Riley bit her tongue to keep it from the ulcer. The room felt clinical, antiseptic. There was no sense of shock, no empathy, no sorrow. Something had been scrubbed clean.

O'Neil crossed his arms. He had a foot in height on the politician. "What's your role with the school?" he said.

"Just a parent," Bishop said. "Got the kids here."

O'Neil nodded slowly. "Not nice, losing a child."

Preston cleared his throat.

Bishop patted his chest pocket and looked at O'Neil. "That was the premier on the phone," he said. "She worked for me, back in the day. You need anything, you give me a call."

A cloying drawl. Repulsion slithered in Riley. Who had whom in whose pocket? Sydney was a corrupt town, and Canberra would be worse. It was a slimy game, and Bishop was a player.

"Well"—Bishop bent to retrieve his hat—"I'll let you get back to work."

O'Neil's hand went inside his suit jacket to his pocket—and came out with his notebook. "There is one thing," he said. "Before you go."

Bishop fingered the brim. "What's that?"

"Could you tell me where you were on Wednesday? And Wednesday night?"

Riley marveled at the politician's jaw muscles. It had been a while since someone had told Hugh Bishop to get fucked.

"Call my office," he said. "They'll give you my diary."

Call the office. Put in a call. Bishop could end O'Neil's career by picking up the phone. The calls to the Satyr hotline had claimed Preston had the board in his pocket. Bishop would be in on that. They'd walked into a snake pit, and Riley knew how it worked—networks of influence, the peddling of favors, stretching through politics, big business, construction, sport, media, the law.

O'Neil stared him down. "I'm happy for you to provide a statement at a later stage," he said. "But we need to clear this one thing now. Wednesday—where were you?"

Bishop's face was stony. You could rappel down the motherfucker. "I was at home with my family in Blayney. Now, if you'll excuse me." He nodded to Preston and headed for the door. The headmaster followed him out.

O'Neil cocked an eyebrow at Riley. "Checking in on Philip? Philip seems fine."

Riley watched through the window as Preston walked Bishop to the Caprice. Neither man had shown any real concern for the dead girl or her parents. Bruce Dunlop had been Preston's colleague for more than a decade.

"They didn't even mention Marguerite by name," she said.

The politician got into the back seat, already on the phone.

O'Neil watched beside her. "Why now?" he said.

Good question. Riley pictured Marguerite's face. Why were two men meeting over the body of a dead girl?

Preston returned and sat in an armchair with a headmasterly wave. "Tell me what you need."

"Wednesday," O'Neil said. "You were here alone all day?"

Preston blew air through his nose. "I went through all that with your officers last night."

O'Neil studied the bookshelf. "A teenage girl has been killed at your school. That means anyone at the school is a person of interest, and we need to eliminate them from the investigation. The easiest way to do that is with an irrefutable alibi."

"But you know who you're looking for," Preston said. "This BMK."

"That's a good point you make. We're going to need a download of your smartphone and a photocopy of your diary, going back three months. Of particular interest are two dates at the beginning and end of November—as well as Wednesday. You've got a secretary?"

"Of course." Preston's nostrils flared. "What are you implying?"

"I'm not implying anything." O'Neil turned. "I'm stating a fact. You don't have an alibi. That's a problem."

"I don't believe this." He smiled with hurt disbelief. "I've told you where I was." He held his hands out. "Right here."

In his statement, Preston had said that he and his wife had spent Christmas in Adelaide with his mother-in-law. His wife had stayed on while he had returned to Sydney on Boxing Day, to get some work done. They had no children.

O'Neil took a seat to take Preston through his statement. As soon as the headmaster answered a question, O'Neil asked another. Why hadn't his wife returned home? His hosts in Roseville—did they know Hugh Bishop? Did his wife know about the Roseville dinner? Did his wife know Bishop? Was there anything he wanted to get off his chest?

Preston's voice got faster as O'Neil stripped him down. Had Preston made any calls on Wednesday? Could anybody vouch for him? How well did he know Marguerite Dunlop? Had he been in her house? Were the Sheridan or Chatfield families from Gladesville associated with the school in any way?

O'Neil had him rattled. The detective had been careful not to use the word *arrest*, but he'd made it clear things could get out of hand. The police could fixate on Preston, get a crime-scene warrant for his house, take him in for questioning.

Riley stood to the side. What were they dealing with? Vanity—in the voice, the hair, the insistence on his title, the proximity to the politician. Bishop was a trophy: fame and power. What else did Preston covet? Five years in Homicide meant she knew that a man like Preston could kill a child and try to ride it out—his personality would allow it. But while that might account for Marguerite, Gladesville was something else entirely. How disordered was Preston's narcissism, and to what else was it coupled? That was Farquhar's territory. They were almost certain Gladesville was acting alone, so what were Preston and Bishop into? Not the schoolboys—if they were molesting at Prince Albert, it would have got out among the other students. Kids always knew that stuff. So not a pedophile ring exploiting schoolboys. But girls? Was Marguerite being shared around?

The tinge of disappointment Riley had felt when she'd first seen Marguerite's body came back to her. She'd wanted it to be Gladesville who'd killed the girl, because that would mean there was only one killer out there, and if he was moving, it gave them a chance of taking him down. The disappointment had been an instinct telling her that Marguerite was not connected to Gladesville. But it was an instinct she had since rejected—it was too concrete, and she wanted to keep open the possibility Gladesville was linked to the school. And the lack of an alibi now allowed for a connection between Preston and Marguerite.

In the silence, Preston's tongue came and went across his moist lips. The headmaster was a man of appetites. He had a greedy mouth.

O'Neil made eyes with Riley and looked down the room. They walked together, and he spoke low. "Stay with him. I'm going to call in Farquhar with Annie and some grunts. They can copy his phone and diary. Farquhar can watch how he responds."

Riley went back to Preston. The headmaster bristled in his chair. "This is absurd," he said. "This is the third murder. Surely you have more to go on than questioning me?"

His long, milky fingers fiddled with his wedding ring. Unblemished hands, good at pointing to the flaws of others, delegating, turning tables. Exhaustion caught her, and she closed her eyes, felt dead hands around her throat. Her eyes came open. Preston was watching her.

"Mr. Bishop described the victim as a 'poor girl,'" Riley said. "We haven't released a name yet. How did he know that?"

"I saw all the police at the chaplain's house last night," Preston said. "I rang Craig Spratt, and he told me."

O'Neil was back. "I'm about to talk to the media," he said. "I'll be identifying the victim as Marguerite Dunlop. I'll also be asking anyone working or living at the school during these holidays to come forward to the police. They'll be asked to give a statement, prints, a DNA swab."

"Would it help if I spoke with the media?" Preston said.

That'd be right. Riley curled her mouth at O'Neil. Media tart.

"No." O'Neil's tone was final.

Riley left first. In the anteroom, the COMCAR driver's empty mug sat on the table like a totem. She turned on Preston. "Just getting back to Mr. Bishop. Why was he here this morning?"

"He'll be chairman of the board when he leaves politics," Preston said. "He's an old boy, his children are here, and the school is an important part of his life. He wants to protect the brand."

Riley gave a nod and spelled it out. "A dead girl's not good for marketing."

"How about you just do your job?" Preston said. "Without the leaks and the gossip."

"We don't gossip," Riley said.

"Well, you're not exactly airtight." Preston went through to the entry hall. "That picture in the paper—how did the journalist get in?"

Riley followed. "Maybe it was an inside job."

There was a map of Canada on the wall. Preston's accent was faint—and not American. "That where you're from?" Riley said.

He blinked. "I was born in Ottawa. We came here when I was young."

She heard vehicles on the drive. Preston opened the door and balked. Farquhar's Volvo, a patrol car, two unmarked Commodores, a Crime Scene van. Annie Tran was standing under the portico in a gray T-shirt, jeans, and joggers, her black hair spiky short.

"Detective Sergeant Tran," O'Neil said to Preston. "She'll oversee your DNA and prints. And she'll have some further questions."

Riley watched as Tran directed traffic and Preston digested the show of force. O'Neil spoke with Farquhar and then walked with Riley to the Calais.

"An inside job?" O'Neil said when they were in the car.

"The journo who got the photo—I caught him poking around this morning."

"And?"

"Kicked him out."

O'Neil glanced across. "You want to use him?"

She pressed the ignition. "He lived here as a kid. He might give us something."

O'Neil frowned out the window.

Something? Riley knew O'Neil would take anything right now. Three dead girls, and they were stuck in first gear, never out in front, always reacting. O'Neil sucked it up, but she sensed the pressure building, coming down on the commissioner from the premier and the press. Command needed results. Without them, they'd spear O'Neil to save themselves. And now a federal cabinet minister had driven onto the crime scene in his limousine. She put the car in gear. A friendly journo could be useful if Bishop were to come at them. Sunlight was the best disinfectant against a man like that. The politician wouldn't like it if a reporter started asking questions, publishing Bishop's name in connection with the investigation into Marguerite Dunlop's murder.

"How do you want to play it?" O'Neil said.

"I could have a chat, see how it feels. He doesn't look like a grub."

"All right. Test him out: spin him a line, and tell him it's off the record—maybe feed him that rape categorization stuff Farquhar goes on about. See how long it is before we read it in the paper. If he's another Benny Beat-Up, I don't want him anywhere near us."

8

Bowman arrived at the office in Surry Hills as O'Neil was speaking to the media at Prince Albert. Benny Diamond was with the pack at the school and would cover the press conference for the paper.

There were more journalists on deck than last night, but the cavernous news floor was still close to empty. Maybe thirty heads, where a decade ago there would have been three hundred. The room swept off into a graveyard of desks and broken chairs and filing cabinets, documenting a lost era. The broadsheet was on its knees and bleeding out, most of its staff laid off or having quit. All that was left were kids on the website, the odd boomer columnist bravely braying on, and a calcified seam of middle-aged timeservers grinding the paper out. Bowman had hung on because he was cheap and did the late shifts: the graveyard in the graveyard.

He put his bag on his desk and looked around. Across the floor, Alexander had stepped out of his office and was waving him over. Alexander was a case in point. He was the editor—he should have been out to lunch while the chief of staff herded the reporters and gathered the news. But the chief of staff was on stress leave, and there was no one left to do her job.

Bowman had never been waved at by the editor, only screamed at and chased around the subs' table. He hurried over.

"Never run in a newsroom," Alexander said. He had a shoe off. Brandy's gout was on the gallop.

The editor limped through his door and sat behind his desk, looking at the television that hung off the wall. Bowman followed. O'Neil was fronting the cameras on the Prince Albert oval. The detective identified the body and offered some details. The postmortem would take twenty-four hours and toxicology at least a week. The school would be sealed for several days. There was a lot of forensic evidence. He finished with a plea for everyone on the campus to come forward: "If you live or work at this school and you don't come to the police, I'll be wondering why you haven't."

"Poor bastard." Alexander turned the volume down and brought his shoeless foot onto the desk. "Trying to get on the front foot."

Bowman glanced at a chair but didn't take it.

"So." Alexander eyed him like a ferret. "Do you know the girl—or the family?"

Bowman didn't know the girl—or the family. But he knew where this was headed. Straight down the ferret hole. Straight to a death knock on the dead girl's door.

"No."

"You reckon you can get to them?"

"What—death knock?"

"Well . . . if we have to. Can't you just ask to sit down with them?"

Bowman didn't think Marguerite Dunlop's parents would be feeling very chatty.

"Good story if we get 'em," Alexander said. "And if we don't, someone else will."

"I'll ask for an interview. But if it comes to a death knock, you can send Diamond."

Alexander made a face. "Haven't the poor people suffered enough?" He looked at the TV. "Speak of the devil."

The network was still carrying the feed from the school. O'Neil's comments had in no way satiated the media, so the television reporters on the oval were doing what they always did: interviewing other journalists.

Beat-Up Benny Diamond loved a chat to camera, oblivious to the fact he had a face for radio. Beat-Up Benny had a body for radio. The armpits of his white shirt were yellow, ambition leaking out of him in primary color. He was overripe, running to fat, but his wardrobe hadn't kept up. His clothes were too tight. His cheeks sheened with perspiration: byline fever. Bowman could smell the Dolce & Gabbana coming through the screen.

Alexander's mouth had fallen open. "Fuck me sideways—I can't even bear to look." He switched it off and winced at his toe. "People live at this school?"

Bowman explained the setup. Maybe a third of the staff lived on-site in houses and cottages and flats, while the rest commuted.

Alexander's eyes narrowed. "And you couldn't find anyone?"

"Holidays it gets empty." Bowman neglected to say he'd walked straight into the Homicide squad. "I'll hit the phones here."

"Who ya gonna call?"

Bowman had one number from the past, an old chalkie who had taught at the school with his parents. It wasn't uncommon for teachers from that generation to regard Prince Albert as a job for life. Some had arrived in their twenties and never left.

"All right," Alexander said. "You work up what you can on the girl, the family, the personal stuff. Diamond'll do the straight news."

At his desk, Bowman got lucky. One call led to another, and the teachers wanted to talk. He spoke with friends of the Dunlops from Prince Albert, people who had known Marguerite as a child and seen her raised. Then he snagged a number for someone at St. Anne's, Marguerite's school, and a fresh cavern of agony opened up. Marguerite was pious, smart, principled—and yet proud and rebellious in her own way. She didn't preen on Instagram or signal her virtue—she rejected the platform outright. She gravitated toward the quiet girls, the humble, the plain, the normal. There was no hypocrisy and no cowardice, physical or moral. She could never have been a journalist, Bowman thought as he wrote.

His left eyelid was quivering as he filed right at 9:00 p.m., the first-edition deadline. The paper would be late off. He'd written four thousand words in seven hours. Adrenaline had got him through, and now he felt it leach out of him. He slumped back, sucking at an empty can of Vanilla Coke. His phone rang.

"Adam Bowman."

"Mr. Bowman. Detective Riley. Rose Riley."

He sat up. "Hi."

"I'm in Rozelle. Have you got time for a beer?"

Another chemical released into his brain. "Nice timing. I've just knocked off."

In a corner of the Bald Rock, Riley caught Bowman's eye as he came through the door. It was cool inside and smelled good—pub food laced with vinegar. She watched him approach, confirming her impression from the morning: his shirt may have been purple, but his life was drab.

"Long day?" she said.

His chin inched up. "Yourself?"

"Feel like I've got jet lag."

She was halfway through a schooner, and he went through the thinning Friday crowd to get two more. His jeans hung loose, no bum to speak of. Riley had a theory about Australian men and their tight arses. She'd seen enough of them now to consider herself an expert, and she'd peer-reviewed it with the girls in the squad. The lack of a backside came from boyhoods spent outdoors, roaming the suburbs, the beach, the bush, from morning until their mothers called them in for tea. It was a way of life lost now—Steve Jobs and Bill Gates had seen to that. The butt end of the information revolution: fatbergs larded with Zucker-tucker.

Riley drained her beer as Bowman put down the new glasses.

"Taken any more photos?" she said.

"Not today. Just wrote a long story, though. Think I forgot to mention you."

"I thought Diamond was your police reporter?"

"I'm helping out."

"I'll bet he's enjoying that." Riley sipped. "You know the lie of the land out there—the school?"

"I grew up there. Till I was fifteen."

She examined him when he wasn't looking. His popping gut, his sleeves rolled between wrist and elbow, his pen-pusher hands. A boyhood spent outdoors—bindi-eye weeds and a BMX. Not so far removed from her own childhood, Riley guessed, though Bowman had a decade on her and a rung up the social ladder. But he wasn't very far ahead, the son of a teacher, part of the help at a place like Prince Albert. Riley had worked a big fraud case on her way out of uniform: it'd been full of slippery private-school stockbrokers, their greed and entitlement physical. They'd been coated in it. There was none of that on Bowman.

"Yeah, so I've been thinking," she said. "If you can play by some rules, we might get along."

"What rules?"

Reel him in slowly. Riley waited while a table of three couples beside them stood and headed for the door. "This is stranger murder," she said. "An unknown serial offender. Very rare, hunts at night. The scary shit."

"Like, only in America?"

She ran a finger around the rim of her glass.

"Are you talking to the Yanks?" he said.

That was Farquhar's job. Read the literature, Zoom with Quantico. "There's a forensic psychiatrist on the strike force."

"What do they reckon?"

Gender neutral. She liked that. "Off the record?"

He nodded, a good head of marsupial hair, dusky streaked to eastern gray. She saw her father in twilight, shooting on the farm. His trigger finger steady, his oil-stained hands. She shifted in her seat. Time to chum up and bait the hook. Farquhar's rape categories. People loved this shit. Until it came through their window at 3:00 a.m.

"They classify four types of rapists," she said. "The ultimate category is anger excitation. That's your sadist. Gets off on causing pain and looking at it."

Bowman sat up straighter, took a gulp.

"So our boy's anger excitation," she said. It wasn't strictly true. Gladesville was beyond rape, if that was where he'd even started. He was into pain, though—that much was true.

She watched Bowman reach into his bag for his notebook and let him scribble something down. "Not a word, remember," she said. "Not even deep background."

"It's just for me." He glanced up from the pad. "To do some research."

Yeah right—a bit of research on anger-excitation rapists. That'd look good in his search history when the tactical boys smashed down his door. Something told her she wouldn't want to see Bowman's search history. Still, she wouldn't want anyone looking at hers either. She'd been horny early in the week—but Marguerite Dunlop had washed that away. One animal urge replaced by another. She was on the prowl now, but it was to fight and kill.

"So why the school?" Bowman said.

"Dunno."

"There's a creek—"

"Listen." She wasn't going there. "Steve O'Neil. You familiar with O'Neil?"

"I know who he is."

"With a case like this, we can't just be following along, so he'll take risks, get creative."

"Sounds like a cliché machine."

Riley drank. It was better than breathing and counting to ten, and smarter than smacking the journo in the mouth.

"When it comes to talking to the media, you'll only see O'Neil," she said. "He's the face of it—it makes it personal. He's trying to goad the killer, get him moving."

"What if he isn't listening?"

"He's listening. He's staging—leaving his mark."

"Yeah? What type of stuff?"

She caught herself, tried to keep the stumble from showing on her face. She'd overstepped, given Bowman something real. "You can't write that," she said. "You can't even allude to it. Nothing on staging or marking. I never said it. You so much as think it, we're dead."

"Circling the wagons?"

Oh sweet Jesus. She stared at the table. *Circling the wagons?* Of course the wagons were in a circle. She picked up her glass to glance over the rim. What was he, an imbecile? Or worse, the opposite? Had he reeled *her* in?

"How much police reporting have you done?" she said. "I'd never heard of you. Neither had O'Neil. No offense."

He didn't like that, she saw. More male inferiority, another journo craving recognition.

"Not much," he said. "Bit of general, some courts."

Maybe that was it, fingers crossed—he just didn't know how the world worked.

"We always hold back details," she said. "It's standard. It weeds out the cranks, for a start. The press, you call him Blue Moon Killer—that's true north for the psychics, the winter solstice at Stonehenge. We've already had a dozen confessions, more, with Gladesville. Hundreds of calls to the hotline. None of them knew anything—except that there's a two-million-dollar reward."

He went to pick up his pen again.

"Nuh-uh," she said. "Look, it's important." She leaned in and lowered her voice. "The marking can't be made public. The holdbacks are strategic. We release bits of detail for a purpose, to get some info flowing or push buttons. We can put things out there to play with his mind."

"So that's where I come in?"

"Yes—and no," she said. "If we want to use the media, we can just shovel it in *The Mirror*, or O'Neil can front up and say it on Channel 9. With you we might be more . . . *delicate*."

"That sounds nice. You fuck me up the arse, and I don't notice."

"Well, you are a little private-school boy."

He held up a middle finger—and his empty glass.

She went to the bar, leaving him to tear at a beer mat. She came back and put the drinks down.

"We bring you into the tent a bit," she said. "You work with us, we work with you."

"Don't you mean *use*?"

"If you like. We all know the score."

"I made a lot of calls today," Bowman said. "I heard who found the body. A kid named Tom Green—and a staff member, Craig Spratt."

"Maybe."

"Thing is, the boy's parents wouldn't talk to me. Neither would Spratt."

"Bit sad."

"How about you give them the green light?"

"I'll think about it." Riley needed sleep. She pushed away her glass and stood.

"Also," he said, "are you guys approaching Diamond as well?"

"Benny Beat-Up?" She scrunched her nose. "Nah. O'Neil can't come at him—too sweaty. Says he's got the look of a chronic masturbator."

Bowman nearly spat his beer.

9

The Strike Force Satyr incident room had been established at the back of the Gladesville police station, less than a kilometer from the two scenes. An image of Marguerite Dunlop in school uniform now had center place on the main wall, among portraits of Lena Chatfield and Jill Sheridan. Pictures of victims motivated investigators, especially these victims—dead young white females had the media salivating, politicians sharking in, and even the hardened cops sitting up straighter. There were banks of computers, whiteboards, photos of the bodies and the kill rooms, timelines, victimology lists, maps. In Homicide, visuals helped a great deal.

At her desk, Riley was waiting for O'Neil and Farquhar. She checked the time on her screen: 7:10 a.m. Saturday, New Year's Eve. Riley would take no part in the celebration and would be glad when it was over—she found the crowds and the mandated bonhomie and the fireworks spectacularly stupid. The drink with Bowman had lit something in her brain and kept her from sleep. Her mind had circled around and around the case until she had been delirious. She didn't like pills—they fuzzed her edge—so at 2:00 a.m. she'd got up and spent ten minutes slugging down Jack Daniel's in front of the TV.

She pushed two Panadol from a sleeve and swallowed them dry. The strike force had grown by one: they'd hooked a detective constable from Parramatta who had attended the scene on Thursday night. "Got a pressie for you" was how the super had put it to O'Neil last night. "Smart, young, tidy. Turning into Charlie's Angels, your mob." There were now fifteen detective constables with Satyr: from Homicide, Sex Crimes, Ryde, Gladesville, Chatswood, Parramatta, and a couple of ring-ins from Gangs. Then Annie Tran with Riley under O'Neil. Plus Farquhar, a team of six analysts . . . and a journo riding shotgun.

The new constable, the Parramatta detective, was first in, sitting at the end of the row of desks with a laptop. Riley had noted her at the school on Thursday and again yesterday and liked what she saw: diligence and intelligence.

O'Neil and Farquhar came through the door with takeaway cups.

"Sleep well?" O'Neil said.

"Don't start," Riley said.

"Green tea and boxing—you should give it a try." He gave her a coffee and looked about. There was no one, save for the new girl down the room. O'Neil considered her for a moment, his head at a tilt. "Oi," he called.

Startled, the Parramatta constable looked up, eyes wide. O'Neil beckoned. She stood, crow-black hair in a ponytail. She was twenty-eight, tops. Riley watched O'Neil avert his gaze as she walked over.

"Patel, right?" he said.

"Sir."

"First name?"

"Priya."

"You seen the note from Crime Scene? Point of entry?"

Priya Patel glanced back at her desk. "I was just reading it."

"Okay." O'Neil gestured. "This is Dr. Farquhar, Detective Sergeant Riley. Pull up a chair."

Riley grabbed her laptop, and the four of them sat at a round table toward the back of the room. "Righto," O'Neil said. "One thing before we get started. The plastic wrapping the body—they found a small amount of an organic brown substance on it. Slightly moist. Results soon."

"Soil?" Riley said.

"Wait and see."

"There's been no rain," Riley said. "They think it got wet when he washed her?"

"Yeah, they think he washed the whole package after he wrapped her. Now, preliminary forensics on the Dunlop place, let's go."

They went through the briefing note. The house was covered in fingerprints and mixed DNA from the family and visitors. But the techs liked the unlatched pantry window as point of entry. No prints had been found on the window frame, inside or out: it had been wiped clean. But the bench along the wall in the pantry had yielded the prints of four fingertips and a thumb. It was where a hand might be put out for balance by someone coming through the window.

"It feels a bit neat," O'Neil said.

"It could be about timing," Riley said. "He doesn't clean up as he gains access. He does it later, maybe under stress. He remembers the obvious—to wipe down the window frame, but he forgets the bench."

"Good," O'Neil said. "Priya?"

"He's not there to kill her," Patel said. "But it goes south."

O'Neil's fingers steepled. "Go on."

"He uses the window to gain access. He's not worried about prints at that stage, or DNA, because he's just there to look. He thinks the place is empty. He's prowling, looking through her stuff. Then it blows up. She comes home from Coles, and he's in the house—in her room—and she confronts him. He lashes out, kills her."

"And?" O'Neil said.

Patel glanced at Riley. "And now he's got a lot on," Patel said. "He's got to move her, he's got to wash her, he's got to dump her. And he needs to cover his tracks."

"He goes to where he came in," O'Neil said. "Wipes down the window frames?"

"Yes. As Sarge says—he wipes where he can remember. But this might be after he's dealt with the body. It could be hours later. He forgets the bench."

O'Neil sat back. Patel glanced again at Riley. The girl had instincts and rapport, a good combination. O'Neil was clicking his tongue. Riley sent a signal—sisterly, imperceptible—to Patel: *Watch this.* O'Neil's eyes were on Farquhar. A decision had been made.

"We're going to take it on, bring Marguerite into Satyr," O'Neil said. "I want to look at all possible links between Gladesville and the school."

Riley sat still. The ruling ran counter to Farquhar's reading of the scene. Marguerite Dunlop's death bore no real resemblance to Gladesville. Gladesville was around domination, subjugation, ritual, possession, control. That wasn't what had happened at the school. Riley thought O'Neil was going along with the psychiatrist, that he was preparing to decouple and push the Dunlop girl elsewhere. Something in the forensic evidence from the house had swayed him.

Farquhar closed his eyes, and O'Neil flashed with annoyance at the passive disapproval. O'Neil didn't do passive—it made him aggressive. The psychiatrist was agile in his thinking, but he could get stuck in a groove and stubborn with his ideas, like anyone else. O'Neil was forever on the lookout for such shortcomings, in himself and others: tunnel vision, blind alleys, wombat holes. O'Neil was paranoid about wombat holes.

"Let me just state some facts," Farquhar said, eyes still shut, "and then you tell me what's on your mind."

O'Neil folded his arms.

"Gladesville," Farquhar said. "Organized psychopath and sadist. Extreme form of antisocial personality disorder. Not mad—bad. No empathy, no moral boundaries. I've never seen one before, and neither have you." He opened his eyes on O'Neil. "The scene at the school just doesn't—"

"I want to wind back," O'Neil said.

Farquhar blinked.

"You've got all our analysts"—O'Neil waved to the banks of computers now filling with officers—"combing through old cases in Ryde, Gladesville, Hunters Hill, Huntleys Point, looking for weird break-ins."

"Fetish burglaries."

"Priya here is new to us." O'Neil nodded at Patel. "She hasn't heard your theories, but she makes an interesting point. You heard her: she said Marguerite Dunlop's death started as a break-in. Maybe by a pervert with a fetish."

"You think he's going backward?" Farquhar said. "De-escalating, trying to stop?"

"I'm saying we might have found something you've had us looking for."

Farquhar's eyes shifted, considering. *Yep,* Riley thought, *have a suck on that.*

Geography. The psychiatrist was obsessed with it, and for good reason. They had no DNA. Gladesville was cleaning up like he'd been trained in a lab or—Christ, please no—as a cop. Forensic sophistication, Farquhar called it. And without forensic evidence, the next best strategy was to find the offender's early forays and build a geographic profile: where he lived or where he worked. Farquhar believed he lived near the scenes, a marauder swinging around his anchor point, his home. O'Neil saw a commuter. He argued the killer worked near the scenes, probably on the river—a fisherman, filleting his catch.

"If they build the school into the geographic model and we're wrong, it'll skew the profile," Farquhar said.

"Agreed," O'Neil said. "But we could have a second profile running. Just to see what it shows."

The de-escalation theory was interesting. If it was happening, it was probably unique. Riley flicked at the desk with her pen.

"Say it's our boy who's done Marguerite," she said. "He kills her, but what's he left out?"

"Binding, torture, cutting, necrophilia, nailing." Farquhar listed them on his fingers. "He remembered to wrap her and wash her. And he was aiming to put her in a creek, but he deviated."

Not just any creek. "A tributary of the river," she said. "He's where his river rises."

"Mm," Farquhar said.

Riley clicked on an image on her laptop and turned it to face the others. "Priya, have you seen this?" It was Lena Chatfield's face on the slab at Lidcombe. Cut into her forehead was the *t* shape, the vertical line with its undulating crossbar.

Patel nodded. "A calling card?"

"Right," Farquhar said. "He carved it on the Sheridan girl too. Same place."

"What's it mean?" Patel said.

"Nothing, as far as we can tell," Farquhar said. "We've sent it out to art historians, cryptographers, language scholars from Sanskrit to Old Norse to Pitjantjatjara. We thought it might be religious iconography. We looked at some Jungian stuff. Our best guess is pseudohistory, self-help, and the men's movement—ideas about setting males free from societal strictures that promote excessive deference to women and cause paraphilias."

"Paraphilias?" Patel said.

"Deviancy," Farquhar said. "Sexual fetishism. People might fetishize feet—God help them, that's lumpen enough. Gladesville is extreme."

"We think the symbol is his ID," Riley said. "Part of the game."

"Okay," Patel said.

"So"—Riley pointed her pen at Farquhar—"we know he likes to play games. Maybe Marguerite is part of that? He's stripped everything out, gone back to zero. It's part of the game. He's still talking to us."

"Saying what?" Farquhar said.

"Saying we're back at the beginning," Riley said. "Saying this is how it starts. He's linking back to the river. The creek is a beginning too, the beginning of the river."

Farquhar frowned into his beard. In the silence, O'Neil grabbed his elbow to stretch a shoulder. "Let's assume for a moment Rose is on track," he said. "Is he de-escalating, gearing down to stop? Or are we at the beginning of a new cycle—Marguerite is the first? Are we looking at the start of a second spree?"

◆ ◆ ◆

At the round table, the meeting broke up as more Satyr analysts and detectives arrived in the room. It was 8:00 a.m. O'Neil had called a full briefing. Riley went to her desk. She never got used to her insomnia, the way it sapped everything else from the day. Panadol wasn't working. She watched as O'Neil counted heads and clapped. "Boys and girls," he said.

The hubbub died down, and O'Neil thanked them and formally introduced Patel. He waited while they settled. The strike force had been running surveillance operations in Gladesville twenty-four hours a day. Officers with night-vision goggles were posted around the area, and cameras had been put in place in people's yards, on streets, in parks, and at the wharves. This complemented the data from existing CCTV, red-light cameras, and number-plate recognition.

"Righto." O'Neil looked to Annie Tran. "Overnight?"

Tran shook her head—there'd been nothing.

"Okay, so, the Dunlop girl," O'Neil said. "It looks different, agreed. But there are still some similarities, and it's landed with us, and I don't want to separate it. Let's see where it leads. And it's a good opportunity for a poke, to see what Gladesville makes of it."

He didn't mention Bowman. Riley would handle the reporter off the books. O'Neil looked at Patel.

"No leaks, no press," he said. "I don't want to read anything about this in the *Parramatta Advocate*. Very important, understood?"

Patel nodded. She was earnest. If details got out, Riley felt sure they wouldn't come from her.

The victimology on Marguerite was still being worked up, and O'Neil walked everybody through it: the scouring of her phone, her laptop, her social media, and the search for any links to the Gladesville victims. Marguerite had no known boyfriend, and there were no suggestive pictures, no dating apps. Her close friends had left town—it was that time of life, the end of year twelve. Satyr detectives were tracking them all down and speaking to them on the phone or in person, listening for any change in tone, any kink in the narrative. Marguerite's brother, two years older and studying in America, was on a plane home. Her parents' movements had been triple-checked: neither of them had slipped back into Sydney in the days before she was killed.

O'Neil held up a finger. "Keep this in mind. Marguerite and her parents were in Fiji from the sixteenth of December till the twenty-third. That was less than a week before. Is that what lured the killer—he thought the house was empty?"

"Unlikely," Tran said. "The family came back for Christmas. The killer would have seen that if he was watching. Marguerite was coming and going in her Mazda after the parents left for Noosa."

True, Riley thought. The girl had been home five days before she was killed.

"But the trip feels wrong," O'Neil said. "Who goes to Fiji, comes home, and then heads straight to Noosa?"

Lots of people. Riley had seen it with her nephews. Parents taking their kids somewhere special after year twelve, usually to divert them from the parties. And the Dunlops went to Noosa every year—they had a shack in the hinterland, passed down through Beverley Dunlop's family. O'Neil was thinking like a cop who never had a holiday. She could understand why—two months at the beach, and he'd fucking kill someone.

"Bruce Dunlop's a chaplain at a private school," she said. "He's got nothing to do from early December till late January. Go to church at Christmas—other than that, he's a free man."

O'Neil frowned and moved on. Marguerite's job was at an eco-design shop in Westfield Parramatta: they were talking to her boss, her coworkers, looking at the footage from the shop and the mall. Had she met someone? Had someone followed her?

Riley doodled as she listened. There had to be a pattern in the details. There were precisely one hundred and ninety-seven employees at Prince Albert, across teaching, administration, and ancillary: maintenance, grounds, kitchen, laundry, and the rest. When the place was up and running with fifteen hundred students, seventy-seven staff lived on-site.

"At the moment, that number is down to eight," O'Neil said. The Green family of four, two Spratts, Preston. And there was a gardener working through the break, single and living on-site. The bursar was coming and going, but he lived in Carlingford with his wife.

O'Neil took a breath. "Where are we with statements, prints, DNA?"

"Everyone has come forward except one," Tran said. "The gardener who lives on-site. We door-knocked him but no answer. He worked yesterday morning, but the property manager—Spratt—didn't see him after about one p.m. He doesn't have a phone, apparently. Seems to have shot through."

"Who did the canvass?"

Riley looked over the room. Patel put up her hand. "Sir."

"And?" O'Neil said.

Patel swiped at her tablet. "Sir, the name is Kevin Gary Lynch. Emigrated from Ireland in '97, from Dublin. He's fifty-two. Craig Spratt said they ran a working-with-children check before they employed him and came up with nothing. He's got no record. His driver's license is clean. No credit cards. He's got Medicare, and he pays his tax."

"And?" said O'Neil.

"We've got uniforms outside his flat at the school, waiting for him to show," Tran said. "If we don't see him soon, we thought we'd invite ourselves in. Grab DNA and prints."

"Fuck waiting," O'Neil said. "We've got a crime-scene warrant. In and out now. Forensics"—he looked at Patel—"then you. Spratt should have a key. Whatever they bag, straight to Lidcombe. Priority one. Just tell them it's Gladesville."

Patel nodded.

He turned to Tran. "Results to me. No Interpol. I'll send them through to Dublin and the Yard myself."

"Sir," Tran said.

"And keep the uniforms at the flat," O'Neil said. "I want to know if he surfaces."

10

At the cottage on Datchett Street, Bowman's phone told the story—his piece on Marguerite Dunlop had hit the spot. Colleagues who'd ignored him for years were texting their approval. He scrolled through the messages. There was one from Riley: I have told the Greens we are happy for the boy Tom to talk to you. Plus Craig Spratt. Both are free this afternoon. Let me know when. Get moving.

Bowman made a face. *Get moving? How's* Get fucked *sound?* He saw Riley in the Bald Rock: eyes hooded, a hawk roosting, out of his league. It had been a while since Emma. She'd dumped him for "lacking drive," for being a loser. Then she'd wanted him back—nothing better on offer. He didn't want to get married, and he didn't want kids, but he went with the flow. Until he didn't.

He got moving. Riley sure worked fast. Last night she'd said she'd think about lining up the interviews. Now they couldn't happen quick enough. In the Nissan, he looked at her message again. Spratt and Green weren't names he recognized from the past. But where they lived—he knew all about that. The Greens lived in Bowman's old house, where he'd been born and raised. He decided to start with Spratt.

At a red light, he texted Riley. Can u tell spratt i'm coming to interview him?

The light went green.

Yes.

He turned right, and his thoughts swiveled with him. The only time he hadn't lied to Emma was when he'd walked away. They had been in Annandale, in another car at another red light. He'd looked across at her from the passenger seat, her brittle mouth, and he'd opened the door on Parramatta Road and walked away for good. His past was pocked with shame, wounds he grimaced to recall, but leaving Emma wasn't one of them. She had been controlling, angry, disappointed. He'd needed to get clear—that was the truth of it.

He turned off Pennant Hills Road and drove up past St. Anne's. Marguerite Dunlop's school occupied an old hospital site on the southwest border of Prince Albert.

Spratt's place sat just clear of the tree line in a scrappy far corner of the property, lantana country, beyond Ghost Gum and more remote. As a boy, Bowman hadn't lingered here—and he felt it still. He didn't envy Spratt his patch of dirt.

He closed the door of the Nissan as a screen door banged and Craig Spratt came out.

"Craig," Bowman said.

"Did ya come through the police cordon?" Spratt's handshake was dry, hard.

"Nah." Bowman's voice adjusted. "Come up past St. Anne's."

"Well, you know your way around." Spratt's chin ratcheted up in approval. He was wearing black shorts and a blue shearer's singlet, black socks, sneakers. "The detective said you'd be comin'. She's comin' too, in a bit."

They walked up the yard into the house. Spratt thrust his chin again. "Have a seat."

Bowman pulled a chair out from the kitchen table. Brown linoleum floor, green doors on the cabinets, the barnyard funk of marriage.

"Terrible business," Spratt said. "Cuppa?"

There was a tin of International Roast by the sink. "You got tea?"

"Yeah." He filled the kettle. "Missus is at work."

Bowman put his bag down. "Where's she work?"

"On the harbor. Hostie on the charter boats."

Bowman's eyes widened. "Yeah?"

"I used to be a skipper—that's how we met. Never want to see another buck's party."

Bowman snorted lightly. "Fair enough. You got kids?"

"Mm-hmm. They're gone now."

"How old?"

"Twenty-two and twenty."

"They grow up here?"

"Pretty much. We come here when the eldest was seven."

"You know I grew up here?"

Spratt's hand paused on the fridge door. "I heard that. Milk?"

"No, thanks."

Spratt moved around the kitchen.

"Your kids," Bowman said, "they like growing up here?"

He shucked a shoulder. "Hundred and fifty acres of bush, plus the rest of the place. They got to run free. Like you, I'd guess."

Bowman felt it—the hot sun, the chlorine from the pool. When school was out, the tight commune of staff families.

"Not that it helped Marguerite," Spratt said.

There was an undertow to his tone, cold and black and running fast. *Get moving.* Had Riley felt it too? Bowman bent for his notebook and digital recorder.

Spratt put the mugs on the table, and Bowman explained what he wanted: to hear from Spratt and then the boy, Tom Green, about how things had unfolded on Thursday. He clicked on the recorder. Spratt eyed the tools of the journalist's trade and stirred two sugars into his tea.

It was a busy time for Jenny on the boats, he said, with Christmas parties and now New Year's. She'd been lucky this week and scored some day shifts. "Lunch tours with Chinese and stuff. She worked on Boxing Day for the Sydney to Hobart. Usual chaos, every idiot on the water."

Then she'd worked Tuesday, had Wednesday off, worked Thursday. "I wasn't doin' much on Thursday. The wind got up all dusty in the afternoon. Thought I was back in Terry Hie Hie."

"I remember," Bowman said. "The dust got into town."

"True? Anyway, Jen calls about six, says she's gonna have a drink with some of the girls, won't be bringin' any dinner."

Bowman jotted in shorthand.

"So I'm caught a bit short with that announcement." Spratt looked peeved. "There's a hamburger joint down the road, at Dundas."

"I know it." Bowman smiled.

Spratt described the route he had driven through the school. "Get the fright of me life when I see Tom jump down from the Hay Stand and start wavin' both hands. I knew it wasn't good."

The boy had told him there was a body on the floor of the stand. He'd said it was wrapped up, but he knew it was a body. Spratt had got out of his car, and the black shape had come into view as he'd walked. He'd gone up the steps. The floor had been covered in fine red dust, and he'd been able to see Tom's footprints. He hadn't needed much of a look. He'd backed out. Then he'd sat with Tom in the car and called triple zero. The cops hadn't taken long—uniforms and then the cavalry.

Spratt trailed off, eyes following Bowman's pen. "That's it."

"It's quiet here," Bowman said. "Had you seen anyone this week?"

"Cops asked me the same thing. We got one gardener on, so I seen him. The bursar, Graham Murray, seen him on Tuesday, I think. On Wednesday, I seen Preston. He was in his car, over round this side, the lord of the manor checkin' his estate. We had a quick chat."

"You get on all right?"

"With Preston? Up himself. Pretty useless. You know the sort."

"All hat, no cattle."

"Yeah. Bit shifty too. Fish rots from the head down." A pause, then: "Don't put that in the paper."

71

Bowman nodded. "I'll need to describe your job at the school. In the paper."

"Property manager." Spratt drained his mug. "I oversee all the maintenance and grounds staff, the gardeners. Keep an eye on the place in the holidays."

"You really from Terry Hie Hie?" Bowman said.

"Worked there for a bit. Grew up round Wee Waa."

"How was that?"

"Old man had a thing for the sugar cane champagne—liked a Bundy with his Coke. Me and me brother knew the buckle of his belt." Spratt stood and picked up the mugs. "Me mum, she knew the back of his hand."

Bowman swallowed. Alcohol, fathers, brothers, mothers.

Spratt was at the sink. "We had some trouble here with our kids," he said. "Stealin', wreckin' shit, bit of fire lightin'. They took me twenty-two once, went shootin' in the bush."

Bowman couldn't see his face.

"They were harassin' some of the girls, daughters of staff."

Bowman studied his notebook.

"I heard about what happened to your family here," Spratt said. "You don't have to say. I'm just tellin' you my story 'cause I heard yours. Seems only fair."

Fair. He had to say something. "Fair enough."

"Thing is," Spratt said, "my two were loving little boys. We raised 'em up right, not like I was raised. I know how that sounds—like an excuse. But this place . . ." He faltered. "There's a bad feeling here . . . you know what I mean?"

Bowman did know what he meant, but he was surprised to hear Spratt raise it—the strange marsh country, the country of the mind, where things bubbled up in the soil. Maybe in grief, Spratt sensed it—Marguerite had led him to the shadows at the school. The Northern Farms of the early settlement had been here, and Toongabbie, stained in the blood of the Black Wars, lay over the rise to the west. Pemulwuy and guerrilla raids for maize—shootings, spearings, clubbings, rapes, beheadings, the dead strung up on gibbets. There were other types of violence. The trees, the immense trees—true grandeur, rifting back to Pangaea—axed and ring barked and poisoned. Prehistory, clear felled, on the Cumberland Plain.

Spratt's phone rang, and Bowman gathered his things to leave. Something the property manager had said had lodged in his brain: fish rots from the head down. Philip Preston hadn't taken Bowman's call yesterday.

11

On the road around Meadowbank, Riley watched as a low-slung purple pickup barreled up in the rearview mirror and slewed past in a super-charged whine.

"Fucking idiot." She was tempted to hit the siren on the unmarked Calais, pull the prick over, and cuff him on the ground.

Beside her in the passenger seat, Priya Patel sat silently.

"Where you from anyway?" Riley said.

"Taree."

Riley glanced over before she could stop herself—the cop bullshit reflex.

"My parents are from Ahmedabad," Patel said.

Ahmedabad to Taree—and a lifetime of explaining yourself to dumb fucks. Riley heard it in the kid's voice. She thought about apologizing, but it'd be just more dumb-fuck words. Patel was smart, and she'd be tough: brown-skinned girls didn't make detective at Parramatta every day. And O'Neil rated her. After the briefing, he'd sidled up and asked Riley to accompany Patel out to look at the missing gardener's flat. "Pump up her tires a bit," he'd said.

"That was good work this morning," Riley said. "On point of entry."

"Thanks. But I was too passive on the gardener?"

Riley blew air. "Did O'Neil say that?"

"No. But I heard him speak when I was at the academy. He came and gave a talk in Goulburn. There was a whole bit on being passive."

Passive policing, right near the top of O'Neil's list of pet hates. "Did he mention concrete thinking?"

"The dead hand of concrete thinking—I think that's how he put it." Patel's phone pinged. "Forensics are done," she said. "Uniforms say Spratt's waiting at the flat."

"All right. So, Lynch," Riley said. "Names come up early in a case like this. Don't wait—that's passive. You have to move on them."

She swung into the school, past the checkpoint, and through the intersection where she'd sat with Bowman. The road curved up to the right, between the maintenance shed and the laundry. Spratt was waiting next to a white Hilux. Riley pulled over and got out, and Patel followed.

"I just been talkin' to your journo," Spratt said.

Riley felt Patel's interest. "Don't have a journo," she said.

"Well, you told me he was comin'. That's why I gave him the time of day."

Fuck, the man could talk. Two uniforms sat in a patrol car up the road. "No sign of Mr. Lynch?" she said.

"'Fraid not."

"Is that unusual?"

"Unusual?" He turned the word. "Hard to know what's usual with Kev."

"Why do you say that?"

"Flamin' mongrel Irishman, for a start."

She didn't react. It would only encourage him. She counted: this was her fourth conversation with Spratt.

"Look, he's a loose bit of gear." Spratt flicked sweat from his brow with a forefinger. "Operates, like, outside society. No phone, no missus, no kids. Keeps to himself, not much to say."

Probably couldn't get a word in. "So it's not odd that you can't find him now?" Riley said.

"Not really." Spratt's face furrowed. "But I haven't actually looked for him. I mean, it's Saturday. I saw him yesterday. He hasn't missed a shift."

Lynch reported to Spratt. In his statement, Spratt had said he'd seen the gardener throughout the week but had been unable to recall exact times. Spratt had attended a medical appointment in Parramatta, confirmed by his doctor, on Wednesday afternoon.

"Lynch worked Wednesday," Riley said, "but you didn't see him— at least after lunch?"

Spratt nodded.

"Did he knock off early yesterday?"

"Don't reckon. Might have racked off at two instead of three. Friday afternoon."

"Cops were crawling all over the place, and a young girl was dead," Riley said. "Just another Friday afternoon."

"Take your point."

She scanned the block of flats, single story and backing onto bush, dead grass on either side of the path. "How many people live here?"

"There's sixteen flats. Workers come and go."

She turned to Patel, taking two packets of gloves from her back pocket. "Let's have a look."

The communal entrance was open. In the corridor, Spratt pulled out a key and unlocked a door to the sour smell of stale sweat.

Spratt and his keys. "Been meaning to ask," she said. "When did you last have the boat out?"

His upper body shied, and she pretended not to notice.

"A week or so?" he said. "Before Christmas anyway."

"Where do you put it in?"

"Kissing Point. Depends."

Kissing Point was three bays from Gladesville. At Spratt's house, she'd noted the boat had a GPS plotter on the helm. It'd store his trips, waypoints, dates. She indicated Lynch's doorway. "You happy to wait?"

"No worries. Get some fresh air."

The stained lime-green carpet from the hallway had crept in and colonized the flat. The place was dank, even against the dry heat of the westerlies. The blinds were down, and Riley elbowed on a light against the gloom. It was tiny—a sitting room with an alcove kitchen and a bedroom with an ensuite. Empties everywhere: brown longnecks, a five-liter cask of red, a bottle of Tullamore Dew.

"Ouch," Riley said. "The grape and the grain."

Patel moved to a desk and opened drawers. There were screws and washers, nuts and bolts, hose fittings. No bills, no forms, no letters, no papers.

In the kitchen was a kettle, a microwave, a two-burner electric hot plate, a saucepan. A mug in the sink, a dirty glass on the bench, a can of tuna in a cupboard. Two-minute noodles, tea bags, sugar. Victoria Bitter in a bar fridge.

Riley went into the bedroom. Soiled green work clothes in a pile. Nothing in the pockets. There were no shoes anywhere. He probably only had one pair. The bed was unmade, white sheets gray with grime. She felt the mattress, put it on its side, felt underneath. A small TV stood on a chest of drawers at the end of the bed. She rifled through the drawers, checked for false bottoms.

No computer, no pictures. She picked up a copy of *The Mirror*. Friday's edition. Thrown together late with coverage of the killing but the body not yet identified. She leafed through it—nothing had been clipped.

In the bathroom, there was toothpaste but no toothbrush. No hairbrush or comb—bagged by forensics. Heartburn tablets, a cracked cake of yellow soap.

Patel came to the doorway and leaned on the jamb.

"Zero?" Riley said.

"Zip."

12

From the road, the house was hidden by a stand of gums and, beyond that, shrubs ringing the lawn. Bowman turned and started up the drive, its curve a time bend into his past. He parked and got out.

The ordinariness of the place dismayed him. Plain, long, red brick with a tin roof—utilitarian 1960s Australia, built to accommodate the workers. The persimmon tree still stood, and the frangipani his mother had planted, but the enchantment was gone. The lawn was green and raked and manicured. In a foul flash of sepia, Bowman saw Chick's tricycle, capsized under the eaves, a wheel spinning slowly in the air.

There was a flicker in a window as he walked up the path. The front door opened, and a man stood, his mustache as clipped and edged as the grass. Behind him stood a teenage boy, head down but eyes on Bowman.

"I'm Adam Bowman."

The man stared at Bowman's outstretched hand. "I know who you are."

He turned and went into the house. Something robotic . . . Bowman realized where he'd seen him. He had been the figure walking by the road when Riley had driven up yesterday.

The boy was still there. Bowman crossed the threshold and chanced his arm again. "I'm Adam."

Tom Green had the limp handshake of a child yet to grasp the mores of a place like Prince Albert. They'd squeeze that out of him. Bowman looked around the hall and its doors to shrunken portals—guest toilet, study, dining room, sitting room, family room.

He followed the boy through to the open-plan family room and tensed as the narrow kitchen rushed in on him. He saw specters from long ago—burn marks up the wall behind the stove, the ivory coin jar, the chunky wireless . . . *A dingo stole my baby . . .*

Tom was gone, and a woman was standing by the table.

"Excuse me," Bowman said.

She wore a haunted look.

"You knew my parents," he said.

"I knew your mother."

There was a dark spot in her mouth, a dead tooth.

"I'm Sarah. I met you—here." She gestured. "There were always lots of people. I was in my twenties. You were just a teenager."

They swapped a furtive glance. Bowman didn't remember her.

"The police said you want to talk to Tom?"

"If I could—just a few words about what happened."

"Scott's not happy about it. He doesn't like the media. But you're here now. I'll see."

She walked into the back hall, toward the bedrooms. Bowman waited a moment and then crossed to the patio doors and went outside. The backyard was swept, the rockery weeded, a black cat curled in a patch of sun. In the carport, things were labeled and lined up on shelves. He was a bench wiper, compulsive, so he knew what he was looking at. Was it Sarah Green or the husband? Or the two of them together, a perfect sterile boot-camp marriage?

Back in the family room, a television was mounted in the corner where one had always been. *Rick Bourke, Larry Corowa, Prisoner, Doctor Who.* Chick was everywhere, bouncing off the walls. Bowman had known joy here, in these very rooms. *Shut the gate, the horse has bolted.*

Sarah reappeared.

"Scott's coming."

Bowman sat at the table with his notebook and Sarah and Scott Green. There was no sign of the boy. They waited. The Greens were going to make him beg. He was a journalist, good at begging.

"I know it's unusual"—he gave a cough—"to involve a child. But I was hoping to speak to Tom. Just to get an outline of what happened."

"Would you show us the story?" Sarah Green said. "Before you publish?"

"I'm afraid we don't do that."

Scott Green made to stand, and Bowman put his hand out. "But in this instance . . . as Tom is a child"—he widened his eyes—"I could read it to you over the phone."

Scott Green sat down. "Shitty job you've got."

Bowman gave a frowning nod. *Morally indefensible.*

"If it was *my* child they'd found, I'd run you off the property," Scott Green said.

There was nothing to say. "How *is* Tom?" he said.

Scott Green's face was like a curtain had come down. The mustache twitched in encore. "You want him to talk," he said to his wife, "you can babysit."

Sarah watched her husband's back as he departed. She was care-worn, etiolated in a chambray shirt buttoned at the wrists and collar. The room felt lighter with Scott out of it. Bowman sought common ground. "The only time I liked living at the school was in the holidays," he said.

"We never go away," she said. "Sam can use the pool without being ogled. Tom likes it too."

"Sam?"

"My daughter."

"It must be hard for her"—Bowman hesitated—"growing up in a boys' school."

"It's the men that piss her off."

"Really?"

She met his eye. "Have you spoken to Preston yet?"

Bowman shook his head.

"He knew your parents—he was here before they left," she said and looked away. "Before you lost your brother."

A change on the air. The nape of his neck prickled.

He turned. The boy waited silently behind him. Bowman stood to greet him.

"Mum said you used to live in this house."

Bowman nodded. "Until I was your age."

"I think you left something." Tom started for the rear hallway. "Come and look."

The boy ushered Bowman into his room as Sarah stood at the door. They went to the built-in timber bench alongside the wardrobe, and Tom pointed to the front edge. Carved into the wood were the letters *AB*.

Bowman whistled. "That's me."

The boy looked pleased. "That's what Mum said. That a family called Bowman lived here. And that you were called Adam."

"You'll have to leave your mark there, next to mine."

"I will," the boy said. "Got a good knife for it."

A laptop sat open on a desk under the window, and next to it was a drone. "That looks fun," Bowman said.

"It's a Phantom 3." Tom paused in homage. "It can go up, like, a hundred meters." He looked uncertain. "The police took the footage."

Bowman's head went on an angle. "It takes pictures?"

"Video."

"And the police took the video?"

"Um—the memory card. And the hard drive." The boy looked at Bowman. "They'll give it back."

"What's it video of?"

"Um. The school. From, like, the Flats. You know, the playing fields?" Tom swallowed. "I was trying to fly it before . . . before I found her."

Bowman took a knee at the desk to scribble down the make of the drone, and to note the Flats, the memory card, the hard drive. Tom sat on his bed watching, Sarah Green still in the doorway. Bowman gazed across the floorboards, every notch in the pine familiar. He heard Riley again at the Bald Rock: *staging, leaving his mark. AB*, carved in the wood. He was short of breath, stifled by intimacy, kneeling in his childhood bedroom, interviewing a boy about a dead girl. Chick was here too, spliced with Marguerite, a compound ghost. Dead boys and girls.

"Could you tell me what happened," Bowman said, "on Thursday evening?"

The boy recounted his movements. He had been on his bike, riding past the Hay Stand, when he saw a black bundle on the exposed raised floor. The account dovetailed with Spratt's.

Tom finished, and Bowman chewed his pen. He had more than he needed. In fact, he had two stories. The first would detail how Tom Green and Craig Spratt had found Marguerite Dunlop's body. The second would say the police had seized drone footage of the school and were analyzing it for clues. Riley wasn't going to like it—the drone footage would be a holdback for sure.

He stood and thanked Tom. Sarah saw him out.

The afternoon blazed with cicada in dry gum. Sorrow stole up the strange bend in the drive. He'd been buoyant this morning, his success on the job outweighing the horror of the crime, but the visit to the house had triggered a slide, a warning not to use Marguerite as a spark for his stalled career. Bowman knew to heed the message—it wasn't just the school the dead girl could haunt.

His phone rang.

"Heard you got to Spratt," Riley said.

"Yeah. Thanks for that."

"When will you publish?"

"Dunno. They'll probably hold it till tomorrow."

"Don't you just slap stuff up twenty-four seven?"

"New Year's Eve—it'd be wasted."

"Wasted on the wasted."

"That's it," he said.

"Don't s'pose you can send it through to me early?"

"Why?" He couldn't keep the surprise from his voice.

"Come on, keep up. Why did we facilitate the interview?"

"He's a suspect?"

"Everyone's a fucking suspect. Tell me again, what were *you* doing on Wednesday?"

"She was killed on Wednesday?"

"I didn't say that."

"How's the drone footage?"

It was a direct hit, a laser-guided bunker buster. He waited for her to stumble from the rubble.

"Christ," she managed at last. "Never work with children or animals."

"Could be a story."

"No way."

"Could be a story that you're even looking, that you have footage. Might rattle someone's cage."

"Not one word, not yet. Got it? You rat-fuck me on this, it's big trouble in little China."

"The year of the rodent," he said. "Happy New Year."

13

At her desk in the strike force room, Riley hung up on Bowman and scratched at her scalp. The journo was going to blow up in her face on day one.

She opened the analyst's briefing note on the drone footage and read it again. Tom Green had flown the drone on the fields below the dump site twice on Thursday. The black shape of the body could be seen on the floor of the Hay Stand at midday on Thursday. Later in the afternoon, he'd launched again, but there was too much wind, and he'd given up. He was heading home from this failed attempt when he had found the body and Craig Spratt had driven past. Tom hadn't flown the drone on Wednesday.

There was nothing to suggest the kid knew anything was out of the ordinary at noon that Thursday. The structure and the indistinct mound of the body were on the periphery of the video, and there was no sense he had noticed them. You could just catch the black hump in a few frames if you knew to look. The analyst had gone through weeks of footage, and Tom often flew from the same spot.

Riley shut the file and called O'Neil. He was at the school with Annie Tran, retracing Marguerite's movements. He talked Riley through it. The girl was on the CCTV at Coles at North Rocks. The checkout boy remembered her from a photo and said she'd been friendly—nothing strange in her manner, behavior, body language. The CCTV at the school gate clocked her Mazda leaving and coming back onto the grounds on Wednesday morning. The cameras did not cover the Hay Stand, nor was there footage of Marguerite or her Mazda elsewhere on the grounds.

"All we get is Spratt and his wife in their vehicles," O'Neil said. "And the times align with their statements. The same with the Greens' car on Wednesday. Other than that, we have Preston leaving and entering on Thursday evening, the Greens' daughter's Yaris on Wednesday and Thursday, and then Graham Murray, the bursar, coming and going in his car on Tuesday and Thursday."

"The killer would have needed a vehicle to move the body," Riley said. "Have we looked at how you could get from the Dunlop house to the dump site without being seen on CCTV?"

"Analysts are mapping it. There are lots of blind spots. It's possible to get on and off the campus and move around the place without being seen if you know the setup. The journo proves that. From what he told you, he walked several kilometers back and forth across the campus, but he doesn't show up anywhere on the CCTV. He's like a ghost."

"He knows the place because he lived there," Riley said.

"Thirty years ago. There was no CCTV then. How does he know his way around it now?"

"Good point," Riley said. "There's something else. Can the analysts check the CCTV from the November dates to see if Spratt was dragging his boat around?"

"Can do."

"One other thing," she said.

"Let me guess. Bowman?"

"You're good."

"What's he got?"

"Nothing. He wants."

"Sounds about right."

She took a breath. "He knows we have drone footage." She grimaced. "From his interview with Tom Green."

O'Neil's silence was nasty. She held the phone from her ear.

His voice was quiet. "Is it online?"

"No, I've told him not to publish."

"Will he go along with that?"

"Not sure. We could expedite. Release that we've got it."

"What's that get us?"

"Say the killer knew about the CCTV and skirted the system. He's been so careful, but he hasn't factored in a drone. We hit him with the fact there's footage, and suddenly he's shitting himself."

"Could work," O'Neil said. "Maybe we even play it up, say it gives the whole game away. Let's sleep on it."

He hung up, and Riley worked at her desk. As the room emptied, she stretched and checked her phone. Nearly 8:00 p.m. Sleep. She'd need a drink first, to block out the revelers at the pub across from her apartment. She packed her things and went out to the Calais and felt the buzz on the streets. A school friend had got in touch on WhatsApp, inviting her to a party at Kirribilli to watch the fireworks. Riley had declined and now felt remorse as the day burned down and she crossed the river at Birkenhead, crowds teeming on the foreshores.

She considered her self-pity and rejected it. FOMO. Marguerite Dunlop had crossed the river as well—she belonged to Riley now. Marguerite Dunlop would see no fireworks. Waiting to turn right on Balmain Road, Riley made a resolution.

◆ ◆ ◆

The morning streets were strewn with New Year's garbage. Riley drove through Rozelle, past the Three Weeds and punters eating pies in the gutter. She'd slept well—nine solid hours. Her phone rang, and she thumbed the button on the wheel.

"We've got a work vehicle in a shed further back behind the Dunlop house," O'Neil said. "Everything scrubbed clean."

"Coming," she said. "Where are you?"

O'Neil was leaving Redfern. They arrived at the school at the same time. A Crime Scene sergeant led them into a paddock that sloped away from Ghost Gum in a series of fenced yards, dotted with lean-tos and outhouses and huts. Riley knew from Spratt that the school had run a small livestock program for country kids here, but it had been shut down several years ago. The area was in disrepair, separated from the Dunlop house by a windbreak of poplars and mulberry, and the gates and shacks and lockups were rusted.

They came to a bigger wooden shed within the maze of fences, its double doors flung open. Two forensic investigators in Tyvek were working inside. There was a concrete slab floor, a bare bulb on the ceiling, a succession of gardening tools propped along a wall—mattocks, shovels, pitchforks, picks, rakes. A hose was coiled and hung above a tap. In the middle of it all sat a green-and-yellow John Deere utility cart with a two-seater cab and a tray on the back—a souped-up golf buggy for farm work.

"You said scrubbed clean?" O'Neil said.

"Not like Gladesville." The sergeant pointed. "It's more haphazard. The slab and the vehicle have been hosed and washed—bleach and detergent. There was a small amount of brown organic matter squashed in the corner of the vehicle tray."

"You think it's a match with what was on the plastic wrapping the girl?" O'Neil said.

"We've sent it off," the sergeant said, "but yes. The samples look identical. We don't believe it's soil. We'll have results tomorrow."

"If it's not soil," Riley said, "then what is it?"

"We think dung."

"Dog?" O'Neil said.

"No, herbivore."

O'Neil circled the John Deere, and Riley went counterclockwise. The tray was big enough to transport a body. The key was in the ignition. "Was this place locked?" O'Neil said.

"No," the sergeant said. "But the doors were closed."

The John Deere was out of place, a well-maintained working vehicle in a disused shed. Riley looked along the wall of mattocks and rakes. Cobwebs and dust—they hadn't been touched in a long time—but gardening tools nonetheless. O'Neil walked down the row.

"Does it strike you as odd?" he said. "Gardening tools and a missing gardener?"

She didn't answer. Kevin Gary Lynch was starting to piss her off. There was no electronic trail, no bank cards, no registered vehicle.

"There's something else," the sergeant said. "Outside."

They followed him down the side of the shed. An orange wheelbarrow was propped against the wall.

"It's been washed too," the sergeant said. "Shoe and Tire have had a look. There are impressions from the wheel between here and the house. We think he used the barrow to get her here."

"What about John Deere tracks?" O'Neil said.

The sergeant nodded. "At the entrance to the shed. We're rechecking at the dump scene. It's more exposed—the ground's drier, and there's dust coverage."

Riley caught O'Neil's tension and concurred: it felt right. Marguerite Dunlop had been killed in her house and wheeled here in the barrow. It was easy and quiet. The killer had used the cover of the shed to wrap and wash everything and then put her in the John Deere to move her to the Hay Stand.

O'Neil sucked his lips.

"The cart looks out of place," Riley said.

"If it was here, ready, it goes to premeditation," O'Neil said. "Otherwise, he had to get it from elsewhere after he killed her. But then why dump her and bring it back and leave it here?"

She looked away, up toward the Dunlop house. There was another question, even more obvious: Who used the John Deere? Lynch? Spratt? The problem was who to ask. They had to keep the discovery tight— they couldn't have it getting out.

14

Bowman woke late, wondering if he was stalking Riley in her sleep the way she was creeping into his. It had been his crawling dream, rippling with rats like the delirium tremens. Swamp things dragging Chick under. And then there was Riley, watching from the trees. Beside her stood Sarah Green.

He sat up, bilious, naked, alone. He reached for his glass with a shaking hand and drank his lemon water. Citrus: good for the liver. He'd gone a bit hard last night.

New Year's Day. He felt the dead air of the house, nothing stirring. He needed a cat or a dog, something alive in the place. A flatmate, a partner, a wife, a child, a hamster on a wheel. He was more of a dog person—he could take a dog to the pub.

He bent for his sarong. He had a hangover that would kill a brown dog. He'd had a hamster as a child. Rodney. He hadn't had a flatmate since . . . Lodge Street in Glebe after university? No, Tooting Broadway in '99. That had worked out well, his journalism career in London. He'd got a job on Fleet Street—at the Pig and Olive, serving warm pints to chinless Oxbridge hacks. In a year of international "freelancing," he'd sold one story, to a wildlife magazine in Kampala, about the repopulation of bloats of hippos in Uganda after Idi Amin had shot them all out from his helicopter gunship. He'd spent months in Africa: Harare, Nairobi, Dar es Salaam.

Looking back, the hippopotamuses had been a high point. He'd leveraged the story into a copyboy job on *The National* . . . and it had been downhill ever since. The glamour rounds on the paper were federal politics or defense or national security—Bowman had been put on education, then real estate, and then shoveled onto the late shift.

And here he was at the start of another year, childless in his empty house. Never have children: his father's favorite line.

He came into the kitchen. He'd cleaned up before bed, as he always did—bottles in the bin, his glass washed on the sink. Last night, full of truth serum, he'd resolved to write the drone story today and not be dictated to by Riley. Now, in the acid light of morning, he put the coffee on and thought, *Maybe not.* He didn't have the footage, only the news that there was footage. But that was just his mind finding a loophole, the same way it justified another drink. The truth was that if he defied Riley, she would cut him off, and he'd be working on his own.

Sipping coffee, he pulled up the paper online. His story on Tom Green and Craig Spratt finding the body was leading the site. He realized he'd forgotten to read it to the Greens first and hoped he wouldn't need them again. Diamond had written a piece, and Bowman skimmed it: there was nothing new in it, no quotes from O'Neil. It was just a reheat, a holding story saying the investigation was continuing.

His phone rang on the bench. Alexander, calling him first thing on a Sunday morning, New Year's Day. The times, they were a-changin'.

"Good stuff with the kid," the editor said. "What've you got for today?"

If he mentioned the drone footage, Alexander would demand he write it straightaway. "Not sure," he said.

"Listen, there's a bit of shit flying," Alexander said. "I've had a couple of calls. From the old man."

Bowman turned his mug on the bench. "Fair dinkum?" It was company lore that the old man in London always backed his editors and never interfered with *The National*'s coverage.

"He's cagey," Alexander said, "like someone's got to him. It must be coming from the school . . . buggered if I know how. A teacher couldn't even breathe at this altitude."

Bowman's hangover shifted and slung a poison dart through his brain.

"Must be a parent with some clout," Alexander said. "I'll get Business to have a look."

"I could try and interview the headmaster. No one's spoken to him yet."

"Yeah, good. Feel him out about who's who in the old boys and the parent body, the heavy hitters. But be careful. If I'm getting calls from London, then Mahogany Row's hearing it too. We fuck up, they'll skin us alive."

Bowman showered and dressed and drove to the school. The police at the gate waved him through. Riley must have cleared his plates. He drove up past the headmaster's house and parked at the administration block. It was a short walk back to Preston's. The Nissan was the only vehicle in the car park, and the venetians on the admin buildings were down, the slats angled shut.

He remembered his visits here to the staff room as a child, drinking cold water from the refrigerated bubbler and looking at the sign above his father's desk: *Golding was right.* You learned that pretty quick at a place like Prince Albert in the seventies: *Lord of the Flies* was a teaching manual. *Never have children.* Bowman's life was the punch line to a dad joke. He'd shirked raising kids, shelved the biological imperative of existence.

His hangover was getting metaphysical. The idea of an interview with Philip Preston was not enticing.

It was humid, the whiff of rain coming. The CSIRO had invented a word for that smell: *petrichor.* Bowman remembered it from an education story he'd written. Before they invented Wi-Fi, the CSIRO had invented a word.

Studying his face in the reflected glass of the administration building door, he saw movement behind him and turned. A man was approaching, manila folder under one arm, clad in shades of elegant gray: tailored shorts, polo shirt, felt shoes with orange laces.

He crossed the forecourt and stopped to face Bowman. "Are you with the police?" he said.

Rotting fish. Petrichor. Bowman had never seen him, but he knew who he was.

"No," Bowman said. "You?"

With a tilt of the chin, Philip Preston deflected the question. "May I know who you are?"

"Journalist. With *The National*."

The headmaster's head lifted another degree. "Do the police know you're here?"

"They let me through."

"I see." Preston looked down his nose. There was a slow whine to the voice. North American or just pretentious? "You must be Adam Bowman."

The stench of history hung between them.

"Tell me," Preston said, "are there things the police tell you that you can't report?"

Bowman paused. "Not much, really."

"I see." Preston ran a thumb along the edge of his folder. "Everything seems to fit with BMK. The plastic, and so on. But one thing puzzles me." His lips formed a vile smile. "The creek. It's strange he didn't put her in the creek."

Bowman blinked as Preston splashed the creek in his face.

There was the sound of a vehicle. Bowman turned and watched a white Hilux pull up. Craig Spratt had an elbow out the driver's window. He killed the engine and looked at Preston. "The gardener that's done the bolt," Spratt said. "Cops want his file."

Preston held up the folder and gestured sharply. "We might discuss that inside."

Spratt got out, nodded at Bowman, and trailed Preston into the administration building.

Bowman dug for his phone and checked the news sites: nothing on a missing gardener. Could be good, but how to stand it up? Preston would be inside sewing Spratt's loose lips shut. Riley? The danger was she would just put the kibosh on another story. He dialed anyway.

"Yeah?" she answered.

"Just writing a piece on a missing gardener. Any comment?"

He could almost hear her mouthing an obscenity.

"My comment is we'd rather you didn't write that," she said.

"My maths isn't very good, but by my count, that's two stories I've found, and you won't let me write either."

"Listen," she said, "I gave you Spratt and the kid and the run of the school grounds. You play by the rules, you get everything, but you have to come along with us."

"What's with the gardener?"

"He's AWOL. We need to find him. We're releasing an image of him for the six o'clock news."

"Oh. Goody gumdrops. Thanks for everything."

"C'mon. We need his face all over western Sydney. That means TV and *The Mirror*. If we give it to you now, they'll get the shits and downplay it later."

Bowman knew she was right but saw some wiggle room. "Okay," he said. "I'm gonna write a story saying the cops are about to request help from the public in locating a gardener who's disappeared from Prince Albert. Police would like to interview the man in relation to the slaying of Marguerite Dunlop by the killer known as BMK at the school on Wednesday night. How's that grab you?"

"No name, no picture," Riley said. "Go your hardest."

Bowman hung up. He'd been walking as he bartered, and now he'd come into the main quadrangle. Buildings designed to flow with life stood deserted around him. He found a shaded corner, sat down, and bashed out the piece. *The National* put it straight online, and Bowman washed his hands of it: Diamond would cover the afternoon police briefing on the gardener.

He put his laptop in his bag and groaned to his feet. Everything was still, the abandoned campus heavy around him. He arched his back and rolled his neck and became conscious of something his body already knew: he was being watched. The limbering and stretching became a display, his spinal cord pinging as it processed surveillance. He scanned the rows of classrooms while pretending to dig for something in his bag. No movement. *Get moving.* He walked clear of the quad and started down the hill, away from his car, his skin prickling with atavistic unease, as if he were deep and alone in the Australian bush.

Somebody had got at the old man in London. That might mean pure power, or it might be more banal, a personal relationship with someone linked to the school. His aunt's cousin's daughter might have a kid here. Or it could be blackmail. Bowman still felt eyes on him. Spratt? Preston? He did a 360 as he walked, but there was no one he could see. Maybe it was a professional, a private investigator. Maybe Riley had a tail on him. Maybe it was BMK, returning to the scene. Maybe he had a paranoid hangover.

He was on a service lane between the back of the kitchens and the laundry, near where Riley had nabbed him on Friday morning. He recalled Scott Green, out for a stroll with his robotic gait, a mustachioed rooster. Where had he been going? Bowman followed the route Green had taken, down the drive and behind the maintenance building. He came into a clearing with a jumble of pipes and bricks and concrete blocks, a pile of builder's sand on a sheet of plastic, broken pallets, a rusted water heater stranded in the middle of it all. He walked to the edge of the site, where it ran into scrub, and turned. No one had followed him. Up to his left were the single-story flats where the workers lived.

Picking his way back through the debris and long grass, he stood over the pile of sand on its bed of black plastic at the base of the building. He heard Alexander's Queensland twang over the Bluetooth in the Nissan on Thursday: *He's used the black plastic again.*

A length of plasterboard was propped against the wall, and Bowman squatted and squinted into the gap. He sucked in air, stood, took out his phone.

"I think you'd better get out here," he said when Riley answered.

15

Riley was driving Patel and O'Neil to the morgue for a briefing with the forensic pathologist and Farquhar when Bowman called. She hit the siren, turned across three lanes of traffic, and headed back to the school. Bowman was waiting for them at the top of the drive to the maintenance block. He nodded at Patel and O'Neil. Riley didn't bother with introductions.

"Where is it?" she said.

Bowman led her into the clearing and over to the wall and pointed. She bent. The end of a large roll of black plastic was just visible, lying under a sheet of plasterboard.

"That'll do," she said. "Don't want to tread all over it. Did you touch anything?"

"No, I was careful."

They walked back to Patel and O'Neil. The detectives stood in a triangle and watched him closely, three pairs of eyes. "What brought you down here?" Riley said.

He wiped at his mouth. "I'm not really sure. After I wrote the story, I wanted to keep moving. I felt someone was watching me."

"Did you see anyone?" O'Neil said.

"No . . . Well, I'd talked to Preston and Craig Spratt." Bowman recounted his morning, before and after his first call to Riley.

"You think one of them followed you?" O'Neil said.

Bowman looked up the drive. "I don't know. I just felt someone watching, at the classrooms. I walked away, but I couldn't shake it. I found myself back here." He pointed to the curb where Riley had picked him up. "The other day I saw Scott Green walking behind the block."

"When was this?" O'Neil said.

"Friday morning."

"How long was he here?" O'Neil said.

"I don't know." Bowman looked at Riley. "I was going to follow him when I ran into you."

A muggy silence fell. Riley watched as two of the vehicles from the Crime Scene section at the John Deere shed pulled up. She walked across the road to the gutter and stood staring up at Lynch's block of flats. Patel followed her.

"I don't like it," Riley said.

Patel glanced back at Bowman, speaking with O'Neil. "Lynch?" she said. "Or the journalist?"

"Lynch," Riley said. "Why? You don't like the journalist?"

Patel shrugged. O'Neil went over to talk with the Crime Scene sergeant, leaving Bowman on his own. Riley had found him here two days ago, and now here he was again, stumbling over a roll of black plastic. "You don't think he's telling the truth?" she said.

"No, he probably is." Patel paused. "Or he's a good liar."

Riley looked again at the Flats. *Where was Lynch?*

"Let's go," O'Neil called. "We'll give Ray Martin here a lift to his car."

O'Neil took his seat in the rear of the Calais beside Bowman. Riley shook her head at Patel as they opened their doors: O'Neil was superstitious. If there were more than two people in a car, he liked to ride back right. No one spoke as Riley drove to the administration buildings and pulled up at Bowman's Nissan.

"That was good work," O'Neil said. "Thanks for the call."

"But—let me guess," Bowman said. "You'd prefer I didn't write the story?"

"Not yet. No plastic, no drones. Rose will talk to you later. Play the long game, and it's all yours."

Bowman climbed out, and Riley watched the reporter cross to his vehicle.

"Priya," O'Neil said. "What do you think?"

"Sir." Patel turned to face him as Riley reversed. "The John Deere among the gardening tools, the organic matter, and now a roll of black plastic on Lynch's doorstep. Everything seems to say gardener."

"Yeah," O'Neil said. "*Burke's* fucking *Backyard*."

Riley raised a two-finger salute at the uniforms in the patrol car at the gate. "You think it's too neat?"

O'Neil's phone rang. Riley turned right onto Pennant Hills Road as O'Neil listened and hung up.

"Pathologist's been called out to a double shooting at Bonnyrigg," he said. "She's briefed Farquhar on Marguerite. He'll walk us through it in a slideshow."

Riley nodded. "Lynch," she said. "You think someone's trying to frame him?"

No answer. In her rearview mirror, she could see O'Neil looking out the window. She merged off James Ruse Drive onto the M4, traffic heading to town from the Blue Mountains. She cut south for Lidcombe, into the valley of death—the coroner had moved from Glebe to the new complex abutting Rookwood Cemetery. The morgue and the necropolis . . . some planning bureaucrat had really thought things through. Riley was still getting used to it.

She drove in and parked in an emergency bay. New Year's Day, a Sunday—the place was on skeleton staff.

Farquhar met them at the main entrance, and they followed him down a white hallway to a conference room, where he brought up an image of Marguerite Dunlop's body on a screen. It was as the forensic pathologist had said at the scene—the girl had been hit over the temple with something smooth and heavy and died of a brain bleed. There were no defensive wounds, nothing under her fingernails. There had been no rape, and there was no semen in the vagina, anus, or mouth.

The psychiatrist held a baton, and his shoes squeaked on the vinyl as he moved closer to the screen to indicate the side of the girl's head. "Extradural bleeding around the brain." He pointed. "Not within the brain but on the surface, between the dura membrane and the inner part of the skull. There's a fracture in the temple location. The trauma has torn the meningeal artery."

"How long did she take to die?" O'Neil said.

"Hard to say, exactly. But minutes. She's hemorrhaging. The blood's got nowhere to go. It causes pressure. Her brain swells, and then it shifts from left to right. That's what killed her."

"What about the blood on her carpet?" O'Neil said.

Farquhar pointed to the laceration at the temple, where the blow had breached the skin.

"She lost some blood from the cut?" Riley said.

"Correct, but not much. The wound bleeds a little, oozes, and then stops. She lost around 150 milliliters."

"How much was in her hair?" O'Neil said.

"About sixty milliliters."

"And on the carpet?"

"You've seen it—the size of a fifty-cent piece. The pathologist says twenty mils."

"So we're missing seventy mils of blood?" O'Neil said.

"Correct."

"And you think it's on his clothes?"

"Not me, the pathologist. She says since it's not in Marguerite's room and not throughout the house as he moved her, then it's been absorbed into the killer's clothes—or into Marguerite's."

"If she was dressed when he killed her," Patel said.

"Correct," Farquhar said. "She was left in her underwear. If she was dressed, it means he stripped her and took what she was wearing. That might indicate the blood was on her clothes."

"What about on the murder weapon?" Riley said.

"Perhaps. They can't say exactly what it is, only that it's something smooth and heavy. Not jagged or rough or sharp. It hasn't punctured her."

"The pathologist said she had been dead twenty-four hours when we got to her," O'Neil said. "We're still saying killed Wednesday?"

Farquhar pressed a button on his laptop and brought a new picture onto the screen. He pointed with his baton. "This greenish discoloration on the abdomen—here, above the pubic line—is a clear sign of decomposition. In technical speak, she's on the turn. The deterioration is on her right side, which is where it usually begins, above the cecum. She was wrapped in plastic, and it was close to forty degrees at the site on Thursday. But the point is, the deterioration hadn't spread. See?"

He brought up another slide.

"Now, she was under a roof, so not in direct sun, but still, she can't have been there for too long, no more than twenty-four hours, or she'd be green across her abdomen, even up her chest. If you look here, you can see some marbling in the upper chest and arms. This dark streakiness of the blood vessels and veins—that's consistent with the time frame."

He paused and looked at Patel. "You're not Homicide, I recall?"

"No," Patel said. "Parramatta."

"Right," Farquhar said. "Well, rigor mortis. By the time they got to her at the scene, she had been through it. Or it was on the wane. The muscles stiffen in death, but that change was giving way to flaccidity. They can't be precise with the timing, but they can be quite accurate. Again, it points to twenty-four hours, maybe a little longer."

Patel nodded, and the doctor turned to O'Neil. "Did you want me to go through the lividity?"

O'Neil shook his head. "She was left lying on her front for several hours after she was killed and then moved? And found a day later?"

"Correct," Farquhar said. "Wednesday breakfast was the last thing she ate. She was killed between early morning and early afternoon and dumped sometime between Wednesday afternoon and late Thursday morning. Best guess is Wednesday night."

◆　◆　◆

O'Neil sat in the unmarked Prado in the back lane of the Redfern unit block and waited for the secure door of the underground garage. As he drove through, he checked in his mirrors that nothing slipped in under the steel barrier as it came back down. This ritual was recent, and it was due to more than superstition.

It was 2:00 p.m., and he needed a combat nap. He'd trained himself to go down into deep sleep for ten minutes and then come back up, no alarm needed. He parked, took the lift to the fourth floor, and walked the spartan corridor to the empty flat. The agent had described it as a one-bedder, but there was no getting around it—it was a one-roomer. The bed was up three steps on a "mezzanine," but it was still in the kitchen. The whole place was in the kitchen. He opened the fridge. Everything was in the kitchen, except food.

He put his laptop bag on the table, pulled the Glock from the back of his trousers, and loosened his tie. Rubbing the back of his neck, he moved down the room to the windows and looked out at the grimy balcony above Regent Street and the view across to the university. It had been interesting to clap eyes on Bowman. There was an expediency about the reporter that O'Neil hadn't liked. But then, O'Neil didn't like journalists on principle—smarmy fuckers, always seeking advantage and then needy for approval.

O'Neil went over the morning in his mind, knowing his subconscious would work while he slept. He was heading for the mezzanine when his phone buzzed. Riley.

"I emailed you a photo," she said. "Because of the resolution, you need to look on your laptop."

O'Neil cradled the phone to his ear and pulled out his MacBook. "What is it?"

She didn't answer, and he could hear the noise of the strike force room in the background. He put the phone on speaker beside the computer and opened the attachment. It took him a moment to orient himself. It was a crime-scene picture, an unfamiliar room shot from above. Pieces of women's underwear on the floor.

"You got it?" Riley said. "You'll need to zoom out a bit to see it."

O'Neil ran his fingers over the pad, and then his hand froze. He looked at the phone. "Where?"

"Tennyson Point, on the river. One bay up from Gladesville."

"When?"

"Two years ago."

"They investigated?"

"Sort of."

"How sort of?"

"Went through the motions, treated it as a burglary—except nothing was taken. They thought it was kids."

He winced. "They get forensics on it?"

"No."

O'Neil sat back and stared at the screen. The bras, underpants, slips, stockings—all different colors—had been arranged in the *t* shape with the undulating crossbar. Farquhar had said it would be out there, and now they'd found it: the forensic psychiatrist's fabled fetish burglary.

He got the address from Riley and hung up, put the laptop in his bag and the Glock in his trousers, and headed for the car. Fuck the nanna nap—he was feeling better already.

◆　◆　◆

The owners of the Tennyson Point house were in their midforties and still cleaning up after New Year's Eve when the knock on the door came. It took about twenty seconds for their post-party bleariness to curdle into horror. O'Neil withheld the words *Strike Force Satyr* as he made the introductions, but it didn't matter. The couple had seen him on the news—they knew what they were looking at.

They stood in their lounge room, jittery as they glanced from O'Neil to Riley and Farquhar and Patel. Riley nodded reassurance as O'Neil talked. They needed these people calm and contained. Word of this could not get out, not even to the couple's two boys, both in their late teens and out for the day.

"It's a routine visit," O'Neil said. "We're looking at all old break and enters in the neighborhood."

The couple weren't buying it. The Gladesville scenes were eight hundred meters downstream from their house. The woman, breathing shallow, looked aghast at her husband, who jerked his head toward the yard, toward the river.

"This is about that," the man said. "You think BMK came to our house first?"

The wife went green, about to hit the deck. Patel got her seated and gave her a warm smile.

Riley smiled too, at the husband. "It wasn't established at the time how the burglar got in—is that correct?" she said. "There was no sign of forced entry?"

"No," the man said, "except a key was missing."

It wasn't in the police report. "A key?" Riley said.

"We didn't notice it was gone for a few days. By then, the cops had moved on. Nothing was stolen, so they didn't seem interested. They were just kids in uniform." He looked from O'Neil to Farquhar, bearded and silent in the corner. "Not like you guys."

"What was the key to?" Riley said.

"A sliding door on the ground floor."

Riley's eyes met O'Neil's.

Patel and Farquhar stayed with the wife while the husband took Riley and O'Neil down. An open kitchen and family room on the bottom floor led out through glass doors to a patio and terraced garden and then a bay dotted with yachts, branched off the river. Absolute waterfront.

"Would you give us a moment?" O'Neil said to the man.

He nodded, and they left him and walked to the low sandstone seawall. The tide was lapping, almost in the yard. Riley checked the angles, how the shoreline was screened from the neighbors. A facsimile of the Gladesville houses. Total privacy.

"Living the dream," O'Neil said.

They walked back to the owner, and O'Neil indicated the sliding doors on the patio. "The key was to these?"

"That's right."

"The key lives in the lock when you're home?" O'Neil said. "You can secure the door from inside without the key?"

"That's why we didn't miss it at first. You can't get in from the outside, but when the door isn't deadlocked, you can open it from inside without the key. Louise and I both assumed the other had moved it, or one of the kids."

Riley looked over the bay. He'd come up the river and watched the family at home, seen them moving in and out of the house, the sliding doors open. He'd lifted the key and then come back when no one was home. Back then, the uniforms had canvassed the neighbors. No one had seen a thing. Satyr would canvass again.

"You change the locks?" O'Neil said.

"Yes."

"Good. Keep things deadlocked, and put the alarm on. You might want to install some sensor lights in the garden."

The man's brow glistened. "You think he's coming back."

"No," O'Neil said. "Even if it was him, I don't think he's coming back."

The man locked the sliding doors and took the key.

"How long have you been here?" O'Neil said.

"Nearly ten years."

"And you own, right? The house hasn't been on the market in the past, say, five years?"

"No."

"You had anyone housesit while you've been away?"

He frowned, thinking. "No."

In the entry hall, Patel and Farquhar and the wife joined them from the bedrooms.

"Look, I know it's been two years," O'Neil said, "but I'd like to send a couple of officers around tomorrow to ask some detailed questions."

"Oh God," the woman said.

"What type of questions?" the man said.

"Just about anyone who may have been at the house," O'Neil said. "Tradesmen, gardeners, anyone at all. If you could please have a think about that."

The wife dabbed at her eyes with a tissue. Riley handed the couple a card each. "If you think of anything, or if you need anything, give me a call."

"One other thing," O'Neil said. "And this is important." He looked from one to the other. "Please don't tell anyone we were here looking at this. Not the neighbors, not your colleagues or siblings or parents. Not even your boys. Not a word, okay?"

The woman gave a gasp, and her husband put his arm around her.

"It's all right," O'Neil said. "As I said, we're just going back over old cases. There will be detectives door-knocking the street over the next few days. They'll talk to your neighbors, but they won't mention you or the break-in. If the neighbors ask, say yes, you were door-knocked too. Everything is routine, so don't be alarmed."

The woman wiped her nose, nodding as her husband reached for the door.

"Thank you," Riley said. "We'll keep in touch."

The four of them walked up the drive to the vehicles. O'Neil called Annie Tran. "I want to see the whole of Satyr in the room in twenty minutes," he said. "Everyone."

16

Riley sipped Coke as she waited for the room to fill. She was concerned that the decision to inherit the Marguerite Dunlop case was splintering cohesion: the bulk of the strike force under Tran remained focused on Gladesville, but she and O'Neil and Patel were tied up looking for links at the school. The Tennyson Point find was a good opportunity for O'Neil to bring it all back together.

O'Neil cleared his throat. "All right, this is what we've got," he said. The team fell quiet, and he went through the break-in. He spoke slowly, repeated details, hammered points home on his fingers. On the blown-up map on the wall, he traced the route from the Chatfield and Sheridan scenes upriver to the Tennyson Point house. There were a couple of headlands in between.

"Dr. Farquhar predicted this," O'Neil said. "He'll talk to you about what we're looking at."

He half turned to Farquhar. The forensic psychiatrist picked up a felt-tip Texta pen from a desk and removed his glasses.

"I believe that what we're looking at," Farquhar said, "is the killer's backyard." He moved to the map and drew a thick red circle on it. "We combine Tennyson Point with Gladesville, what do we see?"

"A confined area," an analyst said. "On the north bank."

"Correct." Farquhar pointed at his circle. "He's hit in here three times—on the north bank. But"—he held up the Texta—"don't rule out the south side." He traced some more. "Rhodes, Mortlake, Breakfast Point, Cabarita, Abbotsford, Chiswick, Drummoyne. Even Birchgrove or Balmain, at a stretch."

Tran raised a hand. "That's a lot of ground."

Farquhar nodded. "To walk or drive, yes. But we think he's moving via the river." He pointed at Breakfast Point on the south bank. "From here, it's less than two hundred meters to the Tennyson Point house." The Texta trailed east to Abbotsford Point. "It's the same from here, less than two hundred meters to the Gladesville scenes."

"What about further north?" Riley said.

"Indeed." Farquhar tapped at the map, listing suburbs as he went: Ryde, Putney, Huntleys Cove, Hunters Hill, and then around to Woolwich and up the Lane Cove River. "Parcel it all up." He drew another, bigger circle and stepped back. "That's his comfort zone. He lives somewhere in there. He may even have grown up there."

"What about the school?" a Chatswood detective said. "Don't we think he just killed at the school?"

Farquhar looked to O'Neil.

"There are possible links to the school," O'Neil said, "but we're still working on them. We'll leave it out for the moment."

Glances were swapped around the room. Riley knew why: the school was a fault line. It made no sense to bring the murder of Marguerite Dunlop into the investigation while withholding North Parramatta from the geographic profile. She considered pressing O'Neil and the doctor, but it wasn't the place.

O'Neil motioned to Tran. "Annie, you'll oversee the Tennyson Point canvass," he said. "Questions?"

Tran nodded at the map. "We're saying he lives here," she said, "so the focus is residential?"

"Start with that," O'Neil said. "Be alive to details. Watch for lines of sight over the river, a large telescope in a bedroom, a kayak in a yard . . ."

Riley looked at Farquhar's red zone. The psychiatrist saw a home base, but Riley couldn't shake it: she still saw a poacher, and she knew O'Neil saw it that way too. The river was his highway, and Gladesville was a truck stop.

If the focus of the canvass was residential, they might miss something. She stood up, and O'Neil gave her the floor.

"Remember," she said, "he might be a commuter. Always think river traffic. With the Tennyson Point couple and the canvass of the neighbors—I know it's two years ago, but do they recall anyone coming in close and hanging around?"

"Such as?" an analyst said.

"Canoes, paddleboards, water taxis, fishermen, jetty maintenance, waterways construction . . ." She stopped. It was another fault line, and she wanted O'Neil to say it.

"Maritime," O'Neil said. "Water Police."

Heads came up, and more glances went around the room.

"Maybe he's using a dinghy," Tran said. "A tender off a bigger boat."

"Go on," O'Neil said.

"The Gladesville attacks were at night," Tran said. "He could be moored up in a bay on a yacht. He launches the dinghy and comes in after dark. He'd be comfy, no passersby, all the time in the world. He could bring his tool kit."

"You've looked at boat owners," Farquhar said.

"Look again," O'Neil said. "This is good work on the break-in—we don't want to waste it."

The briefing broke up. Riley stood with O'Neil and Farquhar. Patel came over. "What was that?" she said.

"Mm?" O'Neil said.

"Water Police?" Patel said.

Analysts and detectives were settling at their desks. "Let's take a seat," O'Neil said. They moved to the round table at the back of the room, and Riley checked over her shoulder. All clear. Patel was taut, trying to read the vibe.

"Gladesville's hypercareful with the scene," O'Neil said. "Very DNA aware."

"And?" Patel said.

"There's a line of thought that he might be trained in forensic investigation," O'Neil said. "It's not in the mainstream of inquiries, but we need to consider it. He *might* be police."

Her eyes were wide and very white. "Jesus."

"Yeah," O'Neil said.

"He leaves nothing behind?" Patel said.

"That's part of it," O'Neil said. "He knows to change gloves."

"He's probably triple-gloved, booties, gown, mask, hairnet," Riley said. "And he's carrying ammonia and bleach. And plenty of wet wipes."

"That's what's happening in practice," Farquhar said. "There's some theory behind the possibility as well."

"Theory?" Patel said.

"Studies show serial offenders are drawn to authority, fascinated by it," Farquhar said. "They might aim high, try to become a police officer, and if they fail, they take the next rung down that allows them to exert some control. A parking inspector, say . . . or president of the church council."

"Or a headmaster," O'Neil said.

Or a skipper on a charter boat. Riley chewed her pen.

"The Americans just netted a big one," Farquhar said. "He'd escalated over years. Prowler, ransacker, fetish burglar, rapist, killer. He'd worked as a police officer until he was fired for shoplifting."

Patel scratched her head with both hands.

"Back on the DNA, or the lack of it . . . the crime-scene sophistication," Farquhar said. "That could point to specialist police training, but it could point to a lot of other places as well. He could be in a lab—industry, university, the military. He might just be reading the internet or watching TV. There are textbooks. Forensic investigation is hardly a state secret."

"But he's smart," Patel said.

"Correct," Farquhar said. "And he's organized. And we have to consider police. And that's tricky."

Riley rubbed her eye. *Tricky* was a nice way of putting it.

O'Neil uncrossed his arms to wave toward the rest of the room. "If we're going to catch Gladesville, we need all our resources. Forensics, the labs, the water rats, the techs, the uniforms, the analysts, PolAir, Highway Patrol." He stopped and stabbed a finger on the table. "If it got out that Satyr was looking internally, it would be seen as betrayal. Morale would die. We'd kill the goodwill. That's not theory—that's a fact."

"We could start by looking at any officers through the Family Court or with domestic violence orders," Patel said.

O'Neil sat back. "Slippery slope."

"The integrity commission would know," Riley said.

"Yeah. But they won't give it to us," O'Neil said.

"But Water Police?" Riley said. "We could start with who has access to boats in Sydney. Check the logs against the nights in November and the date for Tennyson Point."

"Nope." O'Neil stood. "Too risky. Not yet."

A TV in the strike force room was showing O'Neil fronting a press conference outside the Gladesville police station. He released the name and an image of the missing gardener, Kevin Gary Lynch, and appealed for the public's assistance in finding him.

Riley turned the volume down as an analyst handed her a briefing note. Bowman's car had raised no red flags around the school on Wednesday or at Gladesville on the relevant dates in November. She called her contact in police media: nothing had come out in the press on a roll of black plastic being found at the school, or on the drone footage or rape categorization or the marking of the victims. Bowman was toeing the line.

Her tongue probed her ulcer. She packed up for the day and grabbed her keys. In the car park, she texted Bowman and arranged to meet for a beer at the Commercial, near his house. When she pulled up, he was waiting for her outside the pub, sitting on an empty keg. They shook hands, and she smelled beer on him. She followed him in, past a clutch of five florid locals drinking off the night before.

"Adam," one of the men yelled.

"And Eve," said another.

Coarse laughter followed as she and Bowman went to a booth out back.

"Friends of yours?" she said, sliding in.

"The table of knowledge," he said. "The usual?"

She nodded and scrolled through her phone until he returned with the beers. "So I've been thinking," he said.

"Uh-oh."

"The gardener. Doesn't add up."

"You did say your maths wasn't good."

"He's either nothing or you think BMK lives at the school."

"Why shouldn't he live at the school?"

"He could. But if he does, wouldn't it be weird that he's killed there?"

She sipped. It was all very neat around Lynch. "For this guy, weird is normal."

"Yeah, but is he stupid? Killing at the school—he's shitting in his own nest."

"Mm."

"So?"

Had the idea that Gladesville didn't kill Marguerite occurred to him? She glanced at him while he gulped. Stupid? No. Maybe he knew but wouldn't say.

"Lynch has bolted," she said. "It's not a good look."

"Do you know much about him?"

"I know he likes a drink."

He put his glass down. "And he lives on-site?"

"He lives in the Flats," she said.

No microexpression. No surprise.

"You know where I mean?" she said.

"Yeah." He held her eye. "Where we were today."

Patel was right. If he was a liar, he was a natural. Two of the drunks from the main bar came and slid into the booth, reeking and plastered. "So, ya gonna introduce us?" one of them said.

Bowman pushed his glass away. "We were just leaving," he said. He jerked his head and edged out the other side of the booth. They walked through the bar, and he held the door for her.

"Sorry about that." He was awkward on the pavement. "They'll have been going all day. We'd never have gotten rid of them."

"No worries." She felt for her keys. She needed a pad thai and a bottle of white on the couch.

He took a couple of steps down the hill. "You hungry?"

"Nah. I better get moving."

"Come on." He tossed his head again. "My place is here. One beer."

She imagined her empty flat. He was waiting, not quite looking at her. She didn't want to get stuck for hours. "One beer," she said.

They walked twenty meters down the road and left onto a narrow lane with old sandstone buildings on either side. "You couldn't get a horse and cart down here," she said.

"The first wooden house in Balmain was right there. Built in 1840. It used to be dockworkers, timber yards, brothels. Now it's people who put up signs like that." He pointed to a placard in a window: CLIMATE ACTION NOW. "The Water Police are at the end of the lane."

Grog curdled in her stomach. Coincidence made her wary. He couldn't possibly know of the conversation in the strike force room. Bowman stopped in front of a blistered little clapboard and took out his keys.

He held the door. She went into a living room with a sofa and an armchair, a low table and a television. He dropped his bag against a wall.

"Nice," she said. Well, nicer than Lynch's flat.

"Take a seat." He disappeared down a hall.

The place was small—four or five rooms, she'd guess. There was art on the walls—actual framed painted pictures, pretentious blobs of color, a big yellow thing that mimicked road signs . . . someone had never done a shift on Highway Patrol. The room was ordered, spotless. A bookshelf ran down one wall, built to fit, not from Ikea. Hundreds of books. She looked at spines and recognized nothing, which didn't mean much . . . no *Green Eggs and Ham*.

He came down the hall and handed her a beer.

"Thanks," she said. "My mother would say you keep a tidy home."

"OCD. Often accompanies alcoholism. Cheers."

She swigged and nodded at the shelf. "Have you written a book?"

"No. But I play ball, you guys give me everything . . . There'd be a book in that."

She felt her disdain. He was in it for himself—it was all about the story.

"Sure you're not hungry?" he said. "I can make some pasta."

She screwed up her nose. "I'm fine." She could no longer smell beer on him because it was now also on herself. He could have had a beer at home before he left, but she didn't think so. She thought Bowman had been in the pub before she'd arrived. Had he set up the interruption with the drunks, hoping to get her into his house?

"Who are you looking for anyway?" he said. "White, male, loser?" He sat in the armchair and gestured at the sofa.

Rearranging her Glock on her hip, she propped herself up straight on the edge of the lounge. "We don't profile anymore."

"Why not?"

"It's too blunt, and everyone's gone PC. We're in the age of terror, and terrorism profiles always say the same thing: look for an Arab with a beard."

"They've ditched it?"

"Pretty much," she said. "Actually, what they say is, we've got DNA now, so who needs profiling?" Except that they didn't have DNA now, and they were profiling. He didn't need to know that.

"What would they say about BMK if they were profiling?" he said.

She shifted on the lounge. Journalists were dilettantes—no skin in the game. They didn't stand in the slaughter of the kill rooms. Riley had learned to file the images away.

"They'd say he could be functioning in society—he might be in a relationship," she said. "Or that he lives at home with Mummy, or on his fucking yacht."

He studied her and segued. "How'd you become a cop?"

The beer tasted metallic in her mouth. "Started uni, didn't like it."

"What'd you study?"

"Occupational therapy. Speech pathology." She worked at peeling the bottle label. "Mum was a nurse."

"Where'd you grow up?"

"On a farm, in the Hunter. Then Campbelltown."

Bowman asked more questions, and she answered. She had been going to join the army but settled on the cops. Nine months at the academy, and she had a career. And a motorbike. And a gun.

She looked at the bookshelf. "You read all them?"

"They're objects, designed to impress . . ."

"Yeah?" She'd prefer a big V-8 in the garage. Or even if he had a garage.

"Would you say there's something underlying from your upbringing?" he said. "A sense that you want to serve, to give back?"

What was this: Farquhar's couch? No, because his motivation was selfish: he was thinking of his book, how'd he fill her out and write her up. She didn't want to talk about it, how she had no one because she didn't want to head home and talk about her day. No kids. She'd seen too many dead children. Maisie Hall, three years old, blue and broken in her bed—because Riley hadn't listened to her gut.

She drained her stubby. Why did she do it? For the victim. Because no one else was going to take responsibility.

"Another beer?" he said.

She put the bottle on the table. She needed to eat. "Best be going. Thanks." She rose and felt the weight of her new resolution: justice for Marguerite. Bowman walked her to the door.

17

They got Kevin Gary Lynch just before dawn. He was holed up in a shithole motel off the M7 in Mount Druitt. The night woman at the front desk saw his face on the late news and phoned it in. He came quietly when the Tactical Operations Group rammed through the door.

He was taken to Parramatta and put in an interview room at the station on Marsden Street. Farquhar and Patel watched through the glass as O'Neil and Riley sat across from him. He was compact, chipped and wiry, prison ink behind an ear and at the top of a thumb. Calloused hands, mean mouth, brown teeth. Riley announced the time and date for the tape: 9:00 a.m., Monday, January 2.

"You've what, been on gardening leave?" O'Neil said. "Looking at the flower shows in Rooty Hill?"

Lynch didn't answer.

"Maybe a hair of the dog's in order?" O'Neil said. "Detective Riley here's been through your pad, thought you had Boris Yeltsin staying over."

Lynch swallowed. He smelled like a bushpig.

"Want to tell us why you bolted?" Riley said.

His eyes were on a spot on the wall.

"Well, if that's too complicated, why don't we back up a bit?" O'Neil said. "Maybe tell us what you were doing on Wednesday."

"Workin'," Lynch said.

"Where?" Riley said.

"All round top of the grounds. Watering."

"Watering." O'Neil gave a nod. "Makes sense. It's been a bit dry. Anybody see you?"

Lynch kept his eyes on the wall. "I seen Spratt, and he seen me."

"What about Marguerite Dunlop?" O'Neil said. "You see her?"

"I've never seen her."

"But you know who she is," Riley said.

"Do now."

"What does that mean?" O'Neil said.

"I read it." He looked at O'Neil. "About what happened."

"Was that in Friday's paper?" Riley said.

"Saturday. I seen Friday's paper—her name weren't in it."

"Fair enough," Riley said. "You didn't know of her before you read her name in the paper on Saturday?"

"No."

"Do you know her parents?" Riley said. "Her father?"

He shook his head.

"Never seen them?" O'Neil said. "Even with everyone living together out there, one big happy family?"

"There's lots of people there. I keep to meself."

O'Neil slid a sheet of paper across the table, facedown. "Have a look at that. Maybe it'll jog your memory."

Lynch turned it over. It was a police photo, taken at the scene, showing Marguerite Dunlop's face, the black plastic cut away.

"Ring a bell?" O'Neil said.

Lynch studied the image, turned it back over, and pushed it away.

"No?" O'Neil said. "Try this one." He slid a second photo across the desk, facedown.

Lynch flipped it over, took a long glance, and pushed it away.

"Recognize anything?" O'Neil said.

Lynch sat looking at him.

"That second picture—know where it was taken?"

"No."

"Have a guess."

"I got no idea. The room where she was killed?"

"And where would that room be?" O'Neil said.

There was resentment now. "I dunno. How would I know?"

"Mr. Lynch," Riley said, "as you can see, as you know, we have a young girl murdered. We've asked that everyone on the school grounds come to us and give a statement, have a DNA swab, and give their fingerprints. Why did you not come forward? Why run?"

"I didn't run." He looked at the table.

"Why did you leave?" O'Neil said.

"I needed time." Lynch took a breath. "To think."

"Bit of me time?" O'Neil said. "Do some yoga?"

"What did you need to think about?" Riley said.

"I've got things in me past. I done me time."

"What sort of things?" Riley said.

Lynch looked away. "Rape," he said. "In Dublin."

In the corridor, O'Neil closed the door on Lynch and went to the adjacent room. Riley put coins in a vending machine, pressed for a Coke, and followed.

"The rape, of course, is interesting," Farquhar was saying. "But everything else . . . it's not lining up."

"Why not?" O'Neil said.

"Marguerite Dunlop wasn't a sex crime," Farquhar said. "She wasn't raped."

Riley leaned on the wall. O'Neil looked at her and then Patel. "Anyone?" he said.

"He's agreed to come to the station—he hasn't asked for a lawyer," Riley said. "And his record gives him a reason to go walkabout." She popped open the can.

"Breakfast?" O'Neil said.

"If he'd given his DNA and prints, he knows we would've cross-checked with Dublin." Riley sipped. "He was thinking his job's gone—schools don't tend to employ rapists. He was worrying he'd be deported."

"Priya?" O'Neil said.

"There were no discrepancies," Patel said. "The photo you showed of the scene at the Chatfield house—he seemed to have no idea it had nothing to do with Marguerite."

"He ticks some boxes," Farquhar said. "The loner, the rape, the excess drinking. But why kill Marguerite? Where's the motive?"

O'Neil was looking through the glass at the gardener.

"Passion, grog, or money?" Riley said.

The psychiatrist looked doleful. "I see," he said. "Let's run with those." He held up a thumb. "Passion. The irreproachable virgin daughter of upright Anglicans is having an affair with a drunken fifty-two-year-old rapist gardener? She wants to call it off, and he kills her? Or, said Irishman has spied her around the place and developed a fascination that's led to obsession. She's rebuffed him, and he's killed her?"

O'Neil shrugged. "He hits on her—why not?"

"It's possible," Farquhar said. "But unlikely."

"Why unlikely?" Patel said.

"If he'd gone to the trouble, you'd expect sexual assault in those scenarios."

"I think we can discount booze," Riley said. "Lynch is a drinker, undoubtedly. But the scene doesn't show a drunken rampage. It's clean, controlled."

"Agreed," O'Neil said.

"That leaves money," Farquhar said. "Blackmail? Robbery?"

"Kidnap?" Patel said. "It goes wrong? We're seeing more of that at Parramatta."

Farquhar's head wobbled. "Again, it's possible . . ."

"Enough," O'Neil said, looking at his watch and then at Riley. "Let's go."

She followed him back into the interview room and put the can on the table. Lynch was nursing a polystyrene cup. He needed a shower.

"Haven't you got to arrest me or let me go?" he said.

"We'll get to that," O'Neil said.

He shook his head. "You think I'm this BMK? Out on a spree?"

"Funny you should mention it," O'Neil said. "There were some dates I wanted to ask you about. November 30. Where were you?"

Lynch put the cup on the table. "Went to Dubbo in November. Seen me cousin."

"What's your cousin's name?" O'Neil said.

"Aileen."

"That narrows it down," O'Neil said. "C'mon. Aileen what?"

"Aileen Kelly."

"Who'd have thought it. Address?"

Lynch gave an address. "I took her kids to the zoo." He did some counting on his fingers. "Might be that was the thirtieth."

"Mr. Lynch," Riley said, "are you aware of how Marguerite Dunlop's body was found? What she was wrapped in?"

He sipped his water.

"Can you tell me?" Riley said.

"I read they found her over at the Hay Stand. They said wrapped in plastic."

"Do you know what color plastic?" Riley said.

"Black, it said in the paper." Lynch looked at O'Neil. "And in that picture you showed."

"Yes," Riley said. "Builders' film. Do you know if there is any build-ers' plastic on the school property, Mr. Lynch?"

He met her eye. "Yeah."

"Can you tell me where the plastic is, Mr. Lynch?"

"Down behind maintenance."

O'Neil slid another picture across the table, facing the right way up. "Would that be it there?"

Lynch picked it up and studied the roll lying under its plasterboard tepee. "Looks about right. But that piece of Gyprock doesn't go there. I know where it was stored. Someone moved it."

"Moved the Gyprock or the plastic?" Riley said.

"The Gyprock."

"Speaking of moving things," O'Neil said, "how do you do that at the school? What vehicles do you use?"

"Toyota."

"You don't use anything else?"

"Don't need anything else, 'cept me wheelbarrow."

"What about other workers?" O'Neil said. "What do they use?"

"Utes, tractors, Gators."

Riley pictured the green-and-yellow John Deere cart in the shed, the word GATOR stenciled on its back and sides.

"Who uses the Gators?" O'Neil said.

"The grounds staff, on the ovals." Lynch shrugged. "Anyone who needs 'em."

"How many Gators are there?" O'Neil said.

"Couple. Three, four."

"Anyone can use them?" Riley said. "Even the teachers?"

"Yeah. I seen teachers on 'em."

"Which teachers?" Riley said.

"Dunno their names."

"Does Craig Spratt use them?" Riley said.

"Probably."

"What about Dr. Preston?" Riley said. "The headmaster?"

"Dunno." Lynch shrugged again. "Doubt it."

123

O'Neil rubbed his jaw. "What color is your wheelbarrow?"

Lynch's head eased back in surprise. "Black," he said.

◆ ◆ ◆

The gardener's November alibi checked out. The CCTV at Dubbo Zoo showed him there, and Aileen Kelly had photos of his visit on her phone. He hadn't been in Sydney when Jill Sheridan was murdered, which meant he hadn't killed Lena Chatfield either, and there was no evidence linking him to Marguerite Dunlop. They let him go.

At the round table in the strike force room, it was turning into one of those mornings. They'd drawn a blank with the fingerprints on the bench in the Dunlop house—they weren't Scott Green's or Philip Preston's or Craig Spratt's, nor did they belong to Kevin Lynch or Sarah Green or Jenny Spratt or the bursar, Graham Murray.

Riley felt the drift, the dying of momentum. O'Neil looked like he was about to punch a wall. He'd pinned hopes on Lynch, maybe more than she'd realized. Had he taken it upstairs, told the super they were about to make a move?

She didn't want to know.

Where to now? They were lost and groping—passive policing, concrete thinking . . . passion, grog, or money.

"Let's go back a step," she said, "to Bowman finding the plastic."

O'Neil tugged to loosen his tie. "Yeah?"

"On two separate days, Bowman's lurking near the maintenance shed. The first time, I nearly run him over. The second time, he calls *us* in. Why's he down there?"

"He said he saw Scott Green there, walking, on the Friday morning," O'Neil said.

"That's something he saw," Riley said. "But why was he *there*? He's never explained it."

"That Sunday, he said he felt he was being followed," Patel said.

"That's a feeling," Riley said. "But it's not an explanation. And remember, both times he's wandering around in the middle of the school, and the CCTV never picks him up."

"What was Scott Green doing behind the maintenance block that Friday?" O'Neil said. "He's not on the CCTV either."

"Never assume," Riley said.

"Assume what?"

"That Bowman even saw him."

"Jesus." O'Neil made a face. "What's got your goat? There's nothing putting Bowman at the school on Wednesday, or anywhere near Gladesville on the dates."

"We've run his plates," Riley said. "But not his phone."

O'Neil sat forward, elbows on the table. "We wasted time on Lynch. We can't afford to pursue Bowman down a blind alley too."

Next to Riley, Farquhar crossed his legs but didn't speak.

"Let's eliminate the journo from the Dunlop house," O'Neil said. "Get his prints."

Riley held his gaze. It was good—it was *something*. They were moving again.

"All right," O'Neil said. "Still with Bowman: I gave him the Lynch story. *The National* will put it online ASAP."

"Did you give him one of the holdbacks?" Riley said.

"Not yet, but let's face it, we're bogged. I reckon we do one tomorrow."

"Which one?" she said.

"The drone footage, but we target it. We use Bowman. When it drops, we want eyes on Spratt and Preston."

"What about Green?" Patel said.

"Green gave us the drone footage, via Tom," O'Neil said. "It's got no shock value."

Patel's mouth tightened at her error. O'Neil pulled his chair in under the table and looked at her. "We're going to release strategic information through the media. Bowman seems malleable, so we'll stick with him for now. But it's sensitive: he's not sworn, and as you've heard"—he gestured toward Riley—"Rose has some doubts."

"Yes," Patel said.

"Preston has never seen you," O'Neil said. "Is that correct?"

"I think so . . . yes. I've never seen him."

"Rose and I will go and see Spratt in the morning," O'Neil said. "At the same time, I want to send Bowman into Preston's house to do an interview. I want you to go in with him."

Patel's eyebrows went up. "How will that work?"

"Let's figure it out," O'Neil said.

They went through it around the table. They'd give Bowman the drone story but ask *The National* to hold it until midday tomorrow. They would use Preston's desire to be in the press: the journalist would set up an interview with the headmaster for 11:30 in the morning. They'd get a warrant for Patel to go in as Bowman's videographer and film the whole thing. They'd tell Preston the angle was how the school community was faring, what the headmaster thought about the situation, his condolences for the Dunlops. Preston wouldn't be able to resist. While they were in there, *The National* would publish the drone story online, and Bowman would put it in front of Preston while Patel filmed his reaction.

"In the interview, I want Preston on the back foot," O'Neil said, and looked at Farquhar. "Any ideas?"

"The principals at these big schools—they're more like CEOs nowadays," Farquhar said. "Preston's got a bit of that corporate sheen that he'll hide behind."

"He thinks he's a cool cat," Riley said.

"There's a lot of affectation," Farquhar said. "He's modeling himself on the bunyip aristocracy he deals with in the parent body. Trouble is, he's not a natural. He didn't grow up in that milieu. He's not from thirty thousand acres out back of Armidale."

"I ran a check," Riley said. "He was born in suburban Ottawa to a Canadian father and an Australian mother."

"Midnight Cowboy," O'Neil said.

"Exactly," Farquhar said, "but he thinks he's the Sundance Kid. And as you say, he's a media tart. Most normal, intelligent people wouldn't go near the press in a pink fit. But not our Dr. Preston—he can't get enough of it."

"What does that tell you?" Patel said.

"Lord, how long have you got? He's not as smart as he thinks he is, and it underlines his narcissism."

"His file says charming?" Patel said.

"Yes, in an unctuous way. But he'd lash out if cornered. Now, the point is, you'll be in the driving seat tomorrow. Philip Preston will look at you and the reporter and see the masthead. This isn't the school gazette. Preston will regard the interview as himself addressing the nation. He'll want to talk."

"Watch for a chance to duck out for a minute while Bowman keeps him busy," O'Neil said. "There must be an internal door to the garage. Stretch the warrant. See if you can get a peek in there. What's he got stowed?"

18

Bowman was in his bathroom drinking beer. It was 4:00 p.m. and he'd filed the Lynch story. He'd read in a magazine years ago that drinking in the shower was a sure sign of alcoholism. He didn't drink in the shower anymore. He put his stubby down to hop back under the shower to wash off his shaving cream. Drinking between showers was a bit slippery, he knew.

After toweling dry, he applied moisturizer to his face—a dermatology student he'd roomed with in Glebe had instilled in him this one good habit—and rolled on deodorant. A Somac for reflux, washed down with beer. Novasone to stubborn eczema in his elbow crooks. An eye drop in each eye. He blamed the state of his eyes on alcohol—cataracts at forty, a detached retina. He blamed the state of *himself* on alcohol. He didn't smoke, he didn't burn herb—no drugs—he didn't eat shit. But he drank. Sitting at home alone in his clapboard, Bowman could drink a bottle of wine while wondering what to drink that night. Ten, twelve, fifteen drinks a day, every day—that was his habit. He had to be disciplined—any more, and he'd risk a headache. Like the night before last, when New Year's Eve had got away from him.

His phone rang in the bedroom, and he hobbled through in his towel. Riley.

"I'm looking at your Lynch story," she said.

"The boss is happy. Tell O'Neil thanks."

"I will. I'm with him now . . . We wanted to set up a couple of things for tomorrow. You can write that piece on the drone footage."

Bowman placed his beer on the bedside table. "Nice."

"We need a bit of control on the timing. Think you could put it online at midday?"

"Why's that?"

"We want to be looking at a couple of people when they read it."

"Who?"

He felt her hesitate.

"They're nothing," she said. "They're like Lynch. We have to eliminate them."

"Come on. Who?"

She briefed him on the plan for the morning. "Don't read anything into it," she said. "Names come up, we cross them off."

"But Spratt and Preston?" he said. "Haven't they got alibis?"

"Yeah."

Liar. He was getting to know her tones. "Spratt said he saw Preston on Wednesday. I quoted him in the paper. He saw Preston in his car. They had a chat."

There was silence down the line, deep and still. "Got to go," she said and hung up.

Bowman stood in his towel and looked at his phone.

◆　◆　◆

At her desk, Riley sat frozen.

"What?" O'Neil said.

She put her phone down and opened files on her laptop. "We might have something." She scrolled. "Here. This is Spratt from his statement: *Jenny worked on Monday for the Sydney to Hobart. I saw Lynch, told him his jobs for the week. On Tuesday I saw Graham Murray over at admin. Jenny was at work in the day and home for the evening. On Wednesday Jen was off. I had a doctor's appointment. I saw Philip Preston, the headmaster. I was driving. Him too. In his car over here toward our place, near the tennis courts. I was running late, but we had a quick word. Round two p.m."*

"The statements don't match?" O'Neil said.

"The CCTV clocks Spratt in four spots on that drive at two p.m.," Riley said. "That matches up with his statement."

"Spratt says he sees Preston driving," O'Neil said. "We see Spratt on the CCTV . . ."

"But?" Riley said.

"But we never see Preston." O'Neil bent to her screen. "Preston never mentions seeing Spratt?"

Riley pulled up the headmaster's statement. "Wednesday, remember—he says he's at home, working. No mention of a drive, no mention of a chat with Spratt. If he drove to where Spratt says he saw him, then we'd see it on the CCTV."

"Unless he skirted the cameras," O'Neil said. "Either way, someone's telling porkies."

"Shall we pay a visit?"

"Let's wait. See how they react to the drone footage. If either of them is looking sick, we can hit them with this as well."

She sat back as he straightened, looking at his phone. She waited while he read. He clicked his tongue.

"What?" she said.

"The briefing note from Crime Scene just lobbed," he said. "The house, the shed, the plastic, the John Deere."

"And?" she said.

"I thought I'd seen it all, but Jesus"—he shook his head—"there's some weird shit coming back from the lab."

◆ ◆ ◆

Riley sat with Patel and Farquhar at a rectangular conference table in the middle of the Gladesville room. Across from them sat Annie Tran and her top five officers, all detective constables, all male, all Homicide. There were three analysts as well. In all, it was about half the strike force.

"First," O'Neil said, "they've confirmed the blood on the bedroom carpet is Marguerite's and that the killer tried to clean it up."

"With what?" Tran said.

"Bleach and detergent," O'Neil said. "No wet wipes and no ammonia."

"Still," Riley said, "he's cleaning."

"Agreed," O'Neil said. "But there's no getting around it—it lacks sophistication. If this is our boy, it's another change in his MO."

His eyes went around the table. "Now, the plastic," he said. "Listen carefully, and don't be afraid to ask questions."

Crime Scene had got a fracture-fit match of the plastic from the body with the roll at the maintenance block. It was forensic evidence that would stand up in court: the work under the microscope proved that the plastic wrapped around Marguerite's body had been cut from the roll Bowman had found.

"Cut with what?" Tran said.

"A sharp blade—not serrated and not scissors," O'Neil said.

"So again, different from Gladesville," Tran said.

"Correct," O'Neil said.

"Chemical analysis?" Tran said.

O'Neil put a finger up and looked at Patel. "There's another test we're waiting on, from an outside lab. The chemical markers on the plastic from the two Gladesville scenes are identical—they both came from the same roll. We've sent the plastic used to wrap Marguerite out for the same analysis, but the results are days away. Okay?"

"Sir," Patel said.

"Good." He cricked his neck. "So we're looking at a different blade in Gladesville, and very possibly a different roll. Got it?"

Nods all around.

"Right," he said. "Now, let's look at how we think she was moved."

The Crime Scene briefing said the killer had likely carried the body from the bedroom and out of the house, then used the orange wheelbarrow to get her to the shed where the John Deere had been found, a distance of several hundred meters. Assuming the murder wasn't premeditated, the killer then needed to get the plastic, a three-kilometer round trip to the maintenance block that didn't show up on the CCTV. In the shed, the killer had washed the plastic and the body, minus the hair, and washed the whole package again after wrapping her.

Riley fiddled with her pen. There'd been a lot of washing. She made a note: *John Deere.* The questions from Sunday had not been answered. Did he have it waiting in the shed, or did he have to go and get it? And why not leave it somewhere neutral—why return it to the shed? She looked up. "Just on the washing," she said. "He's DNA aware, showing some knowledge of forensic investigation. Do we think Spratt's smart enough?"

O'Neil's bald head caught the light. "I think Spratt's capable. He's rough, but he's neat and organized."

"I agree," Farquhar said. "Spratt's competent—cunning, even. He's more equipped for this than Preston, I would think."

She looked back at her pad. Competent, cunning, capable. And lots of keys. But the key to the John Deere was in the ignition. And the shed doors were closed, not locked.

"Now," O'Neil said, "the victim's blood. There were sixty mils, dried, in her hair. If he'd washed it, there'd have been blood running on surfaces, and we'd have picked it up under the lights. But he doesn't make that mistake. He doesn't try to wash it out. He doesn't even touch it. He washes everything, but not the hair and not the wound."

"They think he's at ease?" Tran said.

"They think he was composed, that he gloved up and probably put on booties too—although maybe just plastic shopping bags around his shoes."

There were unknown fingerprints throughout the house, presumably from friends and guests, and, of course, the prints and DNA of the Dunlop family. The only other match they had was Craig Spratt, probably from the work he'd done on the locks. There was no trace of Jenny Spratt, Preston, the Greens, Lynch, or Graham Murray.

"But there is evidence of wiping," O'Neil said, "which is interesting. It's likely the killer is retracing his steps to mop up what he's touched. Priya, it goes to what you said."

"He doesn't have gloves on when he enters," Patel said. "He's there to snoop. Things get out of hand. That's when he gloves up."

"All right," O'Neil said. "This is where it gets a bit strange. The brown substance found on the plastic around Marguerite and in the tray of the John Deere has been identified as sheep manure."

"Fertilizer?" Riley said.

"Maybe," O'Neil said.

"You said it got strange?" Farquhar said.

"The sheep manure is laced with anthrax."

Everything went still, and Riley's stomach rolled. An Arab with a beard. She studied the tabletop and tried to think back. She'd said it, not him. He hadn't led her up to it.

"Rose?" O'Neil said.

She looked up and around the silent table. "Sorry, it's crazy," she said. "Last night, I was talking to Bowman . . . about profiling—in the age of terror."

O'Neil was nodding. "That was my reaction too—that this was some chemical weapons trace. Turns out it's more ordinary than that."

"Ordinary?" Farquhar said.

"Crime Scene called in Primary Industries. There's an anthrax belt running down the middle of the state—for some reason, it thrives in this narrow corridor." He read from his laptop. "It lives in the soil and forms a spore. Grazing stock eat it. The first outbreak in New South Wales was in 1847. Then it spread along cattle routes. The department says it killed 120 sheep last year."

"How'd it wind up in North Parramatta?" Tran said.

"Let's find out," O'Neil said.

"We could start with Lynch and Spratt," Patel said. "If it *is* fertilizer, they'd be the ones using it."

"We could put it out through the media again," Tran said. "Ask whether anyone has brought sheep manure into the school."

"We'll leave the anthrax out of it," O'Neil said. "Don't want to scare the horses."

19

The dormant communal buildings of the school huddled in a heat haze as Bowman drove a loop of the place, killing time. The big shuttered boardinghouses were spaced at intervals among sporadic trees on the edge of the bush. Blue gums, red gums, scribbly gums. There was no sign of Riley's Calais. Bowman had called her earlier, offering to give Priya Patel a lift to the interview, and again he'd felt Riley's hesitation.

"No need," she'd said. "We're going out anyway, to see Spratt."

He parked at the admin block and looked at the clock on the dash. He still had twenty minutes. The drone story was filed, along with a short clip of the boy's footage and some stills. *The National's* journalists would give it a shove on Twitter once it was up, and Alexander was doing radio interviews to promote it.

Bowman got out and started toward the headmaster's house. It sat in the center of a wide lawn, a castle in an algal moat. Out front, a rose garden was laid out in squares with a circle in the middle, the beds trimmed with sandstone. The residence had been spruced up over the years: the Pebblecrete panels on the facade had been rendered, and the carport walled into a garage and joined to the house, running off it in an L shape.

There was a new portico topped with a pediment over a section of the driveway to the front door, a faux classical fiasco that reeked of Preston.

On the southern side, the garden gave way to open country studded with trees. Bowman could see the main road, and he watched Riley's Calais turn in through the gate and stop to let Priya Patel out.

Bowman walked toward her, and they met on the drive. He had seen her at the maintenance shed on Sunday, but they hadn't been introduced.

They shook hands. "Rose didn't hang around?" he said.

"They didn't want Preston to see me getting out of her car." Patel adjusted a bag slung over her shoulder.

"So you're a videographer," he said, "taking footage for the website?"

"Yeah." They started up the drive toward the portico.

"Far out," Patel said. "It's like British India crossed with Vegas."

Bowman huffed a laugh. Even before the spruce-ups, his mother had referred to the headmaster's residence as Caesar's Palace. In fifteen years living at the school, Bowman had never been inside. Back then, the headmaster had been English and aloof, careful to maintain a distance from the families on campus. Not that Bowman's parents had cared—they'd had no interest in such a man. His mother had been contemptuous of the petty hierarchies of Prince Albert. It had been beer, cask wine, and menthol cigarettes with friends every afternoon at the Bowman house, stirred up with books, newspapers, and arguments about politics. By fifteen, Bowman had been stealing cans of his father's Tooheys 2.2 and quoting John Pilger. He'd left them both behind: the light beer and the groupthink of the left. He pushed the bell and thought about how he sensed something of his mother in Rose Riley—a bit of mongrel, a bit of the underdog.

The door opened. "Mr. Bowman." Philip Preston smiled moistly. "Bright and early."

"Yes, sorry," Bowman said. "We left time to beat the traffic, but there wasn't any."

Preston nodded at Patel, and they followed him through a hallway into a long formal room and across to a pod of leather sofas and armchairs. Patel put her bag on the floor and started to assemble the camera and tripod.

"We can film here," Preston said. "This doesn't go out live, I take it?"

"No," Bowman said. "Priya will video the interview and edit it to run on the website along with the story. You in your own words, as we discussed on the phone."

"Yes." Preston gave his hands a rub.

Patel pointed from the camera. "If you could sit there, please," she said.

Preston sat in the armchair and cleared his throat, his legs planted, an arm on each wing, fists clenched on knees. Get a load of him: moleskins, polished riding boots, and an ultramarine shirt, sleeves rolled neatly above the elbow. The fucker looked like he was off to the polo in Scone. His black hair was lacquered, combed, parted. Bowman heard his mother: *Never trust a man who dyes his hair*. Sarah Green had said Preston knew Bowman's parents, and yet twice now the headmaster had failed to acknowledge that fact.

It was 11:37. Bowman took a couple of shots with his mobile and then pulled up the voice memo app, pressed play, and placed the phone on the coffee table.

The headmaster's eyes tracked from the tripod to the phone to Patel. He was a different person from the man Bowman had encountered on Sunday, his surliness dissolved by the lens. He loved the camera. Bowman felt a cold squirt of revulsion. It wasn't concern for Marguerite Dunlop that animated Preston—it was the media opportunity she provided.

"Philip, thanks for seeing us," Bowman said. "Are you a Philip or a Phil, by the way?"

Preston blinked. "Ah, more a Philip. Some old friends might call me Dr. Phil over a glass of red. Most people call me Dr. Preston."

"Goodo." Bowman tried to imagine what a glass of red with Preston might look like. Wolf Blass with Dire Straits on in the background. "Well, let's start with the Dunlops. Are you in touch with them?"

Preston stared down the camera. "It is a terribly hard time, and our hearts go out to the Dunlop family. We have offered them every support, my wife and I, and indeed the entire Prince Albert community. I understand Marguerite will be laid to rest next week in a private funeral."

Bowman kept him talking. After several minutes, Patel bent to her bag on the floor, and Bowman watched as Preston's eyes ranged over her. She came up with a notebook just as her phone buzzed, and she stood and walked down the room to take the call.

"Are you close to Bruce Dunlop?" Bowman said.

"Yes—we're colleagues of long standing," Preston said. "He runs the chapel and some pastoral care. I am, of course, his boss. But we have a warm relationship."

Patel came back, still on the phone. *Sorry,* she mouthed. *One sec.*

She went through the door. Preston craned to watch her go.

Bowman pointed Preston back to the camera. "Will there be some sort of commemorative service?"

Patel pulled on a pair of latex gloves and forensic booties from her pocket and went down the hall. An internal door led to the garage. She flicked on a light. It was a big space, enough for four cars. A red Fiat Abarth was parked at the far end. There was a workbench, golf clubs, a hand trolley, an extra fridge, cases of wine and whisky, shelving with large plastic containers. No boat, no trailer. She checked the ceiling: no racks, no canoe, no watercraft. There were gardening tools in a corner: a spade and fork, trowels. Bags and tubs of commercial plant foods. She took a picture on her phone and read a label: Top Rose.

She considered opening a tool bag that was zipped shut but thought better of it—she'd touched the light switch, and she couldn't touch anything else without changing gloves. She elbowed the light off and moved back through the house. She could hear Preston speaking. She took the carpeted stairs two at a time, came to a landing with doors off it. Four bedrooms, bathrooms, and an office. She went into the master. A light cotton cover was pulled up over the bed, but it was disheveled, not properly made, and clothes lay in clumps on the floor. The help must be on holiday. She toed the clothes. A sliding door, half-open, led to an ensuite. She hesitated . . . don't touch. She went back downstairs, removed her gloves and booties, stuffed them in her pocket, and glanced at her phone: 11:57. Three minutes till drone o'clock.

Preston looked up as she reentered the room. She smiled, then checked the camera was still recording and Preston was still in the frame.

"Okay, a couple more questions and we're done," Bowman said.

Patel bent to her bag again and pulled out an iPad.

"You mentioned your wife," Bowman said. "Is she here?"

"Uh, no, she's visiting her mother interstate. She'll stay there for now. All this . . ." Preston twirled a hand. "She doesn't like the school when it's empty at the best of times."

"Wow," Patel said. "Look at this."

"What have we got?" Bowman said.

Patel handed him the iPad. *The National*'s website had uploaded the drone story on the terror template—the layout they kept for mass casualty attacks.

DRONE FOOTAGE IN BMK SCHOOL SLAYING, the headline read.

"Oh." Bowman made surprised eyes and waited until Patel was back behind the camera before handing the iPad to Preston. The headmaster's face went still, and his Adam's apple bobbed. Bowman took a picture with his phone.

Preston's tongue flicked out, and color flushed his neck. He scrolled with a finger. "That's good, isn't it?" His voice was reedy. "But what does it mean?"

"There'll be something in the footage," Patel said. "Otherwise, they wouldn't tell us about it."

Preston stood, a little punch drunk, and handed the iPad back to Bowman. "I'll show you out," he said.

Bowman waited for Patel to pack. They found Preston in the entrance hall.

"Nice to meet you," Patel said, smiling.

Bowman followed her into the sunlight and heard the front door close behind him, the crisp click of the lock shooting home.

Patel had her phone out. "Better call O'Neil."

Bowman's byline had been on the story, and he wondered if Preston had noticed. Patel walked with him off the gravel, and they were standing in the shade of the garden when the Calais pulled into the drive.

O'Neil got out. "Is he inside?"

"Sir," Patel said.

Riley slammed the driver's door and scanned the front of the house. "You want to talk here?"

"Fuck it," O'Neil said. "Let him watch. Did you get a chance to look around?"

"Sir," Patel said. "It's a big garage, internal entry, privacy to wrap and load if we're still looking for that. There's a tool bag, but I didn't open it."

"Manure in the garage?" Riley said.

"Shop-bought fertilizers. Gardening tools."

"How did he react to the drone?" O'Neil said.

"Discomfort . . . it threw him. Change of voice." She adjusted the camera bag on her shoulder. "The body language is interesting."

"What else?" O'Neil said.

"Nothing specific." Patel hesitated. "Observations."

"Good," O'Neil said. "That's why you're here."

Bowman, worried O'Neil would banish him, had backed away to a garden bench within earshot. After a minute, Riley came and sat next to him.

"All good?" she said.

"They put my byline on the story."

Her face hardened.

"Sorry," he said. "I didn't think. It's standard—part of the production process."

She gave a tiny nod. "It doesn't matter. We're showing our hand anyway, debriefing in his yard. He'll know we're playing games."

"Can I write it up? That he was disturbed by the drone footage?"

She stared out over the garden. "You can't bring us into it. That we're looking at him."

"Okay," he said. "Well, what now?"

"We'll watch the tape, see what Farquhar thinks."

"How was Spratt with the drone footage?"

"Intrigued—but comfortable."

"What's the story with manure?"

"Just a line of inquiry."

Yeah. He looked skyward. *No shit.*

20

Bowman drove home and ate baked beans on toast and drank tea and transcribed the interview with Preston before heading to the office. He was crossing George Street when Alexander called.

"Drone story's gone interstellar," the editor said. "They're spewing at *The Mirror*. Are you in the car?"

"Yep."

"Pull over. I want you to see something."

Bowman pulled left into a loading zone. "Yeah?"

"Call up NeedFeed."

He hauled out his laptop, searched up the gossip site, and felt his bowels loosen. "Jesus fucking Christ."

"It's blowback," Alexander said. "Don't wig out."

The main image on the website was a picture of Riley and Bowman sitting on the bench in Preston's garden three hours ago. There was a headline over it: WHERE THE HACK DO BMK LEAKS COME FROM?

There were about ten paragraphs of copy. He read the lede: "Have you been wondering how a washed-up hack at *The National* who has never broken a story is getting a serial killer of leaks on BMK? Well, we think we might have the answer."

The picture caption said: "Old journo Adam Bowman snuggles up to Deep Throat Detective Rose Riley."

Bowman peered at the photo. The grounds around Preston's place ran up to a wrought-iron boundary fence along Pennant Hills Road. "It's taken from outside the school," he said. "A long lens from the road."

"Freelance snapper," Alexander said. "Maggots must have paid for it."

Bowman read the next few paragraphs. "Does it say it's at the headmaster's house?"

"Yep, toward the bottom. Fuckin' churnalists—buried the lede."

Bowman took a breath and went through it. There were unsourced complaints about the accuracy of his reporting, as well as claims that he was a drunk with troubled family ties to the school and a chip on both shoulders. There was no byline—everything was anonymous.

"How does it feel to be clickbait?" Alexander said.

"Where's it coming from?"

"Dunno, but it feels pretty smooth," the editor said. "It's a clean hit, and they moved fast. Someone knows how to use the media."

"So . . . ?"

"Like I said, politics or big business. Got some front."

"The same person who called the old man?"

"Has to be," Alexander said. "It's the favor bank. Someone owes someone, and someone doesn't like what you're up to. Congratulations."

"I better call Riley," Bowman said. "Cops won't like the mention of the headmaster's house."

"She your source?" Alexander said. "Michelle Pfeiffer?"

"One of them."

"Saucy. All right, get in here. We need to punch back."

Alexander hung up, and Bowman called Riley.

"We've seen it," she said.

"Do you know where it's from?"

"Preston."

"What? The source?"

"We're pretty sure."

"How?" Bowman said.

"Bits of phrasing. The word *airtight* to complain about your reporting."

"Yeah?"

"They're words Preston used when we spoke to him at his house on Friday. A couple of points are interesting."

"Oh, you think so?"

"First, if it *is* him, he's done it after your interview, while we were sitting on his lawn. We thought he was in the fetal position, digesting the news about the drone, when he was actually working the phones to rain shit down on us."

"Because of my byline?"

"Mm."

"What's the second thing?"

"Motivation," Riley said. "Why's he having a go at you?"

"Again, my byline. He knows we're in cahoots."

"That might annoy him. He sees it as a lack of trust. But would he lash out like this if he has nothing to hide?"

"To damage my credibility. He wants me to back off."

"Right. But why?"

"To protect the school."

"It's more than that. It seems very . . . personal."

Bowman felt her wait: she thought he was holding out.

"You think Preston has something to hide?" he said. "And what—he thinks I'm going to find it?"

He heard her exhale. "Gotta go," she said. "Talk later."

Bowman drove on to the office and fiddled with the interview with Preston, but he couldn't extrapolate on the headmaster's reaction to the drone footage, so he had no hard angle.

The news floor had the clacking early-evening hum of production, as the threadbare staff of reporters, subs, and section editors bent to the edition. At her perch in the middle of the room, Justine hung up the phone and walked across to Bowman's desk with a notebook. She took a seat beside him and spoke low out the corner of her mouth. "Don't look around. Keep typing."

Bowman's eyes darted left and right. Justine's cool intelligence, her cultural literacy and swagger, always made him clumsy. "What?"

Her head was lowered, but she was staring up the room. Bowman glanced over. Diamond was hovering outside Brandy's office.

"I was on my break." Justine's voice was clear and quiet. "There's a sofa round where advertising used to be."

Bowman nodded.

"I go there every lunch, to read—and get away from that god-awful fucking phone."

Bowman knew the sofa. The advertising and marketing staff had been stripped to the bone, and the remaining bodies marched upstairs to merge with their sister department at *The Mirror*. Bowman often strolled the abandoned crannies of *The National* late at night, looking for stationery to pilfer.

Justine had been slouched on the couch, reading in the silence, the nearest coworker forty meters away, when she heard a voice very close. She started and sat still.

"You get it?" the voice had said. "I sent it in a Gmail." It was Diamond, talking on the phone. She couldn't see him. He must have walked across and been sitting at the group of empty desks behind the sofa.

Justine stared over Bowman's shoulder. "I can't remember the exact form of words, but these are the key phrases. I wrote them down as soon as he left." She read from her notebook. *I went hard. Can't fucking believe Riley.* Justine paused and looked at Bowman. "There was a bit of other stuff—*yes, no, be careful.* Then he said, *Thanks, Cat,* and that was it."

"Cat?" Bowman said.

Justine nodded. Catherine Withers, known to all as Cat. She'd left *The National* two months ago—to be deputy editor at NeedFeed.

"You know Cat was tight with Beat-Up Benny?" Justine said.

"Yeah." Bowman scratched some eczema.

"Okay." Justine closed the notebook. "I wanted you to know. You're a good person. In this place, that's saying something."

Through the glass of the editor's office, Diamond was talking with Alexander. Bowman watched them. Justine had been answering the phone for Alexander for six months. She'd know him as well as anyone.

"What about Brandy?" he said.

Justine stood. "Hard to say. He's a snake in the grass. But he hates Benny."

Bowman pinched his lip as she walked away. He went back to writing up the Preston interview but couldn't concentrate, his eyes flicking to Alexander in his office. Diamond had come out and was working at his desk.

At 5:30 p.m. O'Neil called a press conference, and Bowman watched on one of the big screens on the news floor: Strike Force Satyr wanted to know if anyone had been supplying Prince Albert with sheep manure or was involved in any way with bringing it into the school. The appeal was picked up everywhere and led the evening TV bulletins.

Alexander came out of his office and screamed across the floor: "What the fuck is this shit with manure?"

Bowman didn't know, and Riley wouldn't tell him when he called. Diamond wrote the main story—nothing fresh, an omnibus of the day.

Alexander called Bowman in. The editor wanted him to write a secondary piece, pulling together anything he had.

"I could look into the NeedFeed story," Bowman said.

Alexander glanced up from his screen. "What?"

"I could give Cat a call, find out who wrote it."

Brandy's bafflement seemed genuine.

"Diamond called Cat," Bowman said. "He said he went hard, and he thanked her."

Brandy's ferret eyes flashed yellow. "Thanked her for what?"

Bowman didn't answer. He watched the editor. Alexander scanned the news floor. "Fuck me." He stood and strode to the door, then stopped, turned, and held his chin. "Who knows about this?"

"Me and you—and a little bird," Bowman said.

"All right. Keep it like that. We'll deal with it later." He pointed with his thumb. "Go write your piece."

Bowman went to his desk and got back on the phone with Riley, begging for anything on the drone or the dung or the plastic. Riley wouldn't budge, but she promised to get him a couple of exclusive quotes from O'Neil.

In his story, Bowman pushed as far as he dared. He wrote that a piece of physical evidence left behind by the killer was being examined by forensic investigators and that at least three people were helping detectives with their inquiries. He also claimed that the detectives had another piece of intelligence just as critical as the drone footage. Threaded up high in the story were the quotes from O'Neil:

> The killings being investigated by Strike Force Satyr involve a level of sadism. They are sex crimes, but only insofar as they are crimes of impotence. They are not crimes of strength. They are crimes of weakness and cowardice. We believe the person responsible is incapable of performing or sustaining normal sexual relations.

> It is my belief the person involved in the murders is aware of how close we are, and I dare say, someone reading this now might be feeling very uncomfortable.

> If someone close to that person notices that, this is the type of information we would be seeking to be contacted about.

Bowman knew he was being used. O'Neil wasn't holding back—he was making it personal.

◆　◆　◆

In the strike force room, Riley watched the Preston footage again and closed her laptop. It was 8:00 p.m., and she guessed Bowman would have finished writing his story. Patel was waiting. Riley called Bowman and invited herself over for a drink. This time she acquiesced when he offered to make dinner.

"Give me half an hour," he said. "I might get lost in the supermarket."

"Get enough for three," she said. "I'm bringing Priya. She wants to debrief about your Preston interview."

The whole thing had been O'Neil's idea. "Go together," he'd said. "And get his prints."

Riley parked outside the Commercial, and Patel went inside to grab a bottle. Dusk swamped the lane, crepuscular pink and orange, as the detectives walked past cottages and rang Bowman's bell.

The door opened to cooking smells. "How'd the story go?" she said.

"Shit sandwich—without the bread." He acknowledged Patel. "Come through."

In the kitchen, Patel put the wine on the table, and Bowman handed out beers from the fridge. They clinked bottles and stood in the ungainly silence of colleagues gone domestic.

Bowman went to the stove. He was frying onions and chopping garlic, and things were lined up on the bench: capers, anchovies, a lemon, white wine, tinned tomatoes. It was odd for Riley to watch a man cook. She'd had three long-term relationships, all cops, and each of them would have been flat out unwrapping a kebab.

"Smells good," Patel said.

Bowman slid more ingredients into the pan and pushed at them with a spatula. "Vegetarian."

"Are anchovies vegetarian?" Patel said.

"Yeah." Now he had his head in a cupboard. "Everyone knows that."

His phone rang on the bench, and he looked at the number and excused himself to take it. He removed the pan from the heat and walked into the hall.

"Told you it was cozy," Riley said.

Patel ran a finger on the bench. "And you were right about clean."

Riley made wide eyes over her stubby.

Bowman came back. "Sorry," he said. "Editors. Should have been drowned at birth."

He put the pan back on the gas and filled a large saucepan with water and an exaggerated dose of salt. "The water for pasta should be as salty as the Mediterranean Sea," he said, igniting a second burner.

His movements around the kitchen were fluid and precise. Riley timed him . . . About every twenty-five seconds, he wiped the bench. She was glad to have an investigative reason for the visit. She was a garrulous pub drinker, but this was something else, more intimate. She wasn't a good guest. Ottolenghi salads weren't her scene.

Bowman was busily at ease, and Patel seemed relaxed. Riley admired the younger detective's poise—she was well adjusted and whip smart. Riley assumed she came from a big family and had been to university. In this setting, Riley felt the realignment—she was going to have to eat anchovies and talk about something other than the case.

Patel was studying a framed photograph on the wall, and Riley went to join her. It was a bird's-eye view of Sydney Harbour, the geometry of nature tugged out of shape by the clasp of the bridge.

Bowman glanced over. "It's taken from sixteen thousand feet." He came across and pointed with his pinkie. "Can you see where we are? Goat Island, Cockatoo. Birchgrove, Balmain."

Riley looked closer. It was all there, in black and white. Farquhar's comfort zone.

"It gives a good view down the river," Patel said.

"There are three tributaries," Bowman said. "You can't see them. Darling Mills, Toongabbie . . . and . . ."

"Hunts," Riley said.

This time she saw a microgesture, a flick of shadow. "You've done your homework," he said. "Hunts Creek—they dammed it."

Riley sipped. Pretty pictures, clean surfaces. No mess, no family snapshots. Water Police, terrorism, anthrax—things popping up and slotting into place. The NeedFeed article: Bowman had Preston riled. And Lynch wasn't neat—it was just that evidence had lined up around him, the plastic near his flat . . .

"You think the creek's important?" Bowman said.

"Dunno," Riley said. "What do you think?"

"It's a physical link—between Gladesville and the school."

Riley went to the bench and pulled out an orange stool. On a shelf above the sink, an orange teapot had pride of place, and beside it, an orange-handled folding-blade knife hung on the wall by a leather strap, like an exhibit. Color-coded. She bit her tongue—her ulcer was getting worse. Maybe she could gargle some of that salty seawater he had on to boil.

Bowman was at the stove, and Patel was standing by, ready to help.

"Priya," Riley said, "you got siblings?"

"How'd you guess?" A smile to light up a morgue. "Three."

"Where do you fit in?" Riley said. "Let me guess . . . fourth?"

"Close. Third."

"Let *me* guess," Bowman said. "Rose, you're an only child."

Patel laughed with him.

"Fuck you," Riley said. "Pour me some wine."

"Is he right, though?" Patel poured. "No siblings?"

"What do you think?" Riley said.

"No," Patel said. "You have people. An older brother."

Riley raised her glass. "Two older brothers."

"You're close with your family?"

"We get on. I spoil their kids."

Patel passed Bowman a glass. "What about you, Adam? Siblings?"

"A younger brother." He found something absorbing in the pan.

The NeedFeed story was more than brand protection. Riley sensed Hugh Bishop behind it, driving the hatchet job in the press. Bowman had them nervous. But there was another issue—Gladesville watched the media. The NeedFeed article could put Bowman in Gladesville's sights.

He was draining pasta at the sink. Riley waited until she could see his face. "Does the name Hugh Bishop mean anything to you?" she said.

"The politician?"

Riley nodded.

"I know who he is. I've never met him. Why?"

Patel took a stool next to Riley. Orange.

"I just remembered," he said. "I read a magazine profile of Bishop a few years back. He went to Prince Albert."

Bowman filled bowls and passed them over.

"So Bishop's involved?" he pressed. "What? You think a sex ring?"

"Thanks." Riley took a mouthful. It was good, real food. Gladesville was not a sex ring. But Marguerite Dunlop? "Bishop's name has come up," she said. "Like Lynch, it's probably nothing. Keep it in your back pocket. Don't go asking questions, but let me know if you hear anything. All right?"

He took a seat next to Patel. "I heard something today," he said.

"Mm?" Riley forked pasta.

"Diamond wrote the NeedFeed piece," he said. Riley ate silently as Bowman recounted the conversation with Justine.

"Sounds like vintage Benny Beat-Up," she said. "What did you expect?"

"But you said you weren't dealing with Diamond?" There was a hurt note in his voice.

She looked across at him. "We aren't."

"*Can't fucking believe Riley.* Why would he say that?"

"Because I won't talk to him—and there's a picture of me talking to you." She pushed her bowl away. "Listen, Diamond's a fuckwit's fuckwit, and he's burned a lot of cops. He gets everything wrong, and then he turns up the next day and does it all again. I know that's the sacred right of the media, but in any other job, he'd be sacked."

Patel refilled the glasses.

"After the Sheridan murder," Riley said, "Diamond got a half leak out of Satyr. We don't know who, but someone told him the killer had managed to clean things up a bit. Diamond got no detail, but he wrote a story anyway, quoting an anonymous crime-scene source, who was not part of the investigation, on what the killer might have done to cover his tracks."

Bowman nodded. "I remember the story."

"Yeah," Riley said. "So do I. Nine-tenths of it was wrong, and the other bit wasn't helpful."

A thought occurred to her: the cleaning at the Dunlop house was more agricultural than Gladesville. The killer might have read the Diamond story . . . or Gladesville might have read the Diamond story and followed parts of it to fuck with them.

"I told Alexander about NeedFeed," Bowman said. "He looked pretty pissed. I don't think he knew."

"Did he confront Diamond?"

"No. Not yet."

"Good." Riley drank. Diamond must be talking to Bishop and Preston. It would be interesting to let the conversation run. "Tell Alexander to sit tight. I'll talk to Steve."

Bowman picked up his phone to text the editor and then started to clear the bowls. Patel stood to help, and Riley sat and listened as the two of them talked. She learned some details of her colleague's life. Patel was twenty-six, no partner, and lived alone in Harris Park.

Riley poured more wine. The drink was doing its job, dissolving the high-voltage current arcing through her brain and allowing weariness to seep in. After the drone footage, O'Neil had decided to pull back, go covert—listening devices, phone taps, car trackers—on Preston, Spratt, and Green. The Supreme Court had issued the surveillance powers as a precursor to search warrants. The taps would be running by tonight. Riley's mood dipped. What else could they do? The strategy now was to attribute Marguerite's murder to Gladesville in the press, tie him to the school and see how he reacted. They'd fed Bowman the impotence quotes, and as a consequence, coupled with the NeedFeed story, the reporter was dangling, fully exposed. She looked along the row of three orange stools. His books on the shelf next door were coded too—organized by color. His byline on the drone story—that had been disorganized. He'd thrown her words from the Bald Rock back at her: *It's standard.* He'd used the rogue byline to explain the NeedFeed story, to justify Preston's animosity. And now he had more information—an overheard office conversation that pinned the NeedFeed piece on Diamond.

She looked at the pans and the dirty dishes. They'd fed Bowman the quotes, and in return Bowman had fed them as well—something warm and nutritious.

He turned from the sink. "Back in a sec," he said and disappeared down the hall.

Riley slid off the stool. "Let's get out of here," she said. Bowman's empty stubby was on the bench. Riley put her finger in the spout to pick it up and with her other hand pulled an evidence bag from her pocket and waved it open. She put the bottle in the bag as she crossed the room and looked back at Patel.

"Tell him I'm on the phone, something's come up." She went down the hall and out the front door. After a minute, she heard Bowman's voice, and then Patel was outside with her.

Riley put her head round the jamb, her phone to her ear. Bowman was standing in the main room. *Thanks,* she mouthed, and walked away up the lane with Patel beside her.

21

Riley woke to the sound of smashing glass as the recycling truck did its rounds. She reached for her phone and noted the date. Wednesday, January 4. A grim milestone. Marguerite Dunlop had been dead a week.

The mobile buzzed as she looked at it. "Yeah."

"We got a nibble," O'Neil said. "Preston's phone."

She sat up. "That was quick."

"Mm. Panic might be setting in."

"Always useful." She kicked off the sheet and went through to the kitchen. "What'd he say?"

"I'll tell you when you get here. I gotta make some calls. Twenty minutes."

He hung up, and Riley gulped at a bottle of iced coffee from the fridge on her way to the shower.

Thirty minutes later, she was sitting at the long conference table with Tran and Patel.

O'Neil was across from them. "This was 6:03 this morning. Preston makes the call from home on his mobile to a mobile in Orange." He turned his laptop around and clicked.

A man's voice, blurry. *Dr. Phil. So early. Everything's all right?*

No. Preston's voice.

I know, I know. I saw the news.

Well, what do we do? They'll keep going, you realize.

We stay calm. You say nothing, it blows over.

Someone will know. They're looking, and the journalist's got contacts.

You've told no one, right?

Preston was silent.

Look, the man said, *I have to go. Say nothing. I'll call you.*

The call ended.

"That was a Joseph Zabatino," O'Neil said, "also known as Joey Vino. He's been off the radar five years. Upper-level Griffith mafia, top-level douchebag."

"How's he know Preston?" Riley said.

"I had a chat with organized crime just now," O'Neil said. "Zabatino nearly went down for murder six years ago. Tow-truck war got ugly. Jury let him off—judge was filthy with the DPP and the cops. Zabatino pulled his head in. He's been growing grapes and trying to keep it clean. Sends his kids to private school. Thinks he's a pillar of the community."

"He's got a kid at Prince Albert?" Riley said.

"Young Tony, year twelve." O'Neil looked at Tran. "See what you can find out about him. We're on a plane to Orange in forty-five minutes."

Tran went to her desk, and O'Neil turned to Patel. "What are we risking?"

"The phone tap," Patel said.

"Correct. We speak to Zabatino, he knows we're listening to the headmaster. He gets a message to Preston, phone tap's shot. What do we do?"

Patel rubbed an eyebrow. "Marguerite Dunlop doesn't feel like a mob job. If Zabatino had her killed, either for his own reasons or as a contract for Preston, it wouldn't look like this. She'd be at the bottom of a dam somewhere, not lying in state in the middle of the school."

"Agreed," O'Neil said.

"But Zabatino and Preston are involved in something," Patel said. "From the call, it sounds like it's linked to the murder."

O'Neil looked to Riley. "I've got some leverage."

She gave a nod. They had to risk it—sweat Zabatino and then come down hard to make sure he didn't blab.

O'Neil reached for the conference phone on the desk. He put it on speaker and punched a number. An operator answered. "I need Superintendent Paul Madden at Orange," O'Neil said. "On his mobile."

They stared at the speaker in the silence.

"Madden," a voice said.

"Paul. Steve O'Neil, Homicide."

"Steve, been a while."

"Yeah, look, I'm on the move, 'bout to head your way out of Bankstown. One of your regulars that got flushed from Griffith—I need to have a chat."

"Let me guess—name ends in a vowel?"

"Bingo," O'Neil said.

Madden gave a grunt. "Which one?"

"Joseph Zabatino."

"Joey Vino. Thought he was being a good boy?"

"Not sure. We've heard something. But I want to keep it real quiet."

"This Gladesville?"

"Yeah."

"Okay. How do you want to do it?"

Riley listened as they thrashed it out. O'Neil wanted it off the books, not at the station. Madden agreed to find Zabatino himself and keep him under surveillance until the Satyr team landed.

The call ended. O'Neil drummed his fingers on the table. Tran was on the phone and scrolling at her laptop. There were around two hundred staff at Prince Albert, on holidays up and down the coast, interstate, at home, overseas. Tran had supervised the work to track them all down and speak to them. She looked across now and gave a thumbs-up.

Riley pushed out her chair with a glance at Patel. "Let's go." Tran would brief them on the plane.

Patel sat in the back of the Calais with O'Neil. Riley drove south through Olympic Park, listening to Tran beside her speaking to a teacher. At the airport at Bankstown, she parked at the PolAir base, and they headed to a police Cessna on the apron. Orange was an hour's flight west.

"What have we got?" O'Neil said as the plane leveled off.

Tran had her notebook open in her lap. "I spoke with Tony Zabatino's boarding housemaster, on holiday in Terrigal," she said. "The kid's thick as shit, and there was some trouble toward the end of the school year. A boy got expelled from one of the Eastern Suburbs colleges for dealing and lobbed up at Prince Albert in May. These schools swap kids like the Catholics shunt the peds around. This new boy starts teeing off on Zabatino—constant abuse, calling him a wog. Zabatino snaps, beats the crap out of him. Black eyes, broken nose. New kid's parents go apeshit from Vaucluse—lawyers, want to call the cops, the media. Preston works his magic, smooths it all over. The word from the staffroom is Joe Zabatino's got Preston in his pocket, and hush money was channeled to Vaucluse. No one knows what the price was."

"All right. Good work." O'Neil looked at his watch, put his shoulder to the bulkhead and his head against the wall, and closed his eyes. He seemed to go straight off. Riley frowned in awe: everyone was good at something. She tried to rest. Fragments of a dream came back. She'd incorporated the breaking glass from the recycling truck. There was more, further down, deep in sleep . . . She'd met Marguerite Dunlop walking a dog on a beach in Fiji.

O'Neil woke before they landed. Riley watched the pilot bring it in. Ground crew opened the cabin door to the dry air of the tablelands.

In the terminal, they were met by one of Madden's men, who led them to an unmarked Sprinter in the car park. "Engine's running. Aircon's on." He walked away across the bitumen.

The van was fitted with two front seats open to a loadspace with benches running down either side. No windows. Tran drove with Riley in the passenger seat.

O'Neil connected to the Bluetooth and called Madden. Zabatino was at a restaurant on Sale Street in the middle of the town.

"Shouldn't be long," the superintendent said. "He lives northeast. Grass castle out toward Molong. His office is on the property. I reckon he'll be heading there."

"We're leaving the airport," O'Neil said.

"All right. Head through town and then out on the Mitchell Highway. There's a yuppie coffee place on Murphy Lane—duck in there and wait."

"Got it. Listen, we'll pump Zabatino for an alibi. I'll need you to check it out."

"No worries. I'll let you know when we're moving."

The airport was in farming land to the south. Winter rains had broken the drought, and the country still looked good: strong greens in the hard yellows. The sky was cloudless and pale, Mount Canobolas a bump on the range to the left. This was the bush in Riley's bones. She'd been twelve when they sold the farm and bought the service station at Campbelltown.

They came into town: wide avenues and parks, grand squat buildings with balconies and verandas. Every second vehicle was a Hilux with roo bars and spotlights and dust. Tran drove down the main street and right at a roundabout, past a high school and then a golf course and country club. Riley knew the formula. Agriculture, mining, services, government jobs, and then the trifecta—cheese, wine, and tourists. In the Hunter, they'd lived on the edge of such prosperity.

The café was on the northern outskirts. O'Neil bought three coffees. Riley got a pineapple doughnut and a can of Passiona.

"Get out of town," Tran said. "Do you eat anything that isn't yellow?"

"She'd like my mum's dal," Patel said.

They waited in the van. O'Neil's phone rang.

"With you in five." Madden's voice came over the Bluetooth. "I'll stay on the line."

Tran put her coffee in the cup holder, backed up, and signaled to rejoin the highway.

"Go now," Madden said. "Keep at forty."

A Maserati came up fast behind them, followed by an unmarked Falcon. "There's a rest area coming up on the left," Madden said. "I'll send him in there."

There was half a revolution of a police siren. Tran slowed further and signaled left. Riley watched in her side mirror as the Maserati looked to overtake. Madden hit the siren again, and the Maserati braked and followed the Sprinter into the bay.

"I'll bring him over," Madden said and hung up.

Tran left the motor running and moved onto the bench with Patel and her coffee. Riley followed. They could hear car doors slamming, then voices.

"They got you working the long paddock now, Paul?" a man said. "Highway Patrol."

"Someone wants to have a chat, Joe," Madden said.

There was a gust of warm air as Madden pulled open the back doors of the van. "Get in," he said.

Zabatino was plethoric, short, thickset, balding. He looked at Riley, Patel, and Tran on one bench and across to O'Neil on the other, then at the coffee cups on the floor. "What's this?" he said. "Lesbian tea party?"

"I said get in," Madden said.

Zabatino hauled himself up and bent to sit beside O'Neil. Raw sausage hands.

Madden climbed in after him, shut the doors, and sat next to Riley.

Zabatino shifted on the bench. "Who the fuck are you lot?"

"Homicide," O'Neil said.

Zabatino scoffed. "Get fucked."

"Listen, Joe," O'Neil said. "Let's bring you up to speed. First thing you should know is that I had a chat with a Supreme Court judge this morning, name of John Cullen. You remember Justice Cullen?"

Zabatino shook his head.

"Well," O'Neil said, "Justice Cullen remembers you. All that tow-truck bullshit with the Lebs?"

"It went to trial. I was innocent." Zabatino smiled. "Did he remember that bit?"

Riley watched him. Amoral, wound tight.

"Just to fast-forward a sec—we're investigating a murder up in Sydney." O'Neil gestured at his colleagues. "Funny thing is, your name's come up."

Still smiling, Zabatino stared at his hands.

"With that in mind," O'Neil said, "I rang Justice Cullen this morning and gave him some details about my case, sounded him out. Know what he said?"

Zabatino waited.

"Without a word of a lie, he said, 'If you want a search warrant for Joseph Zabatino, I'll sign it right now.'"

"I got no idea what you're talking about." Zabatino's face creased in disgust. "I'm growing grapes. Making table wine."

"That might be so," O'Neil said. "But I've got enough to bring you in. We could take our time getting to the station, go the scenic route. Might take what? Eight hours? That's eight extra hours we've got at your property, looking for wall cavities, while you're in the cop shop. The media would love it."

"I know a bloke at *The Mirror*," Riley said.

Zabatino eyed her, then looked away, dead eyes dead ahead.

"What were you doing last Wednesday?" O'Neil said. "Three days after Christmas."

Zabatino blinked. "I was at Echuca, water-skiing with the family. Boxing Day to New Year's."

Madden opened his notebook. "Who else was there?"

"'Bout thirty-five people. Big fucking family."

"I want their names," Madden said. "Where you stayed, where you went, what you did. Shops, pubs, restaurants."

Madden scrawled notes as Zabatino spat out the information. The superintendent let himself out of the van, waving his notebook at O'Neil as he climbed down. "I'll have it all checked out," he said.

"Specially the Tuesday night and Wednesday," O'Neil said. "Want to be sure there's no chance of a surprise trip to Parramatta."

"Parramatta?" Zabatino said. "What, you think I'm BMK?"

"Joey Vino, catching on fast," O'Neil said.

Zabatino shook his head. "You got to be kidding me."

"What's your relationship with Philip Preston?" Riley said.

She saw him tighten. O'Neil had felt it beside him. "I'll say this one time, Joe," O'Neil said. "You tell us everything, and you get to slide out of here. Otherwise, we haul you into it, and it gets real ugly. The search warrant will be just the start."

Zabatino looked along the line, from Patel to Tran to Riley.

"How much did you pay to make your kid's bashing incident go away?" Tran said.

"It was his idea." Zabatino's voice was flat. "Dr. Phil's."

"What did he want in return for clearing up the problem?" Riley said.

He shrugged. "Usual things."

"Such as?" Riley said.

Zabatino looked at the roof and blew air. "I gave him a case of Scotch when my boy first started at the school. He invited me in. We had a few drinks. It went from there."

"Went where?" O'Neil said.

"Cases of wine. It doesn't cost me nothing . . ."

162

"What else?" O'Neil said.

Zabatino swallowed. "He wanted more. To fix the boy. He's always talking hookers . . . He likes them young."

Silence in the van. "How young?" Riley said.

"Not kiddie stuff." Zabatino looked affronted. "Legal. I put him up here for a weekend, a place out of town, very private."

"This is what you gave to fix things for your son?" O'Neil said.

"Yep, no cash."

"Why no cash?" Tran said.

"Plausible deniability—he always goes on about it. Says he can swear he never took a buck if the shit hits the fan."

"You do anything else for him?" Riley said.

Zabatino considered, weighing odds. "He in a lot of shit?"

They didn't answer.

"You reckon Dr. Phil did the girl?" Zabatino said.

O'Neil's head inched sideways: *Don't answer.*

"I've seen what he does with girls," Zabatino said. "His soul, it's fucking black." He looked at his hands in his lap. "This didn't come from me, right?"

O'Neil stared ahead. Zabatino was on a roll, negotiating with himself.

"After this, I'm gone," Zabatino said. "Drive away, no more to pay. Deal?" He gave a hopeful nod. "I know nothing about the girl at the school—I never met her, never heard of her till I saw it on the news. That's the honest truth. All I done is grease the wheels with my son's boss."

Riley knew O'Neil would make a deal—but only if he had to.

"The manure you're asking about on the TV," Zabatino said. "Dr. Phil's sweating on it. It comes from me. I got some sheep. I get it bagged and take some for the doctor whenever I drive up. He puts it on his rose garden. He's obsessed with his roses." Zabatino shook his head. "Like the fucking Godfather."

It was quiet, just the whir of the air-conditioning.

"Right," Zabatino said and made to stand. Riley put her hand up to sit him down.

"Anyone else know about the manure?" O'Neil said.

"Nah. I back the car up to the garage, and we unload. Manure, Scotch, wine."

"When was the last drop?" O'Neil said.

"A month ago"—Zabatino frowned—"first week of December."

"You know where he stores the manure?" O'Neil said.

Zabatino shook his head. "I know he composts it. You gotta age it."

"Okay," O'Neil said. "Two more things."

Zabatino crossed his arms.

"One, if Preston calls you—don't answer. Ever. Let it go straight to voice mail. If he texts, you text back once and tell him you're dealing with some heavy shit and will be off the air for a while. There's to be no other contact. Capisce?"

Zabatino nodded.

"I get any sense you or anyone you know is in touch with Preston, I'm down here waving Justice Cullen's warrant."

"Yeah," Zabatino said. "I get it."

"Good. Second thing. We need to get Crime Scene to your place now. They'll be discreet. We need samples of your sheep manure. Do you bag it in a single place?"

Zabatino winced. "Yeah."

"Good. You go straight home now. Detective Sergeant Tran here will be along with Crime Scene."

Zabatino climbed down from the van. Riley got into the driver's seat. O'Neil called Madden and requested the forensic investigators and a pickup for Tran. "We're going to head off," O'Neil said. "Annie can fly back commercial."

"Zabatino's alibi is checking out," Madden said.

"I expect it will," O'Neil said. "You might have a mob brothel operating here. You know that?"

"No."

"Keep a lid on it. We'll talk later."

"Thanks. Tell me—you really have a promise of a warrant from this judge?"

"Justice Cullen?" O'Neil said. "Never spoken to him in my life."

22

At the school gate, Riley wound down the window to talk with the uniforms on duty. The only civilian traffic through had been a couple in a Mercedes at 8:20 a.m., there for a scheduled meeting with Preston.

She thanked them and drove on, glancing at the dash: 9:05. Preston's Range Rover wasn't in the driveway when she pulled up. O'Neil got out and rang the doorbell.

He came back. "Not here. Let's go for a stroll."

Riley and Patel followed him across the lawn to the rose garden, five raised stone beds forty meters from the house. The bushes were staked, some in tight bud, some with drooping flowers. The beds were hard, with a tatty cover of dry straw.

"Anyone got green fingers?" O'Neil said.

"Doesn't smell like shit," Riley said.

"Sheep shit doesn't smell," Patel said.

They looked at her.

"I read the internet," Patel said, squatting to poke the mulch. "Nothing's been put on here for a while."

They walked down the side of the garage. Hot-water systems and air-conditioning units were mounted on the wall. A low hedge of rosemary ran parallel.

"There." Patel pointed. A compost bin sat under trees past the edge of the back lawn.

"Hiding in plain sight," Riley said.

"He'd have had no reason to hide it," O'Neil said. "Until the night before yesterday."

A red wheelbarrow was propped against a tree, and there were thick-tread tire tracks around the bin. Riley bent closer. "Not a car," she said.

Patel pulled a glove from her pocket and lifted a corner of the lid. The tub was full of dark pellets breaking down into something fibrous.

"Careful with your feet," Riley said.

They heard a vehicle and turned to see Farquhar's black Volvo coming up the drive.

O'Neil called Crime Scene as they walked back to the Calais. Farquhar greeted them and followed as Riley drove to the administration block. There were two vehicles in the car park—Preston's Range Rover and a Mercedes sedan. Farquhar pulled up beside Riley. They waited until the front door of the building opened, and a man and a woman emerged, trailed by Philip Preston.

"This should be fun." O'Neil got out.

Riley and Patel came up as he intercepted Preston and the couple on the asphalt.

"*Mr.* Preston," O'Neil said. "Good morning."

"Detective." Preston gestured. "Some prospective parents, just flown in from Singapore."

O'Neil put his hands on his hips.

"They only have this morning," the headmaster said. "I need to show them the facilities. I'll be with you in half an hour."

"We haven't got half an hour."

Farquhar came over from the Volvo and smiled at the couple. The woman was bottle-blonde North Shore blue blood, pearls and diamonds.

Preston put a hand on her lower back. "As I was saying, the police are still on-site. You might need to excuse me."

O'Neil looked at the admin block. "Somewhere we can talk in there?"

Preston took a moment to shunt the expat parents toward the classrooms for a little self-guided tour. Once they were out of earshot, he rounded and got up close in Patel's face. "Still working with the newspaper?"

Patel stood her ground.

"She's multitalented," O'Neil said. "Does a bit of police media."

"Talking of media," Riley said, "that NeedFeed article was interesting."

Preston stepped back.

"You don't know anything about that, do you, Dr. Phil?" Riley said.

His eyes went around the four of them.

"Can we call you that?" Patel said. "Or do we need a glass of red first?"

"Or a Scotch," Riley said. "Hear you've got plenty of Scotch."

"This is beginning to resemble harassment," Preston said. "If it continues, I'll have to call the lawyers."

"Lawyering up." O'Neil grimaced.

"In our experience," Riley said, "only the guilty call their lawyers."

"What is it you think I'm guilty of? Murdering three girls?"

"Let's start with one," O'Neil said. "Let's start with Marguerite Dunlop."

The headmaster tried for a smile. "You're being ridiculous. I've never so much as touched Marguerite Dunlop."

"Yeah?" O'Neil said. "I hear you like touching girls."

Fear flashed with loathing. "I can sue you for that."

"Off you go then," O'Neil said. "Call the lawyers. But make sure they know the facts. Make sure they know you like paying for girls."

Preston's head went back. "I have never paid any girls for anything."

O'Neil looked at Riley.

"There it is," she said. "Plausible deniability."

Preston flinched, chickens coming home to roost on his face.

"Is there somewhere we can talk?" O'Neil said. "Out of the sun?"

The headmaster led them across the car park to the admin building. The wandering parents could be seen in the quadrangle in the distance.

"How are enrollments?" Riley said. "Don't they read the news in Singapore?"

Preston ignored her and took them up a staircase and along a carpeted hall to a spacious office. There were chairs in front of a sleek desk and a clutch of sofas around a low table. Blown up on the wall was a photo of Preston standing between the prime minister and Hugh Bishop.

The desk was polished white stone with a large Mac to one side and nothing else. Preston sat behind it. The detectives fanned out and stood. Farquhar took a seat.

"You might have noticed in the press," O'Neil said, "that for reasons pertinent to our investigation, we are interested in sheep manure that has been brought into the school. Do you know anything about sheep manure being brought onto the grounds?"

"My colleague's daughter has been murdered," Preston said, "and of all things, you're interested in sheep manure?"

"That's called not answering the question." O'Neil nodded at the photo. "Those politicians teach you that?"

"We've seen your compost bin," Patel said.

"We've been to Orange," Riley said.

Preston looked as if he'd trod in something. "What has Marguerite Dunlop's death got to do with Orange and compost?"

"Just tell me what you know about sheep manure," O'Neil said.

Preston's brow glistened. "A parent brings it in for me. From his farm in, yes, Orange. I compost it and put it on my roses. End of story."

Riley had her notebook out. "How do you move it around—to the compost bin and to the roses?"

"I borrow a buggy from the grounds staff. I have a wheelbarrow."

"This buggy," O'Neil said. "What does it look like?"

"Like a golf cart. They're green and yellow."

"Do you drive the buggy, or do the grounds staff?" O'Neil said.

"The staff don't work on my roses."

"You said *they*," O'Neil said. "How many are there?"

"I don't know. Two or three."

"Where are the buggies kept?" Riley said.

"All over." Preston shrugged. "At the front oval, at the Flats. There are sheds. You'd have to ask Craig Spratt."

"When was the last delivery of manure?" Riley said.

Preston looked at the wall. "Around the first week of December. Speech Day. The seventh."

"When did you move it to the compost bin?" Riley said.

"About a week later, when the holidays had started."

"And you used a buggy?" Riley said.

"It was eight bags. I drove to the Flats and took a buggy. When I had finished, I drove the buggy back and got my car."

"Well?" O'Neil said from the rear of the Calais. "Wayne?"

In the passenger seat, Farquhar gazed through the windshield. "He was . . . plausible."

They were in the admin car park still, aircon running. "You think he's telling the truth?" O'Neil said.

"I think he's a good liar," the psychiatrist said. "He's not what he presents as—the upstanding headmaster of a school. We know he's a predator, at the very least sleeping with young prostitutes."

"All this payola," O'Neil said. "Zabatino seems to be paying over the odds to fix a problem with his kid."

"There'll be more to it," Riley said. "The politician will be in on it. Zabatino's in Orange. Bishop's a stone's throw away in Blayney. Preston makes the introduction. Zabatino's buying favors. He needs to keep Preston sweet."

"So it's graft?" O'Neil said. "It carries a lot of risk."

"Preston might like risk," Farquhar said. "Zabatino indicated Preston might be rough with the girls. We should check with them about how bad it got. I'd like to ask Preston's wife about their sex life. Is Preston difficult to satisfy? What is he aroused by? Do they even have sex?"

"The wife's still in Adelaide," O'Neil said. "Annie's spoken with her. You could fly down."

"That's odd as well," Farquhar said. "The fact she hasn't returned to support her husband."

"He says he told her to stay away." Riley sniffed. "Reckons she's not comfortable in the empty school—even before this."

"That's convenient," Farquhar said. "Maybe the marriage is too."

"What else?" O'Neil said.

"He's entitled," Farquhar said. "He's in the pocket of the mafia. He's corrupt. He's not ethical—he's expedient. He lies. He manipulates. He sponges off others. It's not a pretty list."

"Where's it pointing?"

"Borderline personality disorder, narcissistic features," Farquhar said. "That's not uncommon. It's a long way from psychopath."

"But could he kill?" Patel said.

"Anyone can kill," Farquhar said. "In a panic or a rage or a corner. The difference is that Preston's type wouldn't fess up and take his due."

"What's his motive?" Riley said.

"Again, as with Lynch, I can only assume a scenario. Say Preston put the hard word on Marguerite, or perhaps it had gone beyond that, and there had been something physical. The girl didn't like it and threatened to blow the whistle. In a corner, his reputation at stake, Preston lashes out."

"He kills her, and then he rides it out?" Riley said.

"Yes," Farquhar said. "In his mind, he's more important than the victim. He has more to offer the world. He'd convince himself he's honored Marguerite, bestowed some special privilege on her with his interest in her. His psychology would allow him to kill her and then live with himself. Nietzsche sums it up: it is easier to cope with a bad conscience than a bad reputation."

"You said he was plausible about the cart," Patel said. "Let's say he's telling the truth. He used the John Deere to move his manure and put the cart back at the playing fields. If that's the case, why didn't he just admit to the manure delivery when he saw us asking in the media?"

"It goes back to risk," Farquhar said. "He rationalized that only he and Zabatino knew. And maybe Bishop. So Preston wants to ride it out. He thinks if he comes clean about the manure, it'll lead us to Zabatino and graft and prostitutes."

"He knows we'll dig into it and that Bowman won't be far behind," O'Neil said. "It'd finish him at this place—it might even send him to jail."

Riley half turned. After they had confronted Preston with Orange and the manure, she had expected O'Neil to go harder, to hit the headmaster with the discrepancy between the CCTV and his statement. "You didn't want to give him both barrels, Steve?"

O'Neil's tongue clicked on the roof of his mouth. "I wanted him broken before we used the CCTV," he said. "The way it played, he managed to stay standing."

"Yes, but he's starting to unravel," Farquhar said. "Rhythmic ambiguity."

"What?" O'Neil said.

"The voice," Farquhar said. "He's all over the place."

"Back in Ottawa," Riley said. She'd heard it too.

"The accent, the pretense," Farquhar said. "It's unraveling under pressure. We should keep it up."

"All right." O'Neil stretched his neck. "Let's bring him in and lay it all on him."

"Now?" Riley said.

"Tomorrow," O'Neil said. "Let's stir him up more first."

"We could tell him we've got a search warrant for his house," Riley said. "The court will grant it if we say manure from his garden turned up on the plastic that wrapped the body."

"Nice," O'Neil said. "What else?"

Patel cleared her throat. "We could play dirty."

"Mm?" O'Neil said.

"There's a book I'm reading," Patel said. "Case studies about the early days of behavioral science at the FBI."

A corner of O'Neil's mouth curled up. "Right."

"At two in the morning, I ring Preston on a burner," Patel said.

"And say what?"

"And say I'm Marguerite Dunlop."

O'Neil's eyes closed. "Let's pretend you didn't say that."

"Sir," Patel said.

"It's hillbilly shit. The court would eat us alive."

"It's got one thing going for it," Riley said. "It's not concrete thinking."

"What are we hoping to achieve?" Farquhar said. "To spook him?"

"It's more pressure—it adds to his stress," Patel said. "The night timing is important. He's home alone, in a big house. Things are ominous at the witching hour. We'd need to have eyes on the place when we call, see if he runs. If we do it right, keep it simple, it will be unsettling, throw him off balance."

"We'd steal some sleep off him, at least," Riley said. "Bring him in tired in the morning."

"Tell me," O'Neil said, "when the feds ran this maneuver, did it work?"

"The case was a few years old and going nowhere with the local cops," Patel said. "The FBI came in and cracked it open."

"How did I know you were going to say that?" O'Neil said.

Farquhar opened his door.

"So let's agree," O'Neil said, "that we never had this conversation."

Patel nodded and got out with the psychiatrist.

"You know what that's called?" O'Neil said.

Patel looked back in at him. "Plausible deniability?"

"You learn fast, kiddo."

◆ ◆ ◆

Riley watched Farquhar and Patel walk to the doctor's Volvo. O'Neil climbed from the back of the Calais and came around to the front passenger seat. She left the car in park.

"Got the briefing note on the carts," he said, bald head bent over his phone.

She waited while he read. Preston's admissions had not changed the fact that the John Deere from the shed behind the Dunlop house remained their best lead. Two of Tran's boys had been digging into the carts since Monday, and O'Neil had ordered them to keep clear of Spratt. Riley agreed—Spratt was a person of interest, and they relied on him too much.

To circumvent the property manager, the Satyr detectives had tracked down the head of the grounds staff to Bermagui, where he'd been since before Christmas, a watertight alibi. The officers had traveled south to question him in person about the carts and then spoken to the bursar, Murray, to confirm details. O'Neil finished reading their findings and looked out the windshield.

"What?" Riley said.

O'Neil summarized. Prince Albert owned three John Deere Gator utility vehicles. They ran on twenty-five-horsepower diesel engines and could carry two people in their cabs, as well as loads of up to 650 kilograms in their trays. They had been bought as a job lot three years ago and were serviced annually. One of them had recently had its tires replaced.

"Where are they kept?" Riley said.

"That's the problem," O'Neil said. "It doesn't matter who you ask—the answer to that question is always the same."

Spratt. She put the car in gear.

"He probably knows we've been looking," O'Neil said.

Riley nodded: news traveled. She drove through the school. Lynch, the bursar, the head of the grounds staff, and now Preston had all been questioned about the John Deeres. Spratt had an ear to the ground.

There was an old Subaru, but no Hilux, outside the Spratt house. They knocked, and Jenny Spratt opened the door. Tanned, thin, late forties, faded short shorts and a singlet, no bra.

"Mrs. Spratt, I'm sorry to bother you again," Riley said. "This is Detective Chief Inspector O'Neil."

"Jenny," she said to O'Neil. "Craig's out. You want to come in?"

They followed her to the kitchen.

"Do you know where Craig is?" O'Neil said.

"Nope, but he won't be far. Cuppa?"

"Sounds good," O'Neil said.

She flicked the kettle on and faced them across the bench. Dirty-blonde hair with the roots showing, lines around the mouth. Party girl. Booze, drugs, sun, smokes—it was written on her face.

"Mind if I use the bathroom?" Riley said. "Been drinking tea all morning."

Jenny Spratt nodded toward the hall. "First on the right."

In the mirrored cabinet over the sink, Riley saw Berocca, face cream, eye drops, Panadol, tramadol, deodorant, Dettol, Voltaren, talc, nail polish remover. Stilnox sleeping pills . . . She picked up the bottle, pushed the lid down, and turned. Maybe twenty tablets. She opened the drawers in the vanity. Toothpaste, toothbrushes, floss, makeup, a hair dryer. A bunch of prescription meds: steroid creams, asthma sprays, birth control pills.

Listening, Riley slipped down the hall, passed the Spratts' bedroom, then a spare room, then a small office with a desk and a bank of four monitors. She went in and brought the screens to life with a click on the keyboard. CCTV footage of the school. There was no movement on the screens, and Riley guessed it was live. She walked to the back door. It was unlocked—three steps down to the yard, brown grass and packed earth. A long hose hung coiled on the side fence. It was done right, no kinks. Not everyone could coil a long hose right. She looked at the boat on its trailer over the fence. If you ran a boat, you learned to coil a hose.

She heard a car pull up at the front. She went back to the bathroom, flushed the toilet, and returned to the kitchen as Craig Spratt walked in.

"Mr. Spratt," O'Neil said, picking up his mug.

Spratt nodded at him and then Riley. "Can *I* have a cuppa?" he said to his wife.

O'Neil started straight in. "The three John Deere carts," he said to Spratt. "Can you tell us who uses them?"

Spratt scratched the back of his neck. "Groundsmen, mainly."

"What about the headmaster?" O'Neil said. "He use them?"

There was a change on the air. Jenny Spratt turned to the sink.

"Preston?" Spratt said. "Yeah, when he's feeding his roses."

"Does he sign the cart out or something?" Riley said.

Spratt looked confused. "Nah. Keys are left in the ignition. Lots of teachers use 'em."

"Do you use them?" Riley said.

"Me?" Spratt squinted at her like she might have a roo loose. He took the mug from his wife. "Not unless I have to. Got me Hilux."

"Do you know where all three carts are now?" O'Neil said.

"In the work huts." Spratt gave an over-yonder look. "At the back of the Flats."

O'Neil's phone buzzed, and he excused himself, stooping through the screen door to take the call outside.

"At the Flats," Riley said. "You know that for certain?"

"Yeah, we put 'em away for the break." Spratt blew on his tea. "Why?"

O'Neil came in, nodding at Jenny Spratt as he put his mug on the bench. "Thanks," he said. "We need to keep moving."

Riley followed him to the Calais and started the engine. "What?" she said.

"Shoe and Tire came back on the vehicle tracks at Preston's compost bin. A match with the John Deere in the shed."

Analysts had also checked the CCTV footage from earlier in the month and confirmed that Preston had picked up a John Deere from behind the Flats and then returned it. "That was on December 13," O'Neil said. "The John Deere is at the Flats, nearly two kilometers from where we find it in the shed on January 1."

Riley drove at a crawl. "On Wednesday, December 28, or the next morning, the killer moves Marguerite's body from her bedroom to the shed," she said. "He's either moved the John Deere to the shed sometime after December 13 or now needs to go and get it. He washes, wraps, and dumps the body, then takes the John Deere back to the shed behind the house and leaves it."

"That's what I still don't get," O'Neil said. "Why does he return to the shed? He'd be better off leaving the cart back at the Flats, or at least somewhere neutral. Why return it to the scene?"

"Because he's obsessive," Riley said. "He knows there's a hose and privacy. He wants to wash the cart again."

"And then what? He plans to come back and move it later?"

"Maybe," she said. "It's the same with the creek. Farquhar thinks he wanted to put the body in the creek."

"He runs out of time."

She saw Spratt's coiled hose and Preston's garage—Priya had said there was privacy to wrap and load. Riley's phone pinged, and she read the text: "Bowman's prints have come back clean."

They were now near the Hay Stand, the police tape still streaming. Riley pulled up and put her window down, and O'Neil did the same. The prints on the bench at the Dunlop house weren't Bowman's. They sat in the warm cross breeze.

"Bowman's obsessive," Riley said. "He's a bench wiper."

"Jesus, Rose."

"I know. But there's . . ." Something? Or just coincidence piling up.

"What about Preston?"

"You really want to get Priya to call him tonight?"

"There's a phone tap running—we'd have to be careful."

They talked it through as Riley drove back to the station. In the strike force room, they briefed Patel. She would be taken to the school by patrol car at 1:00 a.m. She would make the call, watch the house in case Preston ran, and be brought back in the same car. Riley handed her a clean, prepaid mobile. If there was anything urgent, Patel was to call O'Neil on her own phone. Otherwise, she could brief him by email on the ride home. Riley and O'Neil would go to Preston's house at 6:00 a.m. and ask him to accompany them to Parramatta to answer some questions.

At 8:30 p.m., they disbanded. They needed to sleep.

O'Neil was woken in his mezzanine by a call at 4:10 a.m.

"What?" He sat up, fully alert, and listened. "Don't approach the house," he said. "I'm on my way. Call me if it changes."

He threw on clothes and nearly tripped down the stairs to the kitchen. He called Patel's mobile. Voice mail. He went down in the lift, drumming at the handrail, and ran to the Prado. He called Patel's number again as he waited for the garage door. No answer. He was doing 130 through the empty streets of Camperdown when his phone rang again. It was the officer who had woken him, the general-duties constable who had driven Patel to Prince Albert.

"Sir, we got her. We heard her phone ringing. She's okay."

O'Neil braked. "Put her on."

"Steve," Patel said, "we need Crime Scene."

"What happened?"

"Gladesville. He knocked me out, tied me up, said some things."

"Jesus fuck."

"Yeah, it's good. Flushed from his burrow."

"Fucking Christ. Where?"

"In the trees outside Preston's."

"Make a voice memo—what he said, everything you can remember. I'll be there in ten. Put the constable back on."

"Sir?" the constable said.

"Secure the scene and the school. No one steps on a blade of grass. Don't touch Patel. Call an ambulance. Was she gagged?"

"Yes, sir."

"With tape?"

"We cut it, but it's still on her face. She won't let us touch it."

"Good," O'Neil said.

"Sir," the constable said, "she wants to talk to you again."

Patel's voice came back on the Bluetooth. "He said he left a present at Preston's door."

O'Neil went into the tunnel at Haberfield. "What else did he say?"

"'Tell Riley we'll play.'"

23

Riley arrived from the east with the dawn. Crime Scene was under-way, processing the ground where Patel had been attacked and an area around the front door of Preston's house. She parked and got out, and a Satyr detective logged her in through the police tape. Annie Tran was overseeing the canvass. On the gravel, O'Neil was talking on his phone.

"We need to check Opal cards," he was saying, "plus CCTV on buses and trains—stops and stations everywhere. Clyde, Dundas, Telopea, Carlingford, Epping, Beecroft, Parramatta. The whole network, the Northwest Metro. He might have got off somewhere and walked for an hour. He could have come down on the RiverCat last night. Check Rydalmere."

O'Neil hung up and looked at Riley. "He had two and a half hours before we got mobilized," he said. "Could be past Wollongong—Newcastle if he bolted. Goulburn, Canberra, Bathurst. It's too late for a cordon. Chopper's up. Highway Patrol the whole way through. We're looking at speed cameras, red lights, servos on the main arteries out. He might be sleeping in a van around the corner. He could have come in two days ago, and be ready to sit it out for a week."

"What about if he came down on his own boat?" Riley said.

"We're looking." There was CCTV at the wharves all the way down the river.

"Where's Priya?"

"Westmead. Brain scan."

Riley stared at him.

"She's okay," he said. "He only gave her a tap. If he'd wanted to kill her, she'd be dead."

"Same place Marguerite was hit?"

O'Neil's hand went to his skull. "Bit further back."

"She made the call to Preston and then got hit?"

"Yeah. I haven't got it crystal clear yet. I called Preston, said there'd been an incident and to stay inside until further notice. He didn't say a word, just hung up. He hasn't tried to come out."

Riley studied the house. The area under the portico had been taped off, and two forensic investigators were at work in bunny suits. O'Neil had briefed her quickly when he woke her. The t-shaped symbol had been carved in the wood of the headmaster's front door.

"You said he left the knife?" she said.

O'Neil handed her forensic booties, and they scrunched across the drive and under the bunting to the door.

Riley's breath caught, and her head went back, the hairs on her neck standing on end. The knife had been stabbed into the door at the center of the symbol. A piece of thin leather ran through a hole at the end of the orange handle, tied in a loop.

She swiveled away under the police tape and stood on the drive. Bowman's words came back: *Wouldn't it be weird? Shitting in his own nest.* Drunk locals at the Commercial.

Bowman's knife? There was no logic to it. She tried to control her breathing . . .

They weren't his prints on the bench.

O'Neil was watching, giving her space. She pulled out her phone.

Bowman had woken early, first light. A sticky sea mist had settled on the harbor, and a foghorn had sounded for longer than he'd ever heard, almost a full minute—a leviathan's bellow dragging him from sleep.

He'd had a coffee and decided against a second one. He put the kettle on, pulled down a tin of tea, and pinched loose leaves into his orange pot. T2 Canberra Breakfast, made to taste like an Anzac biscuit. Canberra . . . Bishop must be the conduit to the old man. Alexander had assumed business, but it was politics. Had Beat-Up Benny worked in Canberra? Alexander had worked in the gallery—what did he know about Bishop? Politicians and journalists, backscratching away in their bubble. Bowman would take a cop over the lot of them any day. The kettle clicked off as his phone rang. Riley.

"Bit early, isn't it?" he said.

"You're awake?"

"Course," he said. "Been for a jog. I'm on my second cup."

"In the kitchen?"

He caught the warning note. "Yeah."

"You've got an orange knife," she said, "hanging from a nail on the wall by the bench."

"What?"

"Just tell me," she said, "the knife, is it still there?"

Bowman looked at the nail where his father's sailing knife hung. A remembrance of things past. He hadn't noticed it was missing. "No," he said.

"Adam," Riley said, "you have to listen and do exactly as I say."

"I'm listening."

"Get a clean cloth, a Chux, whatever."

He opened a drawer. "Okay."

"Now tread carefully to the front door. Don't touch anything."

He moved through the hall.

"Open the door with the cloth," she said, "and pull it closed in the same way."

"All right," he said. "I'm outside. What's going on?"

"Go to that café down from the pub and wait there. Don't move. I'm sending Crime Scene to your house. I'll see you in an hour."

◆　◆　◆

They wanted Farquhar to view the knife on Preston's door in situ, before it was bagged and barcoded and removed to the lab. O'Neil handed the doctor forensic booties, gloves, and a mask, and the two men went under the tape. Riley waited on the drive. After a minute, they were back.

Farquhar pulled down his mask. "Two triggers, I think. The murderer of Marguerite trying to impersonate him and then Steve's comments about impotence to the press."

"He thinks Preston killed the girl?" O'Neil said.

"He's just following the coverage," Farquhar said. "Reading the tea leaves."

"We haven't said anything in the media about Preston," Riley said.

"The NeedFeed story," Farquhar said. "It mentioned Preston's house. And we know from Priya that Gladesville referenced you after he attacked her. The story had a picture of you and the journalist in Preston's garden."

Riley nodded at O'Neil.

"The knife belongs to Adam Bowman," O'Neil said. "Rose saw it in his house. He kept it hung in his kitchen."

"Really?" Farquhar's eyes grew wide. "He brings in Bowman?"

Riley toed gravel.

"What if this is Bowman bringing himself in?" O'Neil said.

Farquhar's face puckered. "There's nothing to link Bowman to any of this. And why use his own knife?"

"He likes to play games?" O'Neil gave his scalp a halfhearted rub. He was siding with the doctor. Bowman was a blind alley—they had no evidence, and it didn't make sense.

"It's too far-fetched," Farquhar said. "Keep it simple. We prodded him on impotence, and he saw the gossip story. Rose?"

She shrugged. It lined up: Gladesville was playing off the NeedFeed story.

"It shows some swagger," O'Neil said.

"More than that," Farquhar said. "Insouciance. He goes into Bowman's house. And the attack on Priya—it must have been spontaneous. He didn't know she would be here. He's saying he can go anywhere, do anything. He's the opposite of impotent."

"But there's weakness too, in the arrogance," O'Neil said. "For the first time, we called the shots."

"Indeed," Farquhar said. "He's malleable. We provoked him."

"What's it do for the geographic profile?" Riley said.

Farquhar held up his palms. "I don't think it's relevant. He's following us. We brought him here—as Steve says, we called the shots. The school itself isn't important. It could have been anywhere."

Riley bit her cheek. The school wasn't relevant? It sure felt relevant. "Steve?" she said.

"I think Wayne's right," O'Neil said. "You know it too. It's flowing from the NeedFeed story. It's logical."

Riley knew what O'Neil thought about logic. "He feels pretty comfortable, here at the school," she said. "You both noted it. Spontaneous swagger."

Farquhar stroked his beard.

"You need to make the leap," she said. "Have a look at the map. Get out of your comfort zone. We kept the school out of the geographic profile after Marguerite—fair enough. Now we're going to do it again?"

"Leave it for now," O'Neil said. "What do we do with Bowman?"

"He can't stay in his house," Farquhar said. "Rose, you neither. Gladesville's directly threatened you."

"All right," O'Neil said. "Rose, you go to Bowman. Get a statement, and check in with Crime Scene. Annie will oversee the manhunt."

"You still going to bring Preston in?" Riley said.

O'Neil looked at the headmaster's house. Riley knew he wouldn't want to waste Patel's work. Gladesville in Preston's garden with Bowman's knife. Nausea stirred. It made no sense . . . Weird was normal. Fuck logic—you had to think past it.

◆　◆　◆

O'Neil motioned Farquhar to follow him behind the house. He called Preston's mobile as he walked and asked him to meet them at the back door.

Preston hung up without speaking, and O'Neil and Farquhar waited on the patio. After a minute, with no sign of the headmaster, Farquhar tried the door. It was unlocked and opened into a big kitchen, dark and tangy, like a teenager's bedroom. O'Neil turned on a light. There was dirty crockery around the sink and the plastic packaging of microwave meals.

"Even Riley wouldn't eat that," O'Neil said. He heard a noise farther back in the house and put a finger up. "Incoming."

Preston walked in, his bloodshot eyes registering no surprise at finding them in his kitchen. "What now?" he said.

"Now we go for a little drive," O'Neil said.

Preston poured three fingers of Scotch into a glass from a bottle on the bench.

"We need you to accompany us to Parramatta," O'Neil said. "We've got some questions to clear up."

"Am I under arrest?"

"What would we arrest you for?" O'Neil said.

Preston drank the whisky in two slugs. "All right."

They went out the patio door and around to the Prado. Preston got in the back and looked out at the forensic investigators as O'Neil drove.

"Shuffle along to the middle, and keep your head down," O'Neil said. "There's media at the exit." He slowed as he went through the police checkpoint. At the gate, television cameramen and photographers swarmed the car. The light onto the main road was red, but O'Neil eased out and swung right.

"All clear," he said.

Preston brought his head up from between his knees. "Who tipped them off?"

"It's a goat rodeo," O'Neil said. "They pick up on the ruckus."

They took Preston to the interview room they'd used for Kevin Lynch. The headmaster looked half-blotto, rheumy eyes in a gray face. O'Neil gave silent thanks to Patel.

"Philip," he said, "there's something troubling us. It's to do with your original statement, specifically your movements on Wednesday the twenty-eighth."

Preston twitched a shoulder.

"That's the day Marguerite Dunlop was killed. Remember her? Bludgeoned to death at your school?"

"Get to the point." Dutch courage.

"In your statement, you said you worked at home and didn't leave the house," O'Neil said. "The problem is, other people say they saw you out around the school that day."

"What other people?"

"You were seen driving your car through the school on Wednesday. The CCTV footage corroborates the statements we have regarding this. Why did you tell us you didn't leave the house?"

"You didn't see me on the CCTV," Preston said.

"Now, Philip," O'Neil said, "why would you say that?"

"If you say you have CCTV footage showing me driving in the school on Wednesday, then I say you're lying."

"Whoa," O'Neil said. "I didn't say we had CCTV footage of you. I said we have CCTV footage corroborating the statements of others."

"What others?"

"You're quite certain there's no CCTV footage of you around the school on Wednesday?"

"I just said that." Preston looked at Farquhar. "Did I not just say that?"

"Is that because you maintain your statement is true?" O'Neil said. "You didn't leave the house?"

Preston shook his head. "You think I killed Marguerite?"

"There are anomalies in your statement," O'Neil said. "Someone is not telling us the truth."

"I need to change my statement," Preston said.

O'Neil kept his face blank. "Okay."

"I drove through the school on that Wednesday."

"At what time?" O'Neil said.

Preston didn't need to think. "Just before two. I was home by four."

"Where did you drive?" O'Neil said.

"To the Spratts' house."

O'Neil missed a beat. "Why didn't we see you on the CCTV? There are cameras on the route."

"I avoided the cameras."

"Why?" O'Neil said.

"Habit. Spratt monitors the footage. I don't like him watching me."

"It's his job to keep an eye on things. Why don't you like it?"

"Because I've been sleeping with his wife."

O'Neil stared at the table. He turned to Farquhar, and the two of them stood and headed for the door.

"I've got a bad feeling about this," O'Neil said in the corridor.

Farquhar cleared his throat. "Cognitive dissonance."

O'Neil made a fist and tapped the wall. "Just say it," he said.

"The drunkenness amplifies the resignation," the psychiatrist said. "He knows we're onto his secret life. He also knows he's in the frame for Marguerite. The only way out is to tell the truth."

O'Neil already knew it—Preston was cutting his losses. "The affair explains his reaction to the drone footage," he said. "He was sweating on the possibility it captured him beating a path to Jenny Spratt's door."

"His response is understandable," Farquhar said. "How would the school board react if news of this liaison were to become public?"

O'Neil lifted his phone to call Riley. She needed to confirm Preston's statement with Jenny Spratt.

◆ ◆ ◆

They left Preston to find his own way home and drove to Westmead.

Patel's brain scan was clear. The concussion had been slight. She'd discharged herself and was waiting in an ambulance bay when O'Neil and Farquhar pulled up. Both men got out to help her into the Prado, but she shrugged them off.

"It's all right," she said. "Really, I'm fine."

She wanted to talk through the attack as they drove, but O'Neil stopped her. "Let's wait," he said. "Rose needs to hear it too."

Patel handed O'Neil the burner phone, and at a strip of shops in Ermington, O'Neil pulled over. He took a wet wipe from the glove box, got out, snapped the SIM, and ground the mobile into the pavement under his heel. He picked it up, wiped everything down, and threw it into a bin.

"Forensic sophistication," he said as he buckled his seat belt and merged with the traffic.

The strike force room was humming with the hunt for Gladesville. O'Neil ordered in food and coffee, and Tran briefed them while they waited for Riley. Forensics had got nothing from the scene where Patel had been attacked, and nothing from around Preston's door or driveway.

"No prints, no fiber, no hair," Tran said. "No shoe impressions— he's in booties, and the ground's too hard where he hits Priya. He's on gravel on the drive. So just the knife, wiped clean. The tape and cable ties used on Priya were pristine, and he'd poured bleach and ammonia on them for good measure. And he was at it with the wet wipes."

"What about Bowman's house?" O'Neil said.

"Mixed DNA. Prints everywhere."

"How'd he get in?"

"Side window, we think."

Tran went back to her desk, and O'Neil and Farquhar drank tea and coffee. Riley came in and embraced Patel. The four of them sat at the round table.

"Priya," O'Neil said, "start from when you left this room last night. Every detail, nothing is too small. He might have followed you. He might have been watching your place."

Patel took a breath. She'd driven straight to her unit at Harris Park. "I resisted an open bottle of wine in the fridge. It was nine. I counted how many hours until I was on the road again—four hours—so I didn't have a drink."

"Go on," O'Neil said.

She'd showered, eaten a light meal, slept three hours, woken before her alarm. The patrol car was waiting across from her building as arranged, at 1:00 a.m., interior light on. There wasn't a soul on the street. Two general-duty constables sat in the front, one male, one female, both young. Patel had got in the back. The female constable had turned and looked at her as the car pulled away. Patel had met her eyes but said nothing.

"As agreed," she said to O'Neil, "no chitchat in the car."

O'Neil nodded. Strings had been pulled. The trip had never happened.

A police car had been parked at the gate to the school, and they'd pulled up beside it. The constables had been told Patel wouldn't be long—twenty minutes. She got out, acknowledged the officers in the second car, and started up the slope toward Preston's house, two hundred meters away. The ground was lightly wooded, and it had been completely dark. No moon. She had moved slowly, picking her way through the trees. There was a night-light mounted on the corner of the garage, throwing a glow over the drive and the portico. At the edge of the lawn, next to the rose bed, she had stopped and listened. Nothing. She had pulled the disposable phone out of her pocket and pressed it into life. Preston's number had been programmed. He had taken a while to pick up.

She had just said, "It's me," and waited. Preston's voice had been thick with sleep, saying, "Who is this?" She had said, "It's me, Marguerite," and left him dangling on the line for ten seconds before she hung up.

A light had come on upstairs, then more lights across the top floor and then downstairs as well. "He was moving through the house," Patel said.

"Probably looking for a bottle of Joey Vino's best Scotch," Riley said.

Patel smiled. She'd stayed watching the place to see whether Preston was going to leave. The lights had remained on, and he hadn't come out. After fifteen minutes, she had headed back into the trees, debating whether to use the flashlight on her phone to navigate, ultimately deciding against it. She had been in the thickest group of trees when she'd sensed something.

"You saw something, or heard something?" O'Neil said.

"I couldn't see a thing, it was that black. And it wasn't a noise. It was more I felt it, like a ripple. My skin crawled, my training kicked in, my hand went to my Glock. And that was it. Next thing I know, I'm lying on my side, bound hand and foot and gagged. I could taste tape and bleach. My head was aching."

She had managed to wriggle onto her back, the bindings cutting into her skin. Cable ties, she knew. She had felt twigs under her and heard a truck gearing down. Air brakes. A red light.

"I thought, *It's the road, Pennant Hills Road,* so I knew I was still in the school. Then I thought, *Cable ties, bleach.* There was another smell, and I realized what it was. *Ammonia.* I lay still, concentrated on my breathing, through my nose. My heart was thumping."

Then he had been there, his face a foot from hers, a balaclava, goggles.

"Night vision?" O'Neil said.

"Yes."

"Had he spoken yet?" O'Neil said.

"Not at this stage. He pricked my throat with a knife." She touched her jugular notch. "And then he was gone."

She'd lain on her back, completely still, listening, for a long time, several minutes. The muscles in her arms had started to relax, and her fists, clenched tight, had loosened. She had moved slightly. "That's when he put the toe of his boot into my ribs."

"His particular sadism," Farquhar said. "He enjoyed taking away your hope."

"He was back with the blade, across my stomach, my chest. He turned it on my pubic bone."

"You felt he was making a decision?" Farquhar said.

"He was weighing it," Patel said. "Whether to kill me."

The psychiatrist nodded. "But that would have been a departure."

"Too random?" Riley said.

"He's assiduous," Farquhar said. "He surveils. He's obsessive with the choosing of the victim, the planning, the scene."

"But he was tempted?" Riley said.

"Of course," Farquhar said. "Priya is desirable—she's vulnerable, she's available. But he's methodical, not impulsive. He wants to do things at his pace, with time to watch, even record it, so he can relive it. That's the whole point."

"He knows there's police at the gates," O'Neil said. "It's too risky to try and move Priya."

"Yes," Farquhar said. "But also, she's nothing to him. He builds a fantasy around whomever he's chosen."

"You don't think he followed Priya?" O'Neil said.

"Certainly not. I think he stumbled on her. He was there to put the knife in Preston's door. We know that was premeditated—he had to go to Bowman's house and take the knife. That's why he was at the school. Priya was random."

"And the knife is a response to us?" Riley said. "To our provocation?"

"Theatrics," O'Neil said. "A flourish. He's inserting himself into the investigation."

"Correct," Farquhar said. "But it's a retaliation as well. To kill in the way he does takes severe rage. His arrogance is wrapped up with anger—power and control—but it's also a mask for his insecurity, his total inadequacy. They're the buttons we push."

O'Neil nodded at Patel. "Can you finish? He has the knife on you . . ."

"He stood up, and that was when he spoke. He said, 'I left a present at Preston's door.' Then he said, 'Tell Riley we'll play.' That was all. He was gone. Eventually the constables found me after you called my phone."

"His voice," Riley said. "Can you describe it?"

"Muffled. There was the mask but something else too, in the mouth, to disguise it. Deliberately flat and low."

"Think on it," Riley said. "If there's anything that chimes with a voice you've heard."

"Sleep on it," O'Neil said. She needed to get some rest.

"I don't like the focus on Rose," Farquhar said. "That's not random. But I think we need to move Priya too, for safekeeping."

O'Neil sighed and stretched a shoulder. Homicide had the lease on two apartments in a secure block near police headquarters in Parramatta. They used them for sources and snitches and visits from interstate colleagues. Bowman could go in one, Rose and Priya could share the other.

"Fuck's sake," Riley said.

"And you need to swap out of the Calais," O'Neil said. "There's a white SS in the car park." He tossed her a key. "Tell us about Jenny Spratt."

Riley turned the fob in her fingers. "I went to meet her in Darling Harbour, before she started a shift on a party boat. I put Preston's claim to her, and she got flustered. Wanted to know how we knew— and she wanted to know if Craig knew. I told her he didn't, and there was no reason he would have to if she was truthful and told me everything."

Jenny Spratt had corroborated Preston's story. "She said Preston had been at her house from two till four p.m., and they'd had sex and a couple of vodkas. She was certain of the time because it was arranged around Craig's medical appointment."

"That fits?" O'Neil said.

Riley nodded. Craig Spratt had mentioned his appointment in his original statement, and it had been confirmed by his GP. It was while driving to the doctor that Spratt had seen Preston's car. Spratt had run slightly late, so their paths had crossed.

"You believe her?" O'Neil said.

"There was nothing to suggest she was lying," Riley said.

"How long's it been going on?"

"Couple of months. Jenny had noticed Preston eyeing her off for a while. She was pissed one night after a school function, and he came on pretty strong. She went along with it. It's very casual—when they're bored and the coast is clear. She didn't react to the mention of Orange, but she said she knew Preston would have others on the side."

O'Neil frowned at Farquhar. "Does it ring true?"

"With Preston, yes. He's an opportunist. Sexually compulsive. He'd try it on with any female anywhere. A secretary in his office, a maid in a hotel, a cleaner at his house, the mother of a son at the school, a teacher in an empty classroom, a waiter in a restaurant, the wife of a friend—"

"The seventeen-year-old daughter of his colleague," Riley said.

"Indeed," Farquhar said. "Striving, seeking, conquering."

"A hard dog to keep on the porch," O'Neil said.

24

Riley drove in the white Commodore. All the roads leading to Preston had converged in a dead end. The headmaster had looked good as a suspect, but she wasn't surprised the evidence had fallen away. Why? Because Preston was capable of killing Marguerite, but no one was putting him in the kill rooms at Gladesville.

If Preston had killed Marguerite, then Farquhar was right, and the cases weren't linked. But Farquhar was wrong. Riley could feel it—the cold tug of a missing link.

At the school gate, she slowed past the checkpoint and the scene at the headmaster's house and kept to a crawl through the campus. Gum trees dun green against a cerulean sky. Bowman had grown up here. Had something gone wrong? The NeedFeed story had hinted at troubled family ties, but she'd dismissed that as Preston and Bishop trying to smear. Could she see Bowman in the rooms at the Chatfield and Sheridan houses? Truthfully, she didn't know. She'd tried to follow instinct, but the orange hilt in Preston's door was proving indigestible.

She had arranged to meet Spratt at Ghost Gum. The homestead lost some of its majesty from the rear, its lines weakened by the tacked-on kitchen jutting into the yard. She parked and walked around to the alcove window where Crime Scene had found the open latch. It was Friday. They had hauled Lynch in on Monday and then spent the rest of the week chasing Preston. Hindsight was pointless, but Riley knew their focus had drifted too far from the Dunlop house. Geography. This was someone's comfort zone.

Spratt's Hilux pulled up in front of the double doors of the stand-alone stone garage, and she went to meet him.

He slammed the door of the pickup. "Used to be a barn," he said, nodding at the garage.

"I see. The whole place—it's quite something."

"Oh yeah. I'm not one for ghost stories, but I tell ya, up here on me own sometimes . . ."

"Are you up here on your own a lot?"

"Bit." He shrugged. "Fixin' stuff."

"Yeah. The alterations you did"—she scratched her cheek—"to make Marguerite more comfortable here on her own. Can we go through them again?"

"Sure."

This time she had a key from Crime Scene. Spratt followed her into the kitchen and took her through the bottom level, the space he'd sealed off.

"See what I mean?" He put his hands on his hips. "You can lock yourself away and pretend the creepy bits aren't here."

Riley stood at the door of the old pantry and looked at the alcove window. She felt Spratt's eyes on her, didn't like having him behind her. She turned into the kitchen, took a seat at the table, pulled her laptop from her bag, and scrolled through Bruce Dunlop's statement.

"You installed the locks in late November?"

"That's it." He stood holding the back of a chair. "Bruce and Bev were getting organized. With the locks and Tatters, Margy was happy to stay here."

Riley glanced up. "Tatters?"

He gave her a watchful look. "You don't know about the dog?"

Riley closed her laptop. "Tell me about the dog."

"Not much to tell. Went missing. Bad timing, that was all."

"Bad timing how?"

"Well, right before Margy was to stay here on her own. Having the dog was a big part of it. That and closing off downstairs."

"What happened?"

Spratt's mouth turned down. "School broke up round the seventh, eighth. The next week, the Dunlops went away with Margy."

A horrible stillness. Riley swallowed. Fiji.

"Anyway," Spratt said, "the bloody thing vanished while they were away. The Green kids were feeding it. They went looking everywhere. We checked it hadn't got in here and couldn't get back out. Poor Margy—she lost her security blanket."

Riley had risen from the table and was walking out into the yard, dialing as she went.

"Steve," she said when O'Neil answered, "the Dunlops had a dog."

He was quiet on the line.

"Spratt just filled me in," she said. "It disappeared while the family was in Fiji. The Green kids were looking after it."

She waited.

"Go on," he said.

"You were right. The Fiji trip. Someone comes and kills the dog while they're there."

"And?"

He knew, but she said it anyway. "And a week later, he comes back and kills the daughter."

"Talk to the Greens, talk to Bruce Dunlop," O'Neil said. "Find out whatever you can about the dog."

Spratt was still in the kitchen. Riley sat and indicated for him to do the same. "If I could just ask about the dog," she said. "You said the Green kids were feeding it?"

"Yeah. They always did when the Dunlops were away. The Dunlop kids used to return the favor."

"The Greens have a dog?"

"Nah. A cat."

"When did you learn the dog was missing?"

Spratt eyed the ceiling. "Hmm. Jeez."

"The family went to Fiji on the sixteenth, a Wednesday," Riley said. "For eight days."

"Yeah. Let's say after that weekend. Prob'ly the Monday. I'll firm it up."

"Okay. What happened, exactly?"

"I got a call from Tom. He said he hadn't seen the dog for a day or two, had ridden all over but couldn't find it. He was worried it'd snuck into the house. Wanted me to open up and look."

"The Dunlops hadn't left him a key?"

"S'pose not. Dog food was left in the shed by the garage. Dog slept in there too. There's a tap to fill the water bowl."

"All right. So you came into the house?"

"Tom ran through the place, callin' out."

"Did you come in?"

"Nup. Don't like dogs."

"How long was Tom in here?"

Spratt's shoulders jigged. "Coupla minutes."

"Two minutes?"

"Yeah. Three minutes."

"All right, thanks." She stood. "That's all."

In the yard, Spratt pointed out the dog's shed. It was swept and tidy. Two bowls hung on nails on the wall. There was dry food in a plastic box and a folded rug on a shelf. She would check the briefings, but she guessed Satyr detectives searching the property would have noted the family had once owned a pet.

"Have to keep it clean," Spratt said. "Rats."

Black birds wheeled overhead as Spratt drove off. A murder of crows, omens in flight. Riley walked in circles on the lawn, round and round. There had been no mention of the dog in anyone's statement—not the Dunlops', not the Greens', not Craig Spratt's. It was understandable—confronted with the murder of Marguerite, the missing dog had seemed insignificant.

She got into the Commodore and called Bruce Dunlop. No answer. She drove to the Greens' house.

"We weren't expecting you," Sarah Green said at the door. "I'm the only one home."

"May I come in?" Riley said.

Sarah led her through to the family room. "I hear you've been giving Preston a hard time," she said.

"You've spoken to him?"

Sarah scoffed. "Not likely."

"Why's that?"

"You will have figured it out," she said. "He's one of those men. He takes what he wants, over and over. And he gets away with it."

"You've been subjected to this?"

"No." They sat at the table. "But I've seen him looking at my daughter."

"Tell me about her," Riley said.

Sam Green was Marguerite Dunlop's age, but they hadn't been close. They had gone to different schools. Sam had a job in a bar in the city and spent a lot of nights on friends' sofas in the eastern suburbs.

"She was here, though, the evening Tom found Marguerite's body?" Riley said.

"She's here every few days. Does her laundry, eats and sleeps."

"Two weeks ago—before Christmas. The Dunlops were away. Was Sam feeding their dog?"

"No." Sarah gave her head a shake. "Not anymore. Tom does it."

"And what happened when the dog disappeared?"

Her face creased, puzzled. "Goodness. I'd forgotten about that."

"Was Tom upset?"

"Not as upset as the Dunlops."

"Where's Tom now?"

"He's gone to Carlingford to buy trainers."

"With his dad?"

"No, not with his dad."

Riley heard bitterness and held her eye.

"Want to hear another Preston story?" Sarah segued.

"Go on."

"That Adam Bowman you sent around here the other day—it involves him."

The feather gust of a black bird's wing. Omens in flight. Riley pulled out her notebook.

Sarah Green started to talk. When the Greens had first arrived at Prince Albert thirty years ago, they were just married, childless, and lived in a two-room flat attached to one of the boardinghouses. Sarah had been lonely, unable to connect with the other wives on campus, all of whom seemed to be evangelical Anglicans, dowdy and judgmental. Then she'd met Cath Bowman and her husband, the ribald center of a subterranean social circle, hard drinking and disdainful of the flat-earthers around them. Cath was older than Sarah and a bit wild—she lived on cask wine and Alpine menthols, and she had pulled Sarah into her orbit. Philip Preston had also just arrived at the school, single and svelte in his twenties, and Cath had drawn him in too.

"Cath Bowman and Preston started having an affair." Sarah looked out the window. "They couldn't meet in either of their places, so they'd rendezvous in the bush."

"In the bush?" Riley said.

"They had a spot, a hidden clearing on a ledge over the creek. They'd take a picnic blanket. Cath never minded giving me the details."

Details. Riley stared at her notebook.

One day, Sarah said, Cath's eight-year-old boy had tailed her into the bush, like he did when he played a spy game with his big brother. Cath was straddling a naked Preston when she looked up and saw Chick staring at her from the rim of the ledge.

"She screamed—she couldn't help it. Chick recoiled, lost his footing, and went over the edge backward."

"Cath told you this?" Riley said.

Sarah nodded. "The horror on his face was the last thing she saw of him alive."

It was five or six meters down, rocky outcrops to a stagnant water hole. He didn't make a sound, not a ripple—the creek swallowed him whole. No one ever swam in that black pool under the canopy, not even schoolboys on a dare. Cath had scrambled down and dived under. She had come up frantic, sobbing, diving again and again until she found him. She had dragged him out dead and wouldn't let go of him.

"They left the school," Sarah said. "Cath died a year later."

Riley's tongue found her ulcer. She could taste anchovy. Thirty years ago, Bowman would have been fifteen.

"What happened to Adam?" she said.

"He left in year ten," Sarah said. "He never came back."

"Was Preston linked to the drowning?"

"Never," Sarah said. "After Cath pulled Chick out, she sent Preston away and carried her son home. She told the police she'd been playing hide-and-seek with Chick in the bush, and he'd slipped. She never mentioned Preston."

"Were there ever any rumors about what really happened?"

"No, nothing. I told you—he takes what he wants and gets away with it."

"What about Adam? Does he know the details of his brother's death?"

"No way. Cath made me swear never to tell him."

"But she told you?"

"After they'd left, she rang one night and confessed to me. Every detail. That's what it was—a confession before dying. I never spoke with her again. She was so ashamed. That's what killed her—guilt and grief and shame."

"How did she die?"

"An overdose. Pills—in the bath."

"Do you know who found her?"

Sarah looked at her. "Not Adam. Her husband, I heard. John."

"Can I get your number?"

Sarah gave the number, and Riley entered it into her phone and called. Green's phone rang on the table.

"That's me," Riley said. "If you need anything."

Sarah saw her out. Riley drove clear of the house and pulled over. If Bowman had learned of his mother's affair, it gave him a motive to take revenge on Preston. Motive. Now that one had shimmered into view, it underlined how elusive motive had been with Marguerite. All they'd had was the idea that Preston's personality would allow him to kill the girl and ride it out. That wasn't motive—it was an explanation to back up a hypothesis. Homicide meant looking into backgrounds, yet they hadn't done it properly, not with Bowman.

She unpacked it all again, sieving fact from coincidence and jotting in her notebook. Bowman had twice been at the maintenance shed— the plastic and sighting Scott Green. It was neat but led where, exactly? Bowman killed Marguerite in order to frame Preston?

She called O'Neil. "Steve, is Wayne there? I need him to hear this."

"One sec . . . ," O'Neil said. "Go ahead, you're on speaker."

She took them through it.

"Wayne?" O'Neil said when she was finished.

Riley heard the psychiatrist exhale. "Well," Farquhar said, "there's motive for vengeance, I agree."

"But?" Riley said.

"It's a big *but*," Farquhar said. "The revenge would be on Preston. Why would Bowman avenge his brother by killing an innocent girl?"

Riley's voice sounded strange in her own ears. "Because he's insane. The cases are linked."

She heard a cough and knew they were trading glances.

"You think Bowman's Gladesville?" O'Neil said.

"Why not?" she said. "He was damaged young, at fifteen. He's endured the death of his brother, the suicide of his mother. He hasn't exactly made a brilliant career for himself. He's alone—no partner, no kids. He sheets it all home to Preston."

"Gladesville's psychopathy wasn't made," Farquhar said. "It's not nurture. There's something wrong with him, a developmental problem in the brain."

"So even if Bowman knew about his mother's affair with Preston," O'Neil said, "it wouldn't correlate with what we see at Gladesville?"

"Correct," Farquhar said. "If Bowman is Gladesville, he has an underlying neurological problem. He's predisposed to psychopathy. His family history with Preston would be incidental. Or coincidental, actually."

"Coincidences do happen," Riley said. "They happen all the time. Look at psychiatrists—they're *all* fucking crazy."

"Very good," Farquhar said. "You've been to Bowman's house twice now, I think? Tell me what you saw, what you felt."

"Wiped down, ordered. Art on the wall, neat, framed . . . structured. He's obsessive-compulsive. His books are categorized by color. He drinks a lot."

"Did you feel any sense of threat?"

She told them about the drunks in the bar.

"You felt manipulated?"

"I didn't feel in danger. It was more I thought he may have arranged it. He's a pleaser. There's empathy but . . . emptiness."

"He might be lonely."

"Maybe. There's a void, like he's hollow."

"Books, you say? Reading and drinking can do the same job," Farquhar said. "You fall into them, they fill the void—"

"If you think it's necessary," O'Neil cut in, "you can go and toss Bowman's house. Crime Scene is still there."

"You don't think it's necessary?" Riley said.

"I can see the logic," O'Neil said. "But it doesn't add up."

"It doesn't add up because it's *not* logical," Riley said. "I started with motive and then made a leap."

"You extrapolated," Farquhar said.

"Yeah, what you two are meant to be doing—putting logic aside and thinking past it."

She waited in their silence. There was another point she hadn't mentioned. "Something else to think about. The river. It leads to the creek, which leads to the water hole where Bowman's brother drowned. It's called geography."

She hung up and pressed the ignition. Everything was connected.

25

Bowman sat in a hired Hyundai outside a car rental yard in Zetland. O'Neil had instructed him not to return to his house and to ditch the Nissan. Alexander had been told that a threat had been made against Bowman but was given no details. If the editor knew BMK had been to Bowman's house and stolen a knife, he would demand it be written up as a story.

Alexander had agreed to hire a car for Bowman on one condition—that Bowman try to interview the Dunlops. Marguerite's parents were staying with Beverley Dunlop's sister. No media had tracked them down. Bowman had called a colleague of the Dunlops and, claiming he wanted to send a card, extracted the address in Beecroft.

Bloody death knock. Bowman thought about shunting it off to Diamond, but he knew Alexander was hot to trot and the story would make the front page. And he didn't owe Beat-Up Benny any favors. He entered the street name and number into the GPS, sighed, and swung onto the Eastern Distributor. He crossed the bridge, picked up the M2, and called *The National*'s picture desk to get a photographer to meet him at the house.

"Just tell them to wait in the car and text me their number. I'll let them know if the parents agree to a photo."

The sister's place was a dank Federation, dark brick set back from the street. Bowman opened the gate and followed the path up the middle of the lawn.

The bell chimed in the depths. After a long time, a man opened the door. Slight, bearded, pale like a wraith.

"I'm sorry to bother you," Bowman said.

Bruce Dunlop stood vacantly.

"My name is Adam Bowman. From *The National*."

Dunlop focused for a moment and shuffled aside to let him into the hall. There was a vegetative smell that conjured memories: in a room to the left, a dining table was buried with bouquets—death and its many attendants. They went down the corridor into an open-plan living area spanning the rear of the house.

"Beverley is resting," Dunlop said. "We've had many visitors."

"Of course." Bowman looked around the room.

"Our friends, from the school, said that you had called them." Dunlop's eyes were pools of sorrow. "I recognized your name. You would like to talk about Marguerite?"

"If that's possible."

Dunlop gestured to a table. Bowman took a seat and put his bag on the floor.

"I did my practical training at Prince Albert many years ago," Dunlop said, sitting. "I was still at Moore Theological College, not long out of school myself. That time occurs to me now for a reason. It involves your family. I'm sure you know why."

Bowman felt the table turning.

"I arrived at the school a few months before your brother, Charles, was lost," Dunlop said.

"Chick," Bowman said.

"Yes." Dunlop's head bowed. "I sat with your parents in the chapel, on the evening of the accident, after the police had left. I was twenty-two . . . I'd never seen grief."

206

He'd seen it now. Bowman knew grief. It was looking at him.

"In grief, you come to understand the grief of others," the chaplain said.

"I've spoken with Sarah Green," Bowman said. "She said she knew my parents. And that Philip Preston knew them too?"

"I rang Inspector O'Neil today, after I saw the news," Dunlop said. "He told me he had interviewed the headmaster but that no charges have been laid."

Bowman reached for his notebook. "Do you hold Preston responsible?"

"I have been disappointed with Philip for many years. For his impropriety, the way he runs the school."

Bowman wrote in shorthand. "How does he run the school?"

"By sowing discord," Dunlop said. "His immorality—it invites evil in through the gates."

Good quotes. Bowman could see the story. He kept his voice flat. "Do you think Philip Preston killed Marguerite?"

Too much: Dunlop caught his eye. "This is my wife's sister's house," the chaplain said. "Our son is staying here too."

"He's here now?" Bowman glanced down the hall.

"He's out with his aunt. Melanie has proved . . . formidable in the circumstances. They're organizing some things for the service. Marguerite is to be released to us."

"And Beverley, um . . ."

"Beverley is not well. She is in agony. So much regret."

"Regret"—with his pen hand, Bowman scratched at eczema on his inner arm—"is that what you feel as well?"

Dunlop stared at the table. "For everything. For the fact we weren't there, that we'd gone away and left her. That I didn't hug her more, spend more time with her. That I didn't play with her more when she was a child."

Bowman scribbled.

"Beverley had been ringing and texting Marguerite and sensed she was starting to get annoyed. Then when it went quiet, when there was no response from her, we thought she was busy—perhaps enjoying having some space from us."

"Mm."

"We should have known. Marguerite isn't like that. She would always respond, even if she felt crowded by her mother. When it mattered, we underestimated her—her love for us. Marguerite is selfless. A beautiful soul."

Bowman had what he'd come for and felt an urge to get clear of the house. He brought his bag to his lap. "Thank you," he said. "I'm sorry to have disturbed you."

The chaplain trailed him down the hall. The door was on the latch, and Bowman pulled it open. "Oh, one more thing," he said. "Do you think we could take a quick photo?"

Dunlop was blank, retreating into grief. Bowman guided him over the threshold into the light at the top of the path and moved away to call the photographer.

"Mate," he hissed into the phone, "just the father. He's here now, out front. Be quick."

The snapper emerged from a parked car and shot from the gate with a big lens. Bowman stood out of frame on the edge of the lawn. It took fifteen seconds. The photographer nodded at Bowman and disappeared back to his car. Dunlop blinked in the sun. Bowman gave a stilted wave and went down the path to the Hyundai.

He drove a few blocks, then pulled over and sat in the car to tap out the story. Thirty minutes later, he filed and arched his lower back. It would take more than a shower to scrub himself clean. There had been some heavy currents in the house. Chick had got him through the door, and then Bowman had posed Dunlop for a photo like a chimp at Taronga.

Alexander called. The editor loved the whole package—the piece and the pictures. "He looks like Jesus," Alexander said of the forlorn father. "He looks like he's been crucified."

Bowman rubbed and patted at his spreading rash. The death-knock coverage would look strong and exclusive splashed across the broadsheet. Bowman's treachery wouldn't show up on the page—it was a matter for his soul. That was the trade and the trade-off, the journalist's compact. You'd sell anything—then you had to sell everything.

He was traveling south on Beecroft Road when the phone rang on the CarPlay. Not one of his contacts.

"Adam speaking."

"Miss-ter Bowman." A good country drawl. "Hugh Bishop."

Bowman squinted into the traffic.

"Been reading your coverage," Bishop said. "Prince Albert—you're way out in front."

The car air felt thick with sleaze. Bowman had to swallow. "You're connected with the school, I think?" he said.

"Yeah, long way back. I've got kids there."

Bowman put his window down to breathe. Things were moving too fast. He wasn't the type of reporter federal cabinet ministers rang out of the blue.

"Anyway, look, I've got to jump on a plane," Bishop said, "but I wanted to touch base, see if we can schedule a meeting."

"A meeting with me?"

"About the mess we're in, out there at Parramatta."

He braked for a light. "The investigation?"

"The whole show. There's some talk, a feeling Preston's out of his depth on this one. I thought I might arrange for you to meet with me and a couple of the board. Old boys, like you. Try and recalibrate. Get you what you need, of course."

Bowman sensed tendrils in the shadows of the politician's words, the mycelium network feeding into Bishop. Old boys, the old man, Diamond, Preston. He could hear flights being called in the background.

"I've got to get this plane," Bishop said. "Listen, one of the board's at Qantas. We could fly you up for a night, first class, get you in the chairman's lounge. Ongoing membership. Good tucker—and they're not pouring Yellowglen. I'll call you when I land."

"Fly me up where?" Bowman said.

"The Whitsundays. Hamo. I'm there for a week."

26

Riley had arranged for Crime Scene to leave her a key to Bowman's house. She let herself in, glad to have the place empty and quiet. Pulling on booties and gloves, she started with the bedroom. She flipped the mattress, went under the bed, sifted through drawers and the wardrobe, patting down jacket pockets and looking in shoes. She went through the bathroom cabinet and then the kitchen.

She worked methodically, but it didn't feel right, going through Bowman's things. What was she looking for? Trophies? She didn't know—she just figured she'd know when she found it.

In the living room, she stared at the bookshelf. Her eye was drawn to a block of blue spines. *A History of the World in 100 Objects*, *A Suitable Boy*, *The River Capture*. Drinking and reading . . . Bowman had a world below the surface. For Riley, it was just drinking and TV. And homicide—always homicide. It was homicide that had brought her here now.

She pulled down the river book and leafed through it. It was about the Sullane, in Ireland. There was a farmer named Lynch. There was a quote at the start: "In theory, there is a gravitational attraction between every drop of sea water and even the outermost star of the universe."

Everything was connected. She put the book back. The danger was in trying too hard, imagining connections that weren't there.

She knew O'Neil was only tolerating her diversion, giving her room to work through her suspicion and doing his best to expedite the process. If Bowman had taken his knife to the school and stabbed it into Preston's door, how had he got there? There was no electronic trail from the Nissan plates or his phone. Satyr detectives had canvassed Balmain East, door-knocking Datchett and Duke and Darling Streets, seizing the CCTV at the pub and the ferry wharf. No one had seen anything.

O'Neil called. Bowman had arrived at the Parramatta unit and then gone shopping for supplies. They had a tail on him.

"What'd he buy?" Riley said.

"Alcohol and cleaning products," O'Neil said. "Plus salad and three steaks. Must be tea for you and Priya."

Jesus, Mary, and Joseph, another fucking dinner party? Riley could only shake her head. She went to the front door and peered at the shadows assembling in the lane.

"You should go and get some rest," O'Neil said. "I've got a detective in the apartment with Bowman, plus another in yours. We've told Bowman it's for his protection. We'll keep them there on a roster so you can get some sleep."

She locked the cottage and drove to her flat in Rozelle, one of a dozen in a 1970s white-brick block with chocolate trim, as shabby inside as it was from the street. She hauled a suitcase from the hall cupboard, opened it on the bed, and threw things in from her wardrobe and drawers and bathroom.

A bottle of Jack Daniel's stood on the coffee table between her beige leather couch and the widescreen TV. She sipped, felt the burn in her throat and the warmth as it hit her empty stomach. She swigged again and then again, screwed the top back on, and put down the bottle.

At this hour, in holiday traffic and with a hefty slug of Tennessee diesel on board, it took twenty minutes to get to Parramatta. She toggled between the commercial FM stations, blasting music, enjoying the release brought on by the first drink of the day.

The Homicide apartments were in a secure midrise block overlooking the river. A new development, ugly, although Riley knew they hadn't been leased for their looks. She rang Patel to open the garage and parked underground.

Bowman had his door ajar and must have been listening for the chime of the lift, because he stuck his head out as she wheeled her suitcase down the corridor.

"I'm cooking dinner if you're hungry." He pointed next door. "That's you. Priya's in there."

He was enjoying it: the commotion, the company. "Thanks," she said.

Riley knocked, and a young female detective opened the door. "Sarge," the constable said. She wasn't Satyr, but Riley knew her face from the squad. Homicide was based a block away, at police headquarters, and O'Neil would be raiding the place for plebs to put on an eight-hour babysitting roster.

"It's Needham, right?" Riley said. "Jane?"

"Sarge," the constable said.

"You here overnight?"

"No, till eleven. Then Dawson's here till seven."

Riley looked around. "Patel's here?"

The constable indicated the hallway. "In the shower, I think."

The unit was all chrome and glass and blonde wood, with odd blocks of matte color that hammered home the soullessness. The bedrooms were identical, all with ensuites. Patel's stuff was in one. Riley chose another and closed the door.

She unpacked and showered. She was dressing when she heard a knock. "Yeah?"

Patel opened the door. "Hi."

"Water pressure's good." Riley looked up from her shoes. "You up to speed?"

"Steve briefed me on the dog and the Bowman story. You went to his house?"

Riley stood. Patel was in a gray T-shirt and black trousers, her hair pulled back and still wet.

"No gun?" Riley said.

Patel's hand went to her hip. "We're going next door for dinner. Do I need it?"

Riley picked up her Glock from the bed and clipped it onto her belt. "You tell me."

"I'll tell you one thing. Whoever attacked me this morning, it wasn't Adam Bowman."

"How can you be sure?"

"Height, weight." Patel paused. "Inflection. It wasn't him."

"So you did hear something in the voice."

"I hear something in Bowman's voice. They're different."

"He was wearing a mask and something in his mouth. How can you be sure?"

"Aura." Patel held her eye.

Riley pouted. You couldn't argue with that. "Let's go."

Needham had her laptop open on a table. "We'll be just down the hall," Riley said.

A young male constable opened Bowman's door. Riley greeted him and sent him off to wait with Needham.

The apartment had the same layout, the same chrome and pale wood. Bowman had his back to them, working at the bench as they came into the kitchen.

"Evening," Patel said.

He half turned and acknowledged them with a sip of wine. "Christ, I forgot to ask." He looked at Patel. "Do you eat beef?"

"No sacred cows in Taree."

"Phew." He raised his glass at Riley like a mincing TV chef. "How are your new digs?"

"Nicer than my place," Riley said.

"Never seen your place."

She saw herself at his house, rifling through drawers.

He pushed two glasses and a bottle of red toward Patel and turned to the stove. "Won't be long." Meat spat in a pan, and he upended a takeaway container of salad into a bowl. They sat around an oval green glass table to eat.

"Cheers," Patel said, and they clinked.

"Tell me"—Riley looked at Bowman—"on your travels, have you ever heard the Dunlops had a dog?"

Bowman chewed. "Nup. Did they?"

"Yeah," Riley said. "No one mentions the dog."

"What of it?" Bowman said.

"It's missing."

"To the curious incident of the dog in the nighttime," Bowman said.

"To the what?" Patel said.

"It's a Sherlock Holmes plot," Bowman said.

Riley pinched salt onto her steak. "Do tell."

"If you think the same person killed the dog and Marguerite, you might want to use Sherlock Holmes's logic, which would mean the person who killed Marguerite didn't know the dog."

Logic and extrapolation. "Go on," Riley said.

"The point is," Bowman said, "if the person who killed Marguerite knew the dog, then the dog wouldn't bark at them. So they wouldn't need to get rid of it beforehand. That was the curious incident in the story. The dog made no sound at the house on the night the crime was committed, so Holmes deduced that the dog knew the person who committed the crime."

Riley speared a piece of her salad. Her first thought had been that someone had removed the dog to have a clear run at Marguerite. O'Neil's instinct had told him there was something amiss about the trip to Fiji, and he'd been right—something had happened at the Dunlop house while the family was away. It pointed to someone local—someone who was watching the family and knew their movements. But she found Bowman's point interesting.

He wiped at his mouth with a napkin.

Riley took a chance. "I heard about what happened to your family at the school," she said. "To your brother."

Time stopped. Bowman's cutlery was suspended over his food. "Okay," he said after a while. "It's no big secret."

Patel's voice was gentle. "You didn't think to tell us?"

"It was thirty years ago."

"What happened?" Riley said. "I heard a version. It might not have been accurate."

Bowman put down his knife and fork and told the story with his eyes on his plate. His brother had been playing hide-and-seek with his mother in the bush. He'd slipped and fallen off a rock ledge. His mother had pulled him out of the creek, but he was already dead. She had carried him home.

"No one else was there?" Riley said.

He looked up with consternation. "Like who?"

Riley waited, willing him to answer. She couldn't say Preston, but maybe he would.

He looked from her to Patel. "I can't believe you're asking me this, as if it's relevant," he said. "Is this coming from Preston again?"

"Why would you say that?" Riley said.

"He's smeared me once, remember? With Diamond."

That was true. The NeedFeed article had poked into Bowman's past. It hadn't gone so far as to mention his brother's death, but it had insinuated that disgrace and alcoholism had destroyed the family. It was beyond grubby that Preston was the source for the piece, given his role in it all. And that Diamond had beaten it up on the sly.

"Look, there was no scandal," Bowman said. "Plenty of people know the story. Bruce Dunlop wanted to talk to me about it this afternoon. Spratt's heard it. Sarah Green told me she knew my mother."

"You spoke with Bruce Dunlop?" Riley said.

"Yeah." Bowman looked sheepish. "I went to visit."

"For a story? Well—that's a dog act."

"Editor's orders," he said. "Anyway, if Preston is saying things about my past, it's a distraction. He must have something to hide."

"Like what?" Patel said.

Bowman looked at Riley. "Your mate Hugh Bishop called me today."

Riley rubbed an eye. Bishop was in damage control. He'd be linked to Zabatino and knew Preston was exposed. It was a side issue. "What did he want?" she said.

Bowman recounted the phone call.

"How did you leave it?" Riley said. "Did you agree to meet?"

"No. He hung up to catch his flight. What's his story?"

Riley glanced at Patel. They needed to put Bishop and Preston behind them.

"Off the record," Riley said, "we know Preston is involved in some low-level graft. Bishop is probably in on it and has figured out Preston's dead meat. I think Bishop is scrambling, trying to figure out what you know. He might try and use you to cut Preston loose and save himself."

"Graft?" Bowman said. "Is it about Marguerite?"

"No," Riley said. "I might be able to give you more soon."

She pushed some salad around. She felt certain Bowman was unaware of Preston's role in his brother's death. It wasn't much of a motive if he didn't even know he had it. She thought about what he had said, about how talk of his past would be a distraction. But it hadn't been Preston who had dredged up Bowman's history. It had been Sarah Green.

27

Riley woke in the unfamiliar room to her phone ringing. She had no idea where she was. She slanted her mobile, saw it was O'Neil, saw it was after 8:00 a.m.

"Steve," she said, groggy.

"We found the dog."

Riley rolled over. "Where?"

"In the yards behind the Dunlop house."

She sat up.

"Someone slit its throat, buried it in a shallow grave. Not far from the John Deere shed. Cadaver dog found it. I'm here now. Rise and shine."

She dragged herself to the toilet, splashed water on her face, and brushed her teeth as she dressed. She thought about waking Patel but decided to let her rest. There was a new constable in the main room. Riley grunted at him and went out the door, watching the clock on the dash as she drove. It took nine minutes.

The carcass had been bagged in clear plastic, but there was no bagging the smell, an obscene rancid sweetness. In Homicide, you got used to that smell before breakfast. The area around the grave was taped off. Shoe and Tire was combing the ground.

"Buried about a foot and a half down," O'Neil said. "Pretty amateur, but deep enough to keep the flies away. No maggots, and decomposition was slowed, so you can still see the trauma."

It was a black-and-tan cattle dog, midsize, bit of kelpie in it.

"It turned up one day a few years back, according to Bruce," O'Neil said. "Marguerite started feeding it, and it never left."

Riley straightened and scanned the abandoned yards. Broken fences, lean-tos, outhouses. The shed with the John Deere was fifteen meters away. Ghost Gum was up the hill, hidden by the windbreak of poplars.

"He likes it here, our boy," she said.

O'Neil frowned agreement. "Lots of cover."

"Yeah, but there are people around. St. Anne's is there"—she jerked her head—"and the Spratt house is across there. Spratt's like Mrs. Mangel—sees everything. Whoever this is, he's blending in. Part of the furniture."

"Well, that's not Bowman."

Her mouth was dry. "I asked him point blank last night about his brother's death. He's got no idea Preston was involved."

"Did you tell him?"

"Course not."

"In any case, we ran his plates again," O'Neil said, "just to be sure, given the new time frame of Fiji and the dog disappearing. If he came out here then, it wasn't in his car."

Riley's head ached. She needed coffee.

"The Dunlops go to Fiji, and someone kills their dog," O'Neil said. "Why?"

"They want it out of the way because they intend to come back."

"All right," O'Neil said. "And we think they're local. You said there were sleeping tablets in the Spratts' bathroom?"

"Stilnox."

"Let's ask Jenny Spratt whether she took a tablet on Wednesday night? Plus, did Tom Green see anyone hanging around? You go back and ask him—take Farquhar. But for Christ's sake, get some coffee first."

Riley sneered, but she didn't argue. Not at this hour, not with a tea drinker. In the Commodore, she looked in the mirror, wiped sleep from an eye, and retied her hair. Coffee? No shit, Sherlock. She looked like the Hound of the Baskervilles.

She called Farquhar as she drove out of the school and down the hill to the strip of shops at Kingsdene. She ordered a toasted sandwich and a triple-shot flat white from the deli and ate in the car. With the psychiatrist in tow, she was going to turn up on the Greens' doorstep unannounced. The trick would be not setting off too many alarms with Farquhar's presence. She finished her breakfast, popped the glove box, and took out a packet of antiseptic wipes to clean her hands and her mouth.

Farquhar's Volvo was parked at the school gate. He got out as she pulled up, and they drove to the house together. Scott Green answered the door. Riley hadn't seen him since he was interviewed in the police gazebo at the scene. Nine days, she counted.

"Mr. Green," Riley said. "Sorry to disturb you." He stared at her, a petulance to the mouth under the mustache. Schoolmasters, men dealing with boys all day—perhaps they never grew up. There was movement over his shoulder, and a young woman appeared. Hair out loose, a canvas carryall, dressed for the beach. Maybe eighteen. Just a girl. Riley smiled. "You must be Sam."

The girl nodded and slid past her father out the door.

Riley wanted a look at her, and she felt Farquhar's interest too. "Where are you off to?" she said.

"Clovelly." Sam Green brushed hair from her face. "Have a swim before work."

"Nice. I'm Detective Riley. This is Dr. Wayne Farquhar. He works with us in victim support."

The girl nodded quickly.

"What is it you want?" Scott Green said.

Riley kept her eyes on the daughter. "We've found the Dunlops' dog," she said. "We understand Tom was looking after it?"

Sam Green nodded again. "Yeah, probably."

Sarah Green had come down the hall and was standing in the doorway behind her husband.

"We'd like to ask Tom if he saw anything unusual," Riley said. "We're concerned he might find it distressing. Especially as he found Marguerite."

"Distressing?" Sarah said.

"The dog's dead." Riley half turned to Farquhar. "We thought it would be good if we both talked to him."

"Tatters," Sam said. "That's really sad."

"Tom's out," Scott said.

Farquhar cleared his throat and opened his hands to the three of them. "My role, as you may know, is to help the victims of a crime, where necessary. Do you think we might come in?"

Sam Green looked down the path. "I've gotta go."

Riley walked with her. "Is everything all right?"

The girl looked in her bag for her car key. "Yeah. S'pose."

Riley handed her a card. "That's me, if you need to talk."

"Thanks." She took it. "I talked to the police already."

Riley smiled. "I know. How's your mum?"

Sam opened the door to the Yaris and threw in her bag. "I dunno. The same."

She drove off with a wave, and Riley walked back to the house. Farquhar was sitting with the Greens at the table in the family room.

Scott Green was smiling. "You think we're victims?"

"The whole school community is," Farquhar said, "at both the schools. And your family more than most. I'm sorry not to have visited before." He put his hands together on the table. "It's good to see Sam is getting on with things and going to her work. She seems well adjusted?"

"She works in a bar," Sarah said, "and comes home twice a week."

Farquhar stroked his beard. "Can you tell me how Tom has been faring?"

"Good," Sarah said. "Better."

"Better?" Farquhar said.

"He had grown surly," she said. "Withdrawn."

Riley stood apart, her hip to the bench in the open-plan kitchen. Farquhar asked questions, and the mother answered. Tom had been more open, more helpful in the days following the tragedy, she told him. No, there had been no signs of depression, anxiety, fear.

"And you noted this too?" Farquhar said to Scott. "A change in your son's behavior?"

"He never tries it on with me. He knows I won't put up with it."

The psychiatrist gave the slightest nod. "There's been no, for instance, hiding in his room?"

"He's always hiding in his room," Scott said.

"He's not the only one," Sarah said.

The comment hung. Sarah studied the table. Her collared shirt was buttoned, her arms and neck covered, despite the humid heat. It had been the same yesterday.

Farquhar told the parents it was encouraging that Sam and Tom were coping with the event of Marguerite's death. Scott sat blankly and now let his wife do the talking. Sam seemed disengaged, but Tom was following the BMK case in the media, she said, and she was worried about the effect it might have down the track.

"The drone footage being aired bothered him," she said. "He got hyper. I think he felt responsible."

The psychiatrist consoled her: both children's reactions were understandable in the circumstances. "Does Tom get on well with the kids at school?"

Scott answered. "He's a loner."

"And Sam?" Farquhar said.

"She's finished school."

"She's more sociable," Sarah said.

"Have either of them been in any trouble?" Farquhar said. "Truancy, bullying, shoplifting, things like that?"

"No," Sarah said. "Why would you ask?"

"No arson?" Farquhar said.

The Greens' eyes met.

"Was there some fire setting?" Farquhar said.

Sarah took a breath. There had been a fire, she said, in the bush at the school a year ago, last summer. The fire brigade thought it had been deliberately lit. It was during the holidays. There was no damage to property. No one was injured, and no one was charged.

"But you think Sam and Tom were involved?" Farquhar said.

Sarah picked at a cuff. "Sam was away. Craig Spratt let us know he'd seen Tom in the vicinity," she said.

"I see," Farquhar said. "Did you talk to your son about it?"

"I tried," Sarah said. "He denied it." She looked at her husband.

"Mr. Green?" Farquhar said.

"I think Craig was telling tales," Scott said. "Lighting fires was the sort of thing *his* boys got up to."

Riley straightened at the bench in the kitchen. "Were Spratt's sons living here at the time?" she said.

Scott stared up at her. "Don't know," he said. "They come and go."

"One final question," Farquhar said. "Does Tom have a history of bed-wetting?"

Scott stood abruptly, smiled, and headed into the kitchen past Riley.

His wife watched him. "No," she said. "We haven't had a problem with that."

Riley followed Scott to the sink.

"Marguerite's body was found on Thursday night," she said. "Do you recall what you did the next morning?"

He turned the tap on. "Spoke to you," he said.

"No. We spoke on Thursday night, in the gazebo at the scene."
He drank a glass of water.

"You were walking in the school on Friday morning," she said.

"My morning walk." He smirked again. "Is that a crime now?"

Riley was tempted to ask him about the plastic but stopped herself.
He put his glass on the sink and walked out.

Down the room, Farquhar stood and tucked in his chair. "Thank
you for your time, Mrs. Green."

"One moment." Sarah scuttled off along the rear hall and then was
back. She led them to the door and halted. There was more she wanted
to say.

"I found this"—Sarah spoke low—"when I was tidying Tom's
room."

She stepped close and slipped something into Riley's hand. Riley
held it in her fingers. A USB stick.

"It was on the floor under his desk. There was Blu Tack on it and
on the underside of the desk. I think he'd stuck it up there, and it had
fallen." Sarah looked with anguish at Farquhar. "I don't know what's
on it—more drone footage, I guess. I just thought the police should see
it—they were so thankful when we gave them the hard drive. But I don't
want Tom to know you have this, not after the last time."

"The last time?" Riley said.

"When they played his footage—in the media." Sarah glanced at
the closed doors off the front hall. "As I said, it got him riled."

"Okay, we'll make a copy." Riley felt tentacles of unease. "I'll get
this back to you."

They drove in silence. Riley pulled up beside Farquhar's Volvo,
reached around for her laptop, and connected the USB. Password pro-
tected. "Bugger," she said.

The psychiatrist sat still, a stone druid, lost in thought.

"What's with the bed-wetting?" she said.

"It's part of a theory." He stared ahead. "Highly contentious—you could never use it in court. I've never placed much stock in it, never actually seen a patient present with it."

"The never never never theory. Sounds promising."

"It's called the Macdonald Triad. Published in the US in the sixties. The idea is that if a child presents with three particular behaviors, the triad is a strong predictor of violent tendencies, predatory behavior. Some go as far as to say it's the hallmark of a serial offender."

"And bed-wetting is one?"

"Yes. And arson." He turned to her. "The third is cruelty to animals."

She tilted her head back against the headrest. It sounded good—in theory. "But his mother said there's no history of bed-wetting."

Farquhar ran a finger on the dash.

Riley rolled her neck. "You think Tom killed the dog?"

"I think it's a complicated family."

"Do you reckon Green's beating the wife?"

"Perhaps. He might be beating Sam as well. And Tom."

"Sarah covers up"—Riley ran a hand down her arm—"her limbs and neck. Sam doesn't do that. Or not today."

"With the USB"—Farquhar looked at the laptop—"Sarah doesn't want Tom to know we have it. But she didn't want Scott to know either."

"Look," she said, "you'll think I'm an idiot . . ."

"Go ahead."

"It's about the dog. Something Bowman mentioned, actually, a Sherlock Holmes plot—"

"The curious incident of the dog in the nighttime," Farquhar said.

Riley's eyes popped. "You know it?"

"It's a famous story," he said. "'The Adventure of Silver Blaze.' I read it as a child. In fact, I read it to my children."

Riley frowned. So many books—she was out of the loop. "The point is," she said, "Tom has been feeding the dog off and on for years, whenever the Dunlops went away. The dog would have been used to Tom being up at the house. If he wanted to go there without anyone knowing, he wouldn't have needed to kill the dog to keep it quiet. The dog wouldn't have barked at him anyway."

"That's logical," Farquhar said. "But there's another way to look at it."

"Which is?"

"Think of Tom in terms of the triad. He didn't kill the dog in order to keep the dog quiet . . ."

Riley tapped the steering wheel. "Cruelty to animals."

"Tom liked killing the dog," Farquhar said. "He got off on it."

"Two out of three," she said. "That's still not the triad."

"There are various checklists of behaviors," Farquhar said. "Tom is ticking other boxes."

"What boxes?"

"I would expect a teenager who stumbled on the murdered and dumped body of a girl he knew to show signs of anxiety or fear or worry or withdrawal. To be subdued, mournful, sad—even depressed."

"Hiding in his room," Riley said.

"Exactly. But his actual behavior, according to his mother, has been the opposite. He's been more solicitous at home. And he appears to have been stimulated by events. The drone footage appearing in the media exacerbated this response. Sarah described it as hyper. That sounds as if he's agitated, but it could be in a pleasure-seeking fashion, excited by the novelty of what's happening."

Riley tapped at her teeth. The possibility the boy might somehow be involved had not occurred to her. She wondered if O'Neil had considered it.

"But why now?" she said. "Why kill the dog now, when he's had plenty of prior opportunity? He kills the dog, and then Marguerite is killed a week later. Are you saying that's coincidence?"

"I don't know. I'd like to see the boy."

Her tongue found the ulcer. "Let's suppose you're right, and Tom did kill the dog. What are we looking at?"

"He's fifteen, postpubescent. He's bored, looking for stimulation, lighting fires. He's killed an animal and found a dead body—and his behavior at home *improves*."

"You think he's interfered with the body?"

"I think he's done something else." Farquhar looked again at Riley's laptop. "I think he finds the body and then comes back to his discovery. I think he films it."

28

O'Neil's face was like a sour marriage as he sat across from Riley in the strike force room and listened to Farquhar's briefing in silence. Riley knew what O'Neil was thinking—she could read him like they'd been wed thirty years. The dog and the boy were interesting, but he didn't want to push too hard, not without evidence—and not after Preston.

Preston hung heavy on O'Neil. His actions with the headmaster had lit a political firestorm under Satyr. Riley knew the source of the blaze: Bishop was coming after them. The politician was playing all sides—backstabbing Preston to Bowman even as he used O'Neil's treatment of the headmaster to claim the strike force was harassing people, incompetent, out of control. O'Neil's superiors were holding the line, but they were warning him as well. Bishop had a line into the premier's office, and things were getting white hot.

In the meantime, the techs had taped a call to Preston's phone from Bishop yesterday that made for interesting listening. O'Neil had played it to her and was now weighing giving it to Bowman, but it was risky. If he leaked it to the journalist and it backfired, O'Neil would be burned alive. Riley resented even having to think about it. It was politics, a shabby distraction, and would have to wait.

She listened as Farquhar made his case. The dog was a good lead, and they needed to run it down. But the boy? Farquhar hadn't even met Tom. All they had was a quack theory.

"The McDonald's Triad," O'Neil said. "Did you want fries with that?"

"*Mac*donald," Riley said.

O'Neil put his tea down. Riley held her breath. If he lost his shit, it wouldn't help anybody. She was aware she wasn't helping. Yesterday, she'd had a motive for Bowman, and now she'd come in with the psychiatrist to discuss the kid.

"We're talking about a fifteen-year-old boy." O'Neil looked at Farquhar. "You want to bring him in for questioning about *not* wetting the bed?"

Farquhar opened his mouth to speak, but O'Neil cut him off. "You know, I think I'd be wetting the bed if I had you two coming after me," he said. "Piss myself laughing."

"You finished?" Riley said.

"No." He folded his long arms over his taut chest. "We need to stop with the hypotheticals and do the legwork. It's a fucking shitstorm upstairs. Yesterday, I bring the headmaster of the oldest, most prestigious school in the country in under full media glare. Everyone's waiting for a big announcement, and what do I give them? Nothing. Now, with no evidence, you want to pull in a kid?"

"All right," Riley said. "No one's saying bring him in. Let's do the legwork. Track him down, and have a chat. But I reckon we walk him past the dog's grave and gauge his reaction."

"Where are they with the USB?" O'Neil said.

"It's got some encryption. They need a couple of hours."

She watched him twirl it around in his mind—his thousand-yard stare, his tongue clicking out a sprung rhythm in his head. They wanted the kid on his own, no parents. Speaking to a minor was a gray area, a judgment call, and it depended on the level of suspicion. Riley thought it was legitimate: they were genuine that Tom wasn't a suspect, that they just wanted to have a chat. That wasn't bending the rules—it was applying them in the quest for advantage.

"Okay," O'Neil said. "Get his mobile number and his carrier. The techs can track him down."

◆ ◆ ◆

The technical police triangulated Tom Green's phone to a point in the bush at the back of the school. Riley, Farquhar, and O'Neil drove out together and called Craig Spratt on the way. He met them at the gate, and they showed him the location on Riley's iPad.

"Looks like he's near the cave," Spratt said. "Senior boys go there to smoke and drink. Little dome of rock with a narrow opening."

"Easy access?" O'Neil said.

"There's a fire trail down, and then you follow this path." Spratt pointed on the screen. "The way in is here, easy to spot if you know where to look." He described it for them.

They drove in as far as they could on the trail, parked, and picked up the path on foot. The way was shadow damp, well trod, scruffy and unloved. Spoiled country. The creek was to their left, and the land rose out of the gully, a forested slope on one side, water-carved rock on the other. Riley realized they were passing the ledges Sarah Green had described. She stopped when she glimpsed the water hole down an incline, stagnant under the stone canopy. Farquhar and O'Neil stopped with her.

The bush thrummed with presences beyond their hearing. There was no breeze, just the unruffled surface of black water.

They found the cave a hundred meters farther on, the opening as Spratt had described: two curtains of rock drawn together but not quite meeting, curving back on themselves to leave a gap just wide enough to pass through. They stood at the dark slit: claggy air tinged with burned eucalyptus and a faint scraping noise.

Riley took her phone from her pocket and hit the flashlight. She squeezed sideways into the cave and didn't need the torch. A figure was sitting in the white light of a camp lantern, whittling a stick with a knife.

"Tom," she said. "Police."

The boy's head jerked up, and his hands went still.

"Easy, Tom," O'Neil said, beside her. "We just want to have a chat."

Tom Green's eyes darted between them. "You scared me," he said. "Thought BMK had come back."

"Sorry," Riley said. "We've been looking for you."

She scanned the cave. It was like a domed tent, about five meters in diameter. The remains of a campfire, ringed with blackened stones. A natural chimney in the roof. The walls covered in scratched names. The boy thumbed the sharp end of the stick. "What for?"

Farquhar squeezed through the entrance.

"This is Dr. Farquhar," Riley said. "We just wanted to see how you're going."

"I'm good . . . Wait. How did you know I was here?"

"We followed your tracks," O'Neil said.

Tom grinned with disbelief. "No way."

"True," O'Neil said. "You join the police, they'll teach you."

"Black trackers," Tom said. "I read about them. Good hunters."

Farquhar nodded at the boy's stick. "Do you use that for hunting?"

The boy looked at the stick and the knife in his hands. "No."

There were years of detritus on the cave floor: cans, bottles, food wrappers, a frayed sleeping bag, a sneaker, ripped porn magazines, cigarette packets. Butts everywhere. Newspapers. A pile of kindling.

"You have a fire in here?" Riley said.

"Boarders do sometimes," Tom said. "In, like, winter."

"We wanted to show you something," Riley said. "Come on. We'll go for a drive."

Tom looked uncertain, but he extinguished the lantern and followed her out with the others. They went in single file, Tom between

O'Neil and Farquhar, Riley at the tail. She watched the boy as he walked—his limbs were lean and brown, and his feet, in thongs, were pale, almost white. He had left his stick in the cave and stuck his whittling knife in the band of his shorts.

They put him in the back with O'Neil. Tom was intrigued by the unmarked Commodore and asked questions about engine size, speed, sirens. Riley drove up the access road.

"Can I have a look at your knife?" O'Neil said.

Riley adjusted her mirror and saw Tom pass it. The blade was fixed and about four inches long, handle in mother of pearl. O'Neil held it between thumb and forefinger, careful not to smudge the boy's prints.

"It's a Loveless drop point," Tom said. "Retains its edge."

"Where'd you get it?" O'Neil said.

"On the internet, from America."

"Wow. When?"

"Last Christmas."

"How'd you do that? American credit card?"

"My uncle, um, lives in Texas. I chose it, and he bought it as a present."

"It's sharp."

"Yeah." The boy was pleased. "I freshen it up every night."

They'd come off the access trail and were driving around the edge of the Flats.

"When are you going to catch him?" Tom said.

"Soon," O'Neil said. "He's made too many mistakes."

Tom eyed the knife between O'Neil's fingers. "Like what?"

"With the plastic, for a start."

Tom's eyes flicked to Riley's in the mirror. "What about it?" he said.

"He had to cut it." O'Neil held the knife lengthwise between his index fingers. It was a balancing act—he wouldn't push it. They were just having a chat. Without a suitable adult present, anything Tom said was inadmissible.

"Can I have it back now?"

"You know it's a prohibited weapon?" O'Neil said. "And it's in a school. I have to confiscate it. I'll give it back later."

Tom turned to look out the window. Riley drove up to the Dunlop house and parked at the garage.

"Let's get out here for a tick," O'Neil said, opening his door.

Farquhar and Riley followed, but Tom stayed in the car. Riley popped the boot of the Commodore and pulled out an evidence bag. O'Neil placed the knife in the sleeve, and she zipped it and stowed it. The kid was still in the back.

O'Neil had his hand on the open boot. "You get him out." He spoke low. "But go easy. If he won't budge, tell him we'll have to get his parents."

Riley opened Tom's door and smiled in. "Come," she said. "Won't be a sec."

After a moment, the boy climbed out. He wouldn't look at them.

O'Neil shut the boot. "Let's take a quick walk."

"Nup." Tom stood between Riley and Farquhar. "I don't have to go with you."

They were in the gray area. The kid had to be free to leave. Riley looked to O'Neil. Take the risk. "Come on, Tom," she said. "Otherwise, we have to go get your father."

O'Neil started down to the yards behind the windbreak.

Tom didn't move.

"The Dunlops' dog," Riley said, "what was it called?"

His head cocked. "Tatters?"

O'Neil had turned back and was watching.

"I think you were feeding the dog, weren't you, Tom?" Farquhar said.

The boy nodded quickly—just like his sister.

"Would you tell us what happened," Farquhar said, "when Tatters disappeared?"

"I dunno." His shoulders twitched. "It went missing. I looked for it."

O'Neil walked up.

"It might have been sick," Tom said, "and gone off to die. A dog likes to die on its own."

"Is that right?" O'Neil said. "Do they dig their own grave?"

The boy's eyes slipped down the slope.

"Shall we get your dad here?" O'Neil said.

Tom shook his head. Riley lagged as they picked their way to the police tape around the dog's burial site.

"What happened here, Tom?" O'Neil said.

His face creased. "What do you mean?"

"Did you forget to feed the dog?" Farquhar said. "Leave him tied up by mistake?"

Riley held her breath. The psychiatrist had supplied an excuse . . . The boy didn't take it.

"We dug Tatters up," O'Neil said. "Someone cut his throat."

"With a knife," Riley said.

"The carcass is in a lab, Tom, under a microscope," O'Neil said. "Your knife goes there too. Forensics will tell if the blade cut its throat."

Tom stared at his feet.

The shed where they had found the John Deere was off to the right and still strung with police tape.

O'Neil walked over. "Have a look at this."

Crime Scene had trucked the John Deere away. "The forensic investigators took something from here." O'Neil pointed. "Do you know what it was?"

The boy stood in the doorway, eyes narrow.

"They look for fingerprints, DNA," O'Neil said. "That will tell them who drove it."

Riley stepped through. "Marguerite was here," she said. "Can you feel it?"

Tom shook his head at the floor.

"She was here," Riley said, "but she was dead. She was washed in here."

They stood for long moments. "Tom," O'Neil said, "I don't want you to say anything, not now. But all this"—he waved a hand—"you need to think about it. There was a cleanup in here, but it wasn't thorough. Things got missed."

His mother had said Tom was following the case in the media. "Did you read about how to clean up a scene?" Riley said.

The boy stood completely still.

"Your knife will go under the microscope," O'Neil said, "with Tatters and the plastic."

"We could go find your mum," Riley said, "or someone you trust. Do you want to talk about it then?"

In the silence, Riley could see Farquhar framed in the daylight.

"All right," O'Neil said at last. "Let's get you home."

Tom didn't speak on the way back to the car, or on the drive to his house. He got out without a word and didn't look back as he walked up the path.

Riley drummed at the wheel.

"Drive," O'Neil said.

She drove to the back of the school and onto a corner of the Flats, killed the engine, and put all four windows down. "Well?" She twisted in her seat.

"We got the knife," O'Neil said.

"It feels like a fuckup," she said. "We told him things."

"He showed *us* something," Farquhar said. "His reticence. The way he shut down in the shed, went blank."

Riley turned to her window. The child's silence had surprised her. Kids weren't mature enough to hold back. Even bad kids were vulnerable—they wanted to talk, or they wanted to gloat. "Maybe he doesn't know anything?" she said.

"Then why not say so?" Farquhar said. "Deny everything. Tom didn't do that. He coped. He has an ability to retreat."

"Retreat from what?"

"Typically, exposure to violence as a child," the psychiatrist said. "Abuse, neglect."

"We went to see a boy about a dog," O'Neil said. "And now we think he killed the girl?"

Farquhar didn't answer.

"Well . . . run with it," O'Neil said. "He kills Marguerite. Why?"

"He doesn't mean to," Farquhar said. "He's been watching her, and he breaks into her house. He's thrill seeking. He thinks she's gone to work, but then she comes home. So now he's in a dangerous, confrontational situation. He lashes out, one blow to the head . . . He's nasty enough to clean it up and try to pass it off as BMK. He's been following the case, according to his mother. As Rose asked, did he read about cleaning?"

"He dumps her at the Hay Stand," O'Neil said. "Why then pretend to find the body?"

"That might not have been his intention," Farquhar said. "Maybe he returned to the scene to look, even to film her, perhaps to move her. Then Spratt drives past and forces his hand. Tom's smart. He knows he's leaving footprints in the dust, and he calculates there's a risk Spratt has seen him. There are too many variables, so Tom pivots. He takes the initiative and flags Spratt down."

"There's our fuckup," Riley said.

"How so?" Farquhar said.

O'Neil was already on his phone, calling Annie Tran and ordering surveillance on the Green house, Satyr detectives front and back.

"We know Tom filmed from his drone on Thursday and caught a frame or two of the body at the dump site," Riley said. "Correct?"

The psychiatrist nodded.

"If Tom killed Marguerite, then that footage the next day was a trophy," she said. "If he took something else from her—a trinket, an item of her clothing—then we've just tipped him off to get rid of it."

29

They got the knife to the lab with the dog.

"Priority one," O'Neil said. "Results to me."

Despite the claims they had made to the boy, O'Neil knew the results wouldn't be definitive. The best they could hope for was a finding that it was possible the blade had been used to cut the dog and the plastic. That would be good—better than the lab definitively ruling the blade out—but it was circumstantial. It was evidence. They could dress it up and take it to court, but it was defendable.

There was something else the knife would give them: Tom's prints. They'd printed his father and mother and every other adult at the school, but Tom was a minor.

At his desk in the strike force room, O'Neil could feel it—the prints on the knife would be a match with those on the bench in the Dunlop house.

But there was a problem with that as well. Tom had a built-in defense: he could say he'd left his prints in the house when Spratt had let him in to look for the dog. The prints were evidence, but they were circumstantial too.

"The fucking dog," he said.

Riley, eating a potato scallop at her laptop, raised an eyebrow.

"What are you looking at?" he said.

"Scott Green's movements on that Wednesday."

O'Neil nodded, Farquhar's words in his ears: *exposure to violence as a child*. Scott Green had a strong alibi, but Riley was right to look at it again. "Let's hear it," he said.

On Wednesday, 28 December, Scott Green had been away from the school in the morning and most of the afternoon. His version of events had been verified by CCTV, shop assistants, retail dockets, credit card data, his vehicle registration, and his phone records. His car had been driven out of the school gates at 9:28 a.m.—exactly seven minutes after Marguerite Dunlop had driven in from her visit to Coles at North Rocks. In Northmead, Green had purchased shelving at Bunnings at 10:22 a.m. and a router at Officeworks at 11:09 a.m. He was eating meatballs in Ikea at Rhodes at 12:37 p.m. He'd driven back into the school at 2:44 p.m.

Sarah and the kids all claimed Scott had been in and around the house for the rest of the afternoon and the evening. He had made a forty-four-minute call from his mobile to TPG at 6:48 p.m. Satyr analysts had verified the call with the telco.

"NBN trouble," Riley said. "Hence the router."

O'Neil nodded again. "Busy day." The timing didn't fit. Everything around Marguerite went dark after she'd driven into the school from Coles. She hadn't even put the shopping away. She was in trouble as soon as she got home at about 9:25 a.m. Someone was in the house— just as Scott Green was driving out of the gate.

O'Neil's phone pinged, and he read the text. "Fucking Christ," he said.

"What?" Riley said.

O'Neil gave her the gist of it. The police commissioner had been hauled into the premier's office for a meeting with Hugh Bishop yesterday. The minister had claimed the police treatment of Preston amounted to harassment, and he was advising the headmaster to sue for damages. In the meantime, Bishop wanted O'Neil stood down from the investigation.

"Mother of fuck," Riley said. "Did the boss agree?"

"No, he refused. But Bishop's still circling."

"Unbelievable. Arsehole fucking cunt. Who's telling you this?"

"Madden—in Orange. He's plugged in upstairs."

"Jesus," Riley said. "Bishop . . . It's got to stop."

O'Neil did some breathing. Bishop was dangerous, but they had his measure. The politician was stealing focus from the victims. They had a journalist in their pocket—it was time to use him.

Bowman was sterilizing the sterile kitchen in the Parramatta unit when his phone rang.

"Listen," O'Neil said. "We've had some phone taps running. That's off the record. But there's a call from Preston that makes for intriguing listening."

Bowman put down the Spray n' Wipe. "Who'd he call?"

"Rose filled you in on some dealings Preston had with this Hugh Bishop, the federal minister?"

"Sort of. Bishop called me yesterday."

"Yeah, he was busy yesterday," O'Neil said. "Let me play you our call, and then I need a favor."

Bowman went for his notebook. There was a hiss on the line and then Bishop's wide vowels.

How are things now?

Not good. Preston's voice was flat.

We shouldn't speak on the phone.

Well, come out. You said you would.

I can't. I told you, I'm heading north.

Well, if you're going to run, we'll talk like this.

I'm not running.

If I go down—

Don't talk like that. Why would you go down?

They've been to Orange. They know everything.

What did they say?

The manure linked me to Marguerite. I think they thought I'd done it. They said they knew I liked young girls.

Fucking Zabatino.

He won't take my calls. They must have got to him.

Well, you just have to ride it out.

Preston didn't answer.

They're Homicide, Bishop said. *They're looking for a killer. All this shit is nothing to them. It'll blow over.*

Not if the journalist gets onto it.

I spoke to him. I'm trying to pull him off, get him up for a bit of snout in the trough.

You better.

The audio clicked off, and O'Neil's voice came back. "You get it?"

"Yeah." Bowman stared at his notebook. Young girls, Orange, Zabatino. "What's it all mean?"

"It means Bishop and Preston are on the take with the mafia, and Bishop is trying to save himself. He knows we know about Preston, and he's trying to shut us down before he gets dragged into it."

"Nothing to do with BMK?"

"It's way more ordinary. We looked hard at Preston for Marguerite. We're pretty certain it's not him."

"What's the favor?" Bowman said.

"I need you to get all this ready," O'Neil said, "as a story. But don't publish until you hear from me. I might need you to ring the premier, put to her what you know about Bishop."

"The premier?"

"Yeah," O'Neil said. "I've got to go. We're running something down. Write the bones of it, and sit tight. I'll fill in details later. And tell Alexander to keep an eye on Beat-Up Benny. Bishop might use Diamond to attack me."

O'Neil hung up, and Bowman retied his sarong. "What the fuck?" he said.

◆ ◆ ◆

In the apartment building hallway, Riley raised a fist to knock on Bowman's door and decided against it. She rapped on her own instead, and Needham opened up, back for another shift. Patel was at the table, working on her laptop.

"I bought some fruit"—Patel pointed at a bowl—"so we don't die of scurvy."

Riley needed a beer. "How's your head?" she said.

"All good." Patel touched near her temple.

Riley put her bag on a chair and headed for the kitchen. Someone had stocked the fridge. She broke off two stubbies and went back and took a seat at the table, sliding a bottle to Patel.

"Let's hear it," Patel said.

Riley glanced past her at Needham reading her phone on the couch. "Constable"—Riley tossed her head at the third bedroom—"give us a minute."

Needham got up and left. Riley sipped, then started with the dog and went through the day.

Patel made notes and grunts. "You really think it's the boy?" she said when Riley had finished.

Riley frowned, and her phone pinged—a text from the techs. They'd got into Tom's USB and emailed her a link. She pulled out her laptop and clicked through.

Sarah Green had been right—it was more drone footage, shot from the playing fields below the Hay Stand. Riley left it running, got another beer, and sat back to watch. The perspective had changed, and it took her a moment to orient herself. She stiffened, her mouth open, the stubby halfway to her lips.

"Rose?" Patel said.

Riley blinked. She turned the screen to Patel and pulled out her phone.

O'Neil answered and listened. "On my way," he said.

"Bring Farquhar," Riley said.

Riley and Patel were still at the table with the laptop when O'Neil arrived with the psychiatrist.

"He's got it up pretty high, maybe fifty meters." Riley pressed play and fast-forwarded. The drone was past the Hay Stand now and starting to drop and zero in. It lowered to the level of the Dunlop house and moved toward a window on the ground floor. As the camera focused in, they could clearly see a young woman lying on her bed with headphones on.

"Marguerite," O'Neil murmured.

"Camera sits here for three minutes," Riley said. "He knows he can hover without her hearing. She gets up and moves around. Eventually, she leaves the room, headphones still on."

"This footage was taken when?" O'Neil said.

"Friday, December 9," Riley said. "Before Fiji. But school holidays had started."

"Do we bring him in?" Patel said.

"That's an offense right there"—Riley pointed at the screen—"using a drone like that."

O'Neil sat forward. "We arrest him for the drone offense, then what?"

"We wait on forensics on the knife," Riley said.

"It's all circumstantial, even if it lines up," O'Neil said.

"Right now, he could be busy destroying evidence," Riley said. "He's probably figured out we've got this footage. If we arrest him for the drone, we at least get him out of the house."

"Yeah, but he makes bail." O'Neil exhaled. "He's home in no time."

"But with this"—Patel nodded at the screen—"can't we charge him with Marguerite?"

"It's not enough," O'Neil said. "The strength of good circumstantial evidence is when you piece it together. We need to build it."

Riley got up and walked to the window. Farquhar had said the boy might have killed the dog for kicks. That could be true, but it wasn't why he'd killed it.

"I think he killed the dog for access," she said.

Out the window, the river was silver in the dusk. No one spoke. She turned back to the table.

"It gives him a reason to ask Spratt to open the house," she said, "so he can check that the dog's not got itself trapped inside. Then, while he's in there, he unlatches the window in the alcove. He goes out and tells Spratt no luck, no Tatters. But he's got access now, to come and go when he wants."

O'Neil was nodding. "He's not worried about leaving prints because he hasn't killed anyone. He's not planning to kill anyone."

"No one is ever meant to know he's there," Patel said. "He's a voyeur, obsessed with Marguerite. He wants to come back and snoop."

"Wayne?" Riley said.

The psychiatrist had a hand in his beard. "He's transgressing, just by being in the house. It fits with the scene—that the killing wasn't premeditated, that the murderer was surprised and then panicked."

"He decides to make it look like Gladesville," Riley said. "He has to get the plastic from behind the maintenance shed—a round trip of what? At least three kilometers?"

"He must be on foot, moving through the bush to stay off the road and skirt the cameras," O'Neil said.

"Right," Riley said. "And Scott Green takes the same route on his Friday morning walk."

O'Neil's tongue clicked. "They're working together?"

"Maybe," Riley said. "Maybe what Bowman sees on Friday is the father covering his son's tracks, making sure Tom didn't leave any evidence."

"Does Tom tell his father what has happened and ask for help?" O'Neil said. "Or does Scott find out by chance?"

"Or is it father and son?" Riley said. "They do it all together?"

Farquhar swayed.

"Scott's out of the school on Wednesday," O'Neil said.

"There's another problem with the timing," Patel said. "Scott Green was seen by Bowman at the maintenance shed on Friday morning, but Marguerite was dumped Wednesday evening—or certainly by Thursday morning. If they're covering their tracks, why wait until Friday, when we're crawling all over the place? They had all day Thursday to clean up."

"Perhaps," O'Neil said. "But let's say Scott, however he learns of the death, only does so after we're on the scene—that's why he's checking things on Friday."

"Yes," Farquhar said. "And don't forget Tom is not necessarily in control of the timing of the discovery of the body. As I said, he might have been revisiting the dump site on Thursday evening when Spratt drives past and forces his hand."

O'Neil's mobile rang. He listened and stood. "Arrest him," he said. "I'll charge him. We'll be there in ten."

He hung up and went for his jacket. "Tom Green just tried to slip out his bedroom window," he said. "Our guys grabbed him on the lawn."

30

Riley trailed an ambulance into the school and up the drive to the Greens' house. Tom was cuffed on the grass out front. The arresting detective stood over him, and another Satyr officer waved the paramedics through. "Woman's collapsed inside," he told them.

Patel stayed with Tom while Riley followed O'Neil and the ambos. There were two more detectives in the hall.

Sarah Green lay prone on the family-room floor, one cheek to the carpet, eyes closed. Scott Green moved aside to let the paramedics get to her.

O'Neil turned back to the two detectives. "No one goes into the rest of the house," he said, "including the father. Crime Scene en route."

Scott Green looked from O'Neil to Riley.

"What happened?" O'Neil said.

Scott was calm. "There was a commotion outside. She went to see." He glanced down at his wife. "She came back all white and fainted."

Riley squatted to speak with the ambos. The mother was conscious but in shock. There was no sign of injury, but she may have hit her head as she fell. They would take her to Westmead, and at this hour the doctors would keep her overnight for monitoring.

"Mr. Green," O'Neil said, "we need to take Tom down to the station and ask him some questions. We need you to accompany him."

Scott stared at him. "What questions?"

Riley straightened. Forensics would start with the boy's clothes, looking for the missing seventy mils of blood. They had a warrant, but they needed the father out of the house. O'Neil went through the living room onto the lawn. Riley moved across to Scott Green. "Would you come with us outside, please?" she said.

Tom was sullen on the grass. Drone laws were ambiguous. O'Neil cautioned him and cast the net wide, charging the boy under the Surveillance Devices Act and with breaches of antivoyeurism and antistalking legislation.

"We're going to take you to the station now to answer some questions," O'Neil said. "Your father will come with you."

"Not him," Tom said. "I hate him."

"What is this?" Scott scoffed. "Can we take the cuffs off?"

"I haven't done anything," Tom hissed at his father. "Figure it out."

Scott shrugged at Riley.

"You can ride with your son." O'Neil nodded toward the Commodore. "He needs an adult support person."

"Not him," Tom said.

The ambos came out the door with Sarah Green on a stretcher.

"It's your choice, Tom," Riley said, "but if your father doesn't come, we have to assign someone at the station."

Patel led the boy to the car. Riley stood beside Scott Green. *Figure it out.* If the father knew there was something to dispose of, taking him to the station would only delay him. He could get it done tomorrow, or the next day. The ambulance doors opened in the driveway.

"You should travel to the hospital with your wife," Riley said, "and stay with her there. In the morning, we'll bring you over to see Tom and ask you some questions. I'm sure we can clear all this up."

◆ ◆ ◆

At the Parramatta station, they printed Tom and took a buccal swab. It was close to midnight, Saturday, January 7, and Legal Aid was thin on the ground. The desk sergeant rang around the acceptable persons list, and eventually an old Greek volunteer with clunky English appeared.

"Perfect," O'Neil said.

Patel went into the interview room with Riley. Farquhar and O'Neil watched through the glass.

"Tom," Riley said, "you understand you've been charged with spying on Marguerite Dunlop with a drone?"

The boy shook his head.

On her laptop, Riley clicked the footage of Marguerite and turned it to him. Tom watched for a few moments, swallowed, touched his mouth. "Wait, what? That's not mine. I've never seen that before."

"It was taken by your drone," Riley said. "It was found in your room."

His lip curled. "Nah."

"The footage was shot on your drone about a month ago," Riley said.

His head shook. "Someone must have borrowed it."

"Really?" Riley said. "Someone borrowed your drone, put the video they shot with it onto a USB stick, and stuck it under your desk in your bedroom?"

Tom nodded and stared at the wall.

"The day after Marguerite was killed, you flew your drone again and filmed her body."

"Did not."

"You can see her lying dead," Riley said, "on the footage. You filmed her lying dead."

"Yeah right. So I did that and then gave the police my memory card? Smart."

"You were working up to it. You came back later to do it properly. But it was too windy. So you walked right up to her. You couldn't stay away. You were going to film her. But then you saw Craig Spratt."

His face screwed into teenage contempt.

"Tom," Patel said, "we have a lot of evidence. This is just the start. It'll be much better for you if you tell us the truth. If you lie to us now—well, judges don't like that." She looked at the volunteer.

"It's right," the man said.

Tom studied his hands in his lap.

"Our forensic investigators are going through your room now, Tom," Riley said. "Technicians are going through your laptop. They can tell if the USB has been connected to your computer. They'll find your fingerprints on the stick—and on the Blu Tack you used to hide it."

He sniffed.

"What else will they find in your room, Tom?" Riley said.

"They should mind their own business," he said. "Stop snooping around."

"Snooping," Riley said. "That's an interesting word. You know all about snooping, don't you?"

He rolled his eyes.

"You're a bit of a voyeur, aren't you?" Riley said. "Peeping Tom. You like to watch."

"Retard," he said.

"We know you liked to watch Marguerite." Riley tapped the laptop and leaned forward. "Did you kill Marguerite Dunlop, Tom?"

His head went back. "Are you serious?"

"You didn't mean to kill her, did you? She surprised you in her bedroom, and you lashed out. You hit her hard enough to kill her."

He crossed his arms.

Riley's phone pinged with a text. O'Neil: Come out now.

She motioned to Patel, and they left the room. O'Neil was with Farquhar in the corridor.

"Lab's come back on the knife," he said.

Riley's jaw clenched.

"They got a good print," O'Neil said. "It's a match with the prints on the bench. They're confirming it now against what we just collected from Tom."

Riley found her ulcer. It was on the mend. "What else?" she said.

"The blade was possibly used on the dog. And possibly on the plastic. Too many variables to be definitive."

"Can we charge him with murder?" Patel said.

O'Neil didn't answer. Riley looked at the door of the interview room. If they charged him with murder, he wouldn't get bail. But they didn't have enough to convict. A magistrate might not even commit him to stand trial. The defense would simply argue the prints had been left in the house when Spratt let Tom in to look for the dog.

"Let's keep at him," O'Neil said. "Use the knife and the prints against him. Stack it up, and see if he cracks. We can charge him with animal cruelty if it helps."

Riley reached for the door, and Patel followed her in. Tom had his back to the volunteer.

"You were careful after you killed her," Riley said. "You washed her and wrapped her and washed the whole package again. You read the Gladesville story in the news, about how bleach kills DNA. You used a lot of bleach."

Tom was looking at his spot on the wall.

"Come on," Riley said. "I'm paying you a compliment. You were smart. You did your research. Even before you killed Marguerite, you were following the Gladesville case. BMK. He fascinates you, doesn't he?"

"You washed everything," Patel said, "but you didn't wash her hair. Why was that?"

His eyes widened in derision. "Didn't have any shampoo?"

"You knew if you washed the blood from her hair, it would run everywhere, leave traces," Riley said. "Police are good at finding blood, right?"

"You're the cop."

"Like I said, you were careful, but you were only careful after you killed her."

His face folded closed. Riley wondered what he'd lived through.

"Before you killed her," she said. "Let's talk about that. There's this funny thing with the bench in that room at Marguerite's house where you climbed in. Five perfect prints we found there: a thumb and four fingers of the left hand." Riley arched her fingers and thumb and touched the table with the tips. "You must have gone just like that."

The boy raised his right hand and gave her the finger.

"Do you know where our lab found a match for those prints, Tom? On your knife. See what I mean about not being careful?"

The kid yawned. "What's the big deal? I told you I was in the house, looking for Tatters."

Patel leaned forward. "Tom," she said, "it's not just your prints we have from the knife."

The boy pushed his chair back, straightened his legs out, folded his arms, put his chin on his chest, and closed his eyes.

"The technicians looked at your knife under a microscope," Patel said, "and also the plastic Marguerite was wrapped in, and the roll of plastic behind the maintenance shed—"

Riley raised a hand. They couldn't lie. "The lab used something called fracture fit to compare the cuts and found they were a match. That's irrefutable evidence. The judge just takes it as true."

The room was silent. Riley looked at her watch: 1:15 a.m. Maybe a stint in the cells would shake him up. His eyes were still closed, his legs outstretched. His limbs, his face, his hands, his neck—every part of him was brown from the sun except his feet . . . She remembered him in thongs, walking before her on the path from the cave. Pale feet—he always wore shoes. She looked at the pair he was wearing. Brand-new black-and-white Nikes . . .

His mother had said he was at Carlingford on Friday, buying trainers.

Riley felt the slippage, realization calving. She rose with it, motioning Patel outside.

There were two uniforms stationed in the corridor. "Give us a sec," Riley said.

O'Neil appeared.

"Who have we got at the hospital?" Riley said.

"Annie," O'Neil said, "and two constables."

Riley called Tran and told her what she needed. She hung up and paced the hall. In his story about Gladesville cleaning up, Diamond had speculated that the killer was incinerating evidence. It was rubbish, just another thing Beat-Up Benny had wrong. Tran rang back. Riley listened, then ended the call and walked over to O'Neil and Patel.

"It's his shoes," Riley said.

O'Neil looked past her to the boy in the room.

"Not those," Riley said. "His old ones. I think I know where they are."

Riley trod on the V-8 across the river on O'Connell Street. There was nothing on the roads, and she ran the red lights.

"You think the blood is on his shoes?" O'Neil said.

Riley turned into the school. Sarah Green had told Tran that Tom had asked for money for new trainers early in the week, maybe Tuesday. Sarah had bucked up because she'd only bought the last pair a couple of months ago. Tom had shown her a shoe that was ripped along the instep. He'd said he'd torn it in the bush.

"Sarah says she put it in the rubbish," Riley said. "But here's the thing: she only saw one shoe."

"The rubbish is collected centrally and trucked out," O'Neil said. "We put a stop on it. We've been through it."

They were at the back of the school now, turning onto the access road they'd used earlier. Big gums loomed in the headlights.

"There's something else I want to check," Riley said.

She pulled up, popped the trunk with the button, and passed around gloves, forensic booties, and evidence bags. She clicked on a torch, and they walked in tight single file, with Patel in the middle and O'Neil behind her. It was 2:00 a.m., the same time of night as Patel's attack. The three of them kept up a low murmur to each other as they went, past the water hole to the cave. They gloved up and put the booties on. Riley slipped in first.

"Tread carefully." She lit their way, then played the torch over the debris on the floor.

O'Neil went forward and squatted.

In the beam was a white-striped black Nike. O'Neil opened an evidence bag, and Patel picked up the shoe by the heel, held it between thumb and forefinger in the light. The white of the emblem was stained a rust color. She turned it slightly. The blood had seeped through, marking the green inner sole.

O'Neil pointed at an edge of material on the bottom of the tongue, and Patel pulled it gently. A cloth name tag had been sewn in. It was blotted with blood but readable: Tom Green.

"Don't you just love an organized mother?" O'Neil said.

"Or father," Riley said.

Patel placed the shoe in the bag, and O'Neil held it out. "I don't think we'll call that circumstantial," he said.

They stood, and Riley shined the torch over the campfire and the kindling and newspapers. "The papers are from this week," she said. "He must have brought them down to start a fire. He'd read about incinerating evidence. I think he was going to burn the shoe."

"Then we walked in on him here," O'Neil said. "He must've been going out his window to finish the job."

"But why show one shoe to the mum?" Patel said.

"It mustn't have had blood on it, so he sliced it open to ruin it," Riley said. "He had to make an excuse for getting a new pair."

"But if you think father and son," Patel said, "why didn't he ask his dad for the money?"

Riley's eyes met O'Neil's in the torchlight. *Figure it out.* If Scott Green had been helping clean up, Tom would have gone to him for cash.

"Scott's asleep outside Sarah's room at the hospital," Riley said. "Annie went and checked. She said he was using a vending machine as a pillow."

"If Scott's part of it," O'Neil said, "he missed the memo marked urgent."

31

They drove back to the unit at Parramatta and slept. O'Neil took the spare room. He kept a change of clothes in his car, and at 9:00 a.m. he was showered and dressed and sipping green tea. Riley sent Needham out for a bacon-and-egg roll and coffee.

"Shoe's in the lab," O'Neil said.

She tied back her hair. "You want to wait for results?"

"Nah. Let's do it. See if he denies it."

Riley ate. Patel didn't wake, so they left her and drove to the station. Legal Aid had assigned a lawyer, and Tom Green was brought up from the cells and put in the interview room. He refused to have his father present. O'Neil went in with Riley and leaned against the back wall while she did the honors. She placed a photo of the bloodied Nike before the boy and formally charged him with the murder of Marguerite Dunlop.

Tom showed no emotion. Riley gave him time, but the boy didn't budge. He offered no confession or excuse or apology. He didn't deny the crime, nor did he protest his innocence. He didn't say a word.

O'Neil came up to the table. "Did your father help you with the body, Tom?" he said.

A night in the cells had pinched the boy's face.

"We know you moved her, Tom," O'Neil said. "I'm asking you if your father helped."

"You don't have to answer," the lawyer said. Tom didn't speak.

"You pretended to find Marguerite's body on that Thursday night," O'Neil said. "Why do you think your father was walking behind the maintenance shed on that Friday morning?"

Riley thought about Scott Green, asleep at the hospital. No urgency. Even at the house, bemusement had been his only emotion at the arrest of his son. It was Sarah who had reacted, fainting in shock, as if she gleaned the true horror.

"You asked your mother for money for new shoes," Riley said. "Why didn't you just ask your father?"

The boy stood, walked to the door, and waited. An ability to retreat. But from what?

O'Neil nodded at the lawyer and watched as the uniforms took Tom away.

Back in the Commodore, they drove to Beecroft, where they sat down with Bruce Dunlop and his sister-in-law. O'Neil told them as gently as he could.

Pale and shrunken, the father couldn't take it in. "Tom?" was all Bruce Dunlop could say.

O'Neil warned them the arrest would break in the press within hours, but most of the details would be withheld. Tom Green could not be identified, due to his age. He would be denied bail in court on Monday and held on remand until his committal hearing before a magistrate. That could be some months, O'Neil said.

There was nothing more to say. The detectives took their leave and sat in the Commodore.

"We give it to Bowman?" O'Neil said.

"Seems only fair."

"On the phone or face-to-face?"

She started the engine and turned onto the road.

"Face-to-face it is," O'Neil said.

Bowman opened the door in a sarong and faded T-shirt. "Where the fuck have you been?"

"Taking a break in Bali," Riley said. "Can we come in?"

Bowman peered out and saw O'Neil in the hall. "Is this about Bishop?"

"No," Riley said. "Let's sit down."

Bowman led them to the table off the kitchen.

"We just charged Tom Green with the murder of Marguerite Dunlop," O'Neil said.

Bowman looked from O'Neil to Riley. "*Tom* Green?" he said. "You mean the father?"

"We mean the boy," O'Neil said.

Bowman sat with his mouth open.

"You interviewed him," Riley said. "What did you make of him?"

Bowman blinked. "A bit of a skulker . . ."

"And?" Riley said.

Bowman looked past her, and she felt her allegiance shift. He was a victim, the saddest of all—a victim of his past. A true detective is there to serve the victim: O'Neil's top catechism. She saw her mother in her nurse scrubs, the nobility of her public service. Bowman was a victim, her victim. She stifled an urge to fill him in on his past.

His notebook was on the table. "Got a pen?" O'Neil said. "Story's yours if you want it."

Bowman clicked a Bic. O'Neil was careful. They were giving him the story early, he said, and it was critical that he understood he could not publish Tom's name, age, or photo. The boy was now in the hands of the court, and there would be suppression orders. If Bowman got it wrong, he could jeopardize any hope of a trial.

"You can write that a teenager has been arrested and charged with the murder of Marguerite Dunlop at Prince Albert," O'Neil said. "You can say he's been charged with other offenses and is to appear before a magistrate in Parramatta Children's Court tomorrow. You can say sources allege police have extensive forensic evidence, including new drone footage."

"And you can say that Marguerite Dunlop's parents have been informed of developments," Riley said.

"Is that it?" Bowman said.

"One more thing," O'Neil said. "And this is a direct quote—write it down. 'Detective Chief Inspector Steve O'Neil said the killing of Marguerite Dunlop appeared not to be the work of the killer known as BMK because it lacked his trademarks of cowardice and perversion.'"

They stood while Bowman was still scribbling. "We'll leave you to it," Riley said. "Text me when it's online."

"What about the other stuff?" Bowman looked up. "On Bishop?"

"Don't be greedy," O'Neil said. "We'll talk about it later."

In the corridor, Riley pressed the button for the lift.

"Talking of Bishop," O'Neil said, "Madden left a voice mail from Orange. He showed the girls at the brothel a picture of the minister. A couple of them recognized him. He was there with Preston."

"That's good," Riley said. "Madden can go on the record. Game over."

"I'll set it up," O'Neil said. "You can give it all to Bowman in the morning."

They got into the lift. Riley didn't have the right to tell Bowman what she knew about his mother and the death of his brother. But she liked the symmetry of him getting Preston's head on a platter.

32

Bowman's story of the arrest had gone online on Sunday afternoon, and now, on Monday morning, he updated it to say the accused had been denied a bail application and was remanded into custody, with court orders to protect his identity.

Riley had texted to say she would give him details on Bishop at 10:00 a.m. He looked at his watch, and there was a knock on the door.

Her hair was pulled back damp, and he smelled coconut. "Coffee?" he said.

"Thanks." She sat at the table and waited until he brought the mugs.

As she briefed him, he took notes and sipped coffee, caffeine for his racing heart. The story was better than he could have imagined—a federal cabinet minister in bed with the mafia and consorting with prostitutes. Bishop was finished—that was the big news. Preston was bycatch.

"Take this number down." Riley read out a mobile. "That's Paul Madden, the super at Orange. He's expecting your call, and he's on the record. You work with him."

Bowman scrawled down the number. "This story—is it just a gift?"

"Or what?"

"Does publishing it help you? I know you don't do anything without strategy."

Her lips tightened—almost a smile. "That's true," she said. "He's running interference. We need him out of the way."

She fiddled with her mug. She was holding back, he knew, but something in her face opened, and he glimpsed the girl she must have been—brave, bright, curious. Before the years in Homicide.

"All this"—she waved at his notebook—"it's a sideshow, nothing to do with Marguerite, or Gladesville. But these men need to be held to account. Preston, in particular."

"Why him in particular?"

"Zabatino's mafia, a career criminal running to type. And Bishop—he's a politician, in it for himself. But Preston . . ."

"What about Preston?" Bowman said.

"He shouldn't be near children. At least if you run this, the school won't be able to press the eject button fast enough."

"What happens now?" he said. "With the investigation?"

"We swing back to Gladesville."

He looked around the room. "How long do we have to stay here?"

"Dunno." She drained her mug. "I've got to go."

He watched her leave and leafed through his notes. Then he called Paul Madden and spoke for half an hour. Everything was watertight. Bowman hung up and wrote out a series of questions to put to Preston and Bishop. He was debating which of them to call first when his phone rang. Bishop.

Bowman stared at it before answering. "Minister," he said.

"Saw your story on the arrest," Bishop said. "Wanted to say well done. Bad business."

Bowman's mouth was dry. "Yeah."

"At least that's the end of it," Bishop said. "All quiet on the Western Front."

"How's Queensland?"

"Perfect one day, full of Victorians the next."

"You still gonna fly me up?"

"Ahh, of course . . . if there's any point?"

"To talk about the school."

"There's a kid in custody," Bishop said. "Probably best if we all shut the fuck up."

Bowman braced. "We could talk about Preston."

A longer pause. "What about him?"

"Whether the board still supports him. Does it?"

"Why wouldn't they?"

"You said there was unease, that he was out of his depth."

"Ahh, forget that. Fake news. We're moving forward. School's back in a couple of weeks."

"Can I quote you?"

"On what—moving forward?"

"Nah. Unease. Preston being out of his depth."

"Mate, don't play games." Bishop's drawl was sharpening. "That was off the record."

"Really? I don't recall you saying that. I've got my notes—"

"Fuck your notes. I'm telling you now: it was off the record."

Bowman was conscious of his breathing.

"You print that, I sue," Bishop said. "It's pretty fucking simple."

Bowman sat back. "I'm writing a story."

"Mate." Bishop's voice was quiet. "There's a couple of QCs on the school board who'd love to have a crack. I'm putting a pool in out at Blayney. I don't think your boss in London wants to pay for my swimming pool."

"Gets pretty hot in Blayney," Bowman said.

"Too right. Not this global warming horseshit either. It's called summer. You can quote me on *that*."

"Not as hot as Orange."

Bowman's heart was racing. "Hot tubs in Orange," he said. "That'd make a good headline."

There was menace in the silence. "What are you getting at?" Bishop said.

"That I'm writing a story about Preston."

"Saying what?"

Bowman's hands were shaking. "I'll get back to you on that." He hung up. He needed to regroup. Speaking truth to power—journalists went on about it, as though it were their daily grind, but in truth it didn't happen often. In truth, most journos spent their days sucking up to power. Bowman stood, muttered, shook his arms out.

He called Alexander. The editor listened, speechless. "You are shitting me," he managed at last. "Hugh Bishop in a mafia brothel?"

"It's good, eh?"

"*Good?* Jesus. You know, I'm almost starting to like this BMK." Alexander stopped. "Don't tell anyone I said that."

"How do you want to play it?" Bowman said.

"Have you put it to them?"

"Not to Preston. I alluded to it with Bishop."

"Alluded to it? Fucking how'd you do that?"

"He just called me. He knows I've got something on Preston in Orange."

"All right. Call Preston and then get back to Bishop. Put it to them, and write it up. File it to me, and get in here. I'll get it legalled."

"He mentioned the old man."

"Forget that. A story like this—the old man will sniff the breeze. Bishop'll be swinging in it."

◆ ◆ ◆

The story was up online by 2:00 p.m.

Bishop went to ground in the Whitsundays, and Brandy Alexander went to town. The editor sent *The National*'s Far North Queensland correspondent down to flush out the minister. A reporter and photographer were dispatched to Orange to interview the prostitutes and harass Zabatino. The paper's Canberra bureau was mobilized to stoke the scandal into a full-blown political crisis. The broadsheet's troika of bearded columnists were prodded from January slumber in their South Coast burrows and press-ganged into service. They didn't mind. They each knocked out a thousand-word think piece between their lunchtime Pouilly-Fumé and their afternoon nap. The Anglican archbishop was door-stopped at St. Andrew's Cathedral. Would he sack the whole Prince Albert board? "No comment."

Alexander drove Bowman hard too. The reporter was standing with the editor on the news floor, discussing angles, when Diamond walked in and went to his desk.

Alexander motioned to Justine. "Call security," he said.

Bowman watched as Justine made the call. When she hung up, Alexander said: "Call Diamond."

Down the room, Diamond picked up the phone on his desk. "Brandy wants to see you," Justine said.

Alexander went to his office and came back with a yellow envelope. They watched Diamond walk over.

"How long you been here?" Alexander said. "Twenty years?"

Diamond didn't look at Bowman. "'Bout that," he said.

"You'd be in line for a nice payout, couple of hundred grand"—Alexander handed Diamond the envelope—"if you hadn't been sacked."

Diamond stared at the envelope as two security guards walked up behind him.

"Leave your phone and your pass and your laptop. Just take your bag from your desk." Alexander pointed at the guards. "They'll escort you."

Diamond shrugged. "See you in court."

"You think NeedFeed will back you?" Alexander smiled. "Good luck with that."

Diamond's face glowed scarlet between the white shirts of the security guards. The room fell quiet as he was frog-marched out.

Bowman nodded at Justine and went to his desk. He worked at his story, calling teachers and parents from the school to dig for further details and reactions. By 7:00 p.m. he'd had enough. His phone rang.

"How's it in there?" Riley said.

"Brandy's off the reservation. Think he's falling in love with BMK."

"That'd be right."

"Good for circulation."

"Fuck, I hate journos." She sounded tired. "Beer?"

"Where are you?" he said.

"Gladesville room."

"Three Weeds? Twenty minutes?"

"See you there."

Riley came with Patel, walking through the pub as Bowman arrived through a side door. Patel bought three schooners, and they found a table.

"Alexander sacked Diamond," he said.

"Yeah? Good," Riley said. "How was Preston when you laid it on him?"

"Well, he answered the phone, but that was it. I told him what I was going to write. He listened to it all and hung up."

"Where is he now?"

"Hiding at the house, I think. He got sacked too. The board gave him two days to clear out."

"What about Bishop?" Patel said.

"He's trying to hang on," Bowman said. "We got a pic of him at a six-star resort on Hamilton Island. A real man of the people."

"Madden will haul Bishop in," Riley said. "Preston too. They've opened an investigation in Orange—see what sticks."

A text pinged on Bowman's phone. The prime minister had removed Bishop from the Cabinet and put out a statement saying he believed Bishop's place in the Parliament was "untenable." Bowman felt the rush. His scoop was making waves. Elation, pride, anticipation, greed—it all laced together and coursed through him. He strutted to the bar for another round.

Back at the table, he put the beers down.

"Here's to you," Patel said.

Riley raised her glass with weary collegiality. Bowman realized she was back where she started: Marguerite Dunlop had been a cul-de-sac. Bishop and Preston were mere garbage to be taken out. Out of respect, Bowman made the mental adjustment, came back down to earth.

"So," he said, "there was never any link between Marguerite and BMK?"

Riley drank and ignored him.

"We did consider links between them," Patel said, "but that hasn't turned out to be the case. Tom tried to tie Marguerite's death to BMK."

"When you say *links*, does that include the river?" Bowman said.

"Of course," Patel said. "We have a geographic profile. The school doesn't fit."

There were other geographic facts, Bowman thought. Sydney sat on sand washed down from Broken Hill a quarter of a billion years ago. It happened still—the wind blew the desert in. And the creek fed the river, and the river flowed through Gladesville.

"You're missing the bigger picture," he said. "I reckon you'd be crazy to write off the river."

33

Tuesday went by and then Wednesday, and then the week. Everything had gone quiet, and O'Neil felt the investigation grind down. It was a frustration he knew from experience, and it made him snaky: waiting for something to happen. Waiting for Gladesville to make the next move. Riley was dragging her feet at the Dunlop house, and O'Neil was giving her room. She was caught in a loop, ticking boxes, but it was keeping her going.

The press smelled the city's fear and stirred in tabloid trouble—*The Mirror* was counting down the next full moon.

Satyr's main thrust now was the attack on Patel and the note on the headmaster's door. How had Gladesville got into the school—and how had he got out again? The analysts went to the RTA, the toll road operators, the public wharves, the service stations—and came back with nothing.

By Sunday, O'Neil wanted to rewind a step, back to the Tennyson Point break-in. Police area commands and local stations had been asked to go through their case files and databases over the past three years, combing for anything remotely similar to the fetish burglary. Tran had four detectives making calls, and O'Neil got Patel to help.

He looked at the map on the wall, with Farquhar's circles in red. He studied the suburbs on the northern bank and reread the briefing notes from the detectives who had canvassed the area. Ryde, Putney, Tennyson

Point, Gladesville, Huntleys Cove, Hunters Hill, Woolwich—he was trawling old ground. The focus in the reports was residential, in keeping with the psychiatrist's theory that they were looking at the killer's backyard, that he lived in the area. Nothing stuck out. All O'Neil could think to do was widen the search criteria and canvass again.

Bowman called, asking for a quote, asking for anything. O'Neil thought about it but declined. The timing wasn't right—if he sounded off in the media now, the killer would know they were desperate.

And he was starting to worry about Riley. O'Neil knew that she was still stuck on Marguerite. He'd seen others fold under the weight of their victims. But never Riley. Tom Green was on remand at St. Mary's. The blood on his shoe had come back as Marguerite's, and his prints had matched. Why couldn't Riley let it rest? O'Neil didn't ask, because he feared what she might answer.

He tried to get her to take leave, just a day or two to get out of town and think about something else. As if. He'd known when he said it how stupid it sounded. Riley wasn't even claiming her overtime. The case was all there was, all her days and all her nights. She wasn't going anywhere. She worked methodically through what they'd done at the school and tied off the loose ends. She drilled down into Craig Spratt's boat. She hadn't done it at the time, but she came back to it now. She'd asked the techs to copy the chart plotter and look at where the vessel had been around November 1 and November 30. She'd gone to Maritime and requested the CCTV footage for the boat ramp at Kissing Point, where Spratt claimed to launch.

She chased the outside lab for the incomplete second test on the plastic. Crime Scene had proved the blade used to cut the sheets at Gladesville was different from the one used at the school, but Riley wanted to know what the chemistry showed. Were the chemical markers on the roll at the school a match with the plastic at Gladesville?

O'Neil listened as she harangued the technicians on the phone: Had the plastic used at Gladesville come from the roll at the school?

Her fixation was disturbing. She was beyond ticking boxes—this was tunnel vision in a wombat hole. She couldn't let go. She still thought the cases were linked.

Riley hung up and popped a Berocca with Lucozade. It was one step up from a dingo's breakfast, and O'Neil felt queasy watching her. It was Monday morning, nine days after Tom Green's arrest. O'Neil was ignoring *The Mirror* and its lunar countdown, but he had learned some phrases about phases. Now it was waxing gibbous—and he knew what came next. The room was full, the entire strike force deskbound, moribund, peering at screens or working the phones.

O'Neil's nose twitched, a fizz on the air: Patel was on her feet. O'Neil put his tea down. Patel took a step back and looked toward him, and then he was beside her, bent at her laptop.

"Where?" he said.

"That's what you won't believe." Patel pointed at the screen. "Tallwood Drive, North Rocks."

North Rocks . . .

"Right behind the school," Patel said. "Literally over the fence."

"When?"

"Two and a half years ago," Patel said. "Six months before Tennyson Point."

It was the same story as Tennyson Point. Uniforms had responded to a break and enter. No one had been home at the time, and nothing had been taken. A young couple lived in the house with a toddler. The woman's underwear had been arranged in a pattern on the bedroom floor, the wavy *t* shape. There had been trouble with kids in the area throwing bottles at houses and siphoning petrol from cars. The constables had spoken with them and issued a warning. Things had settled down, and the break-in had been written off as a nuisance crime, a prank.

Riley and O'Neil and Tran and Patel and Farquhar stood at the back end of the long block. The house had sliding glass doors at the rear, but unlike Tennyson Point, there was no river, not even the creek. The yard backed onto bush. Scrub ran hard up to the picket fence. The male owner told them the family left the sliding doors open as they came and went between the yard and the house. And yes, the key to that door had gone missing around the time of the break-in and had never been found.

The detectives and the doctor left the couple at their back gate and walked into the trees. Forty meters down the wooded slope, they came to another fence, chain link, two meters high. On the other side was the desolate rear of Prince Albert, bushland dropping gradually to the creek.

O'Neil grasped the wire. "What in the name of fuck are we doing back here?" he said. "Two and a half years before Gladesville, and he hits *here*?"

No one spoke. O'Neil looked at Farquhar. "Well?"

The psychiatrist frowned at the zigzag pattern of the boundary fence.

O'Neil shook the mesh and swore. For more than two weeks, on doctor's orders, they had resisted plotting the school into the geographic profile.

Instinct, O'Neil thought. *Rose was right.*

"The kid killing Marguerite Dunlop didn't bring Gladesville into the school," he said. "Gladesville was already here."

There was a pulse under Riley's eye.

"But who?" Farquhar said. "It can't be the boy."

"Why not?" Patel said.

"He was twelve at the time of this." Farquhar gestured up the incline. "And then at fifteen, he graduates to Gladesville?"

"He couldn't cover the ground, for a start," Tran said. "He doesn't have a license. Or a vehicle. Or a boat."

"How many staff at the school again?" O'Neil said. "Two hundred?"

"Give or take," Tran said.

"And we've looked at three of them," O'Neil said.

Farquhar's brow glistened. "My thinking was someone living near the scenes at Gladesville, working from an anchor point." He looked from O'Neil to Riley. "You always thought differently."

"A commuter," O'Neil said. "Someone using the river."

"What if he's not using the river to move per se," the doctor said, "but rather for recreation, sailing or fishing, say. The important thing is he's familiar with the river and he has a boat."

"Spratt," O'Neil said. "But we know he didn't have the boat out at the relevant times. Rose, they analyzed the chart plotter?"

She nodded. "He's in the clear on the November dates."

"Come on," O'Neil said. "Let's look—do any other staff own a boat? Are there sailors? We discard Wayne's comfort zone. We plug this place into the profile. What have we got?"

"School, river, boat," Riley said.

Riley sat in the passenger seat as Tran drove to Gladesville. O'Neil had taken Patel and Farquhar to the school to ask Spratt about staff and boats.

"Steve said to discard Wayne's comfort zone," Riley said, "but I don't think that's right."

"Yeah?" Tran said.

"Go back to basics," Riley said. "Opportunity, capability. Remember how with Tom killing the dog, it wasn't what we first thought?"

Tran nodded. "It was about getting future access to the house."

"Correct. Now forget Tom. It's just an example. Think opportunity. It's about access."

"Mm," Tran said.

"School, river, boat."

"And?" Tran said.

"And Wayne's comfort zone," Riley said. "Tennyson Point. Putney."

Tran slowed.

"This last week," Riley said, "I reviewed the Dunlop case. It just occurred to me. The Prince Albert boatshed is in Putney."

"Oh fuck," Tran said.

"Yeah. Your boys, they might have looked at it in the Tennyson Point canvass."

Tran pulled over and took out her laptop. Riley waited while she clicked.

"Here." Tran turned the screen and pointed. "They looked at a boatshed in Putney. There was no signage on-site, but they cross-checked it online. It's labeled 'Rowing Shed 1958' on maps."

Riley peered. It was in the bay past the Tennyson Point scene. "What else?"

Tran scrolled down the briefing note. "It was locked, apparently deserted. Query operational. They wrote it up as a community rowing club and didn't connect it to the school."

"Their focus was residential," Riley said. "They were looking at houses."

Tran closed the laptop. "Fuck, Rose," she said. "Sorry."

"You can make it up to me," Riley said. "Drop me at the Water Police."

Tran signaled to pull out.

Riley rang the Maritime Command at Balmain. They put her through to the super.

"I need to take a look at Putney from the river," she said.

"Thought your specialty was Gladesville," the super said.

"Tide ran out."

"All right. Now?"

"Ten minutes."

She hung up. Tran drove into the tunnel past Strathfield and around the bay at Haberfield, through Rozelle and into Balmain. She pulled up behind the Water Police building, tucked in at the old Jubilee Dock off Johnstons Bay.

Riley undid her seat belt. "Can you get a warrant?"

"Yeah." Tran's mouth was tight.

Riley met her eye. There was nothing to be gained from pointing the bone at Tran's team—hindsight was bullshit. "We missed it too," Riley said. "We knew the school had a boatshed, but we didn't go and look. And we didn't prioritize it for the canvass."

Tran nodded.

"You get the warrant." Riley opened her door. "I'll have a look."

She got out. Bowman's cottage sat up the hill above her. She shook her head. Given the way he'd dredged up the Water Police when they'd walked down the lane, the fucker had been lucky she hadn't shot him in the stomach.

A uniformed constable met her at the front desk. "Sarge," he said, "I'm your ride."

She followed him onto the pontoon and stepped into a ten-meter Naiad. The twin 250s coughed and grumbled, and the constable let go the lines. A double-ended Manly ferry, green and yellow, was out to pasture, tied up at White Bay. The finger wharves of Pyrmont lay to the right, the Anzac Bridge spanned the bay astern, and Barangaroo reared up in front, the glass casino pilfering the sky.

"Putney?" the constable said.

"Yeah. You can drop me. Place marked as 'Rowing Shed 1958.'" Riley stood in the cockpit, holding on to a rail above her head as the Naiad came onto the plane. They rounded Peacock Point, Goat Island off the starboard bow, the Harbour Bridge in their wake, the wind in her hair. They passed Birchgrove and Greenwich and the brackish invisible line into the river proper. Cockatoo Island went past to port, and the Gladesville Bridge was before them.

"Okay," Riley called. "Nice and slow."

They went under the bridge and past Henley, and she looked at the Chatfield and Sheridan houses on either side of the headland. Both banks of the river were built out, brown brick, red brick, yellow brick, white brick—each decade of corruption wore its own color.

The oversight from the canvass was understandable: there was a lot to cover on the river. Riley counted on the helm chart—there were four bays and a dozen rowing clubs just between Putney and Gladesville alone.

They cruised past Cabarita and the *Truman Show* development at Breakfast Point. On the north bank, the Tennyson Point house overlooked an inlet strung with moored boats.

"You move around here at dusk, in the dark, no one would see you," Riley said.

The constable nodded.

They crossed the submerged cables of the Mortlake Ferry and edged into the next bay. There was another mooring field with fifty craft, and a drooping haze of she-oaks in a park to the right. At the top of the inlet, the properties were set back from the river behind a strip of brown sand. In the middle of it all, a flat, gray shed led to a wide pontoon jutting over the water.

The constable pinched the GPS. "This is it," he said. "Did you want to jump off?"

Riley nodded. The constable brought the Naiad alongside, and she hopped onto the floating platform. "Thanks," she said.

The constable came into the cockpit and tied off with the engines running.

Riley took her bearings. Hardwood decking led back to the shed. Three large roller doors, all locked down tight. There was no signage. To the east, a thin boardwalk ran along the exterior of the building to shore, with grimy windows battened down at intervals. Halfway along the wall, she found one of the timber window frames rotting out and starting to give. She went back to the Naiad.

"You got a hammer, or a crowbar—something for leverage?"

The constable dug in a locker and came up with a long screwdriver.

Riley felt the weight of the tool. "Give me a sec to get it back to you."

The constable waved at the screwdriver. "Got three of those," he said and untied the line. "You might need it. I'll see you round."

Riley watched as he maneuvered the boat off the dock. They each gave a nod, and she turned and walked back down the side of the shed to the window. The wood was damp and soft and came away easily. She stuffed the screwdriver down the side of her belt, pulled open the window, and shimmied in. Dropping to the floor, she hoped Tran had the warrant. It was one large open space with rowing boats racked five high in the center. They were sleek eights and fours, shiny carapaces, alien insects at nest in the gloom. Single sculls hung from the ceiling, and oars were bracketed along the western wall.

She held her breath and listened. Five outboards had been hauled up inside the roller doors. *Access to boats.* She pulled out her phone and called Tran.

"There's runabouts here," she said. "Must be for the coaches. We'll need a list of all staff associated with rowing or the shed. You got the warrant?"

"It's coming," Tran said.

"Meet me here. And tell Steve." Riley hung up. There were two doors on the wall toward the shore, and she walked over.

The first was locked. The second opened to an internal stairwell leading down, chipped blue paint on the railing as it doubled back, the smell of the river on the ebb tide. Riley took the stairs and descended to a concrete cube with a swing door. She went through it shoulder first and used her foot to let it settle gently back in place.

She was in a short corridor, leading inland and lit by a dim fluorescent tube. Her eyes adjusted, and she realized she was in a basement built on the riverbed. There was a door half-open ahead to the right. She pulled her Glock, padded over, and with the gun in both hands put her back to the wall and looked in.

It was a storage room, a corner converted to a makeshift office: a trestle table with a lamp, a laptop, a boxy old computer monitor, a chair. There was metal shelving, ropes and fenders, an anchor in the corner, a chest along the wall with its lid up. Mops, hoses, plastic drums for fuel and other fluids. An outboard motor was clamped on a stand, broken oars against a wall.

Riley had flushed to hyperarousal—fight or flight, the hormonal cascade. The bare bulb on the ceiling and the lamp on the desk were both switched on against the dark.

Spratt's Hilux was not at his house, and neither was the Subaru. O'Neil knocked and waited. No one. He went back down the path and climbed into the rear of the Prado.

Patel drove through the school with Farquhar beside her. There was a white pickup truck in the drive at the Greens' place.

"Let's have a look," O'Neil said.

Patel pulled in, and a man came down the front path with a clipboard. O'Neil got out and flashed his badge. "Who're you?"

"Movers."

It was a busy time for movers at Prince Albert. "When are they leaving?" O'Neil said.

"Pack it up tomorrow. Gone by Friday."

The man drove off in the pickup, and O'Neil crossed the yard and rang the bell. Sarah Green opened the door and stared, blank and unblinking.

"I'm sorry," O'Neil said. "I thought you'd moved out?"

She was pale pewter and medicated. "We're in a motel. I had to show the packers."

Patel and Farquhar were behind him. "We just wanted to check in," O'Neil said. "Make sure you had somewhere to go."

Sarah Green stood in the doorway.

"Is Scott here?" O'Neil said.

She shook her head.

Patel stepped up. "Could we come in for a moment?"

Sarah moved aside, and they entered. Four doors were open off the front hall. O'Neil looked in the first one. A man's study. Textbooks waiting to be packed. *Science Essentials*. He went to the next room. There was a table and chair, a lounge, a TV, a daybed along the wall. It had a pillow on it, a sheet and a blanket. He turned.

"Scott's," Sarah said. "He calls it his den."

"He was sleeping in here?" O'Neil said.

The corners of her mouth tugged down. "Nothing new there."

O'Neil looked back to the room. "He always slept here?"

"Not always. A lot. He gets insomnia—up half the night."

"What about you?" O'Neil said. "Sleep all right?"

"I take a tablet."

Crime Scene had listed the pills they found in the house when they processed the place after Tom's arrest: Valium, temazepam, Xanax, fentanyl, Endone. Sarah Green would be lucky to wake up.

Farquhar was in the study, leafing through a textbook. "I imagine the teaching facilities here are first-rate," he said. "The science labs."

Sarah Green considered the psychiatrist. "You know how you were asking if Tom wet the bed?"

Farquhar was studying specimen jars on a shelf. "Yes."

"He doesn't. But years ago, Scott told me his mother used to beat him for wetting the bed. She was a nun who was raped. She didn't even know his name."

Farquhar's eyes went to O'Neil.

"I should have told you," Sarah said. "I wish I'd told you that—and not given you the USB."

"What Tom did," Farquhar said. "You think his father was involved?"

"Involved?" She scoffed. "Try absent."

"But about Tom . . . ," Farquhar said. "Scott knew?"

"Knew?" She shrugged. "Who knows? He lies all the time. Scott doesn't *care*. He came into the motel last night and told me he was going to call Bruce Dunlop to apologize."

"Did he call?" O'Neil said.

"No. It was just another sick game."

"Where's the motel?" O'Neil said.

She scoffed again. "Ryde."

O'Neil's gut clutched.

"I wanted to be out near Tom," she said, "but no."

Ryde. O'Neil looked at Patel. *Why Ryde?* "Is that where he is now?" he said. "At the motel?"

"Doubtful. It's near his"—Sarah Green made speech marks with her fingers—"office."

O'Neil stared at her.

"His office?" Patel said.

"The boatshed," Sarah Green said. "He manages it. That's his extracurricular—instead of coaching sport. He's got some sort of room downstairs. Now he has to pack it up."

In the stillness, O'Neil's phone rang. Annie Tran.

34

O'Neil hung up and went out the front door, calling Riley.

No answer. He started the Prado and had the red and blues flashing as Patel and Farquhar came down the path.

Patel got in the passenger seat.

"Call Rose," he said and sprayed gravel.

"No answer," Patel said.

"Rose went to the boatshed alone. Annie's on the way with tactical." O'Neil looked in the rearview mirror at Farquhar. "Talk to me."

"He's labile," Farquhar said. "It fits."

"Fits with what?"

The psychiatrist grabbed hold as the Prado fishtailed out of the drive. "The other day, when I was here with Rose, she asked Scott why he had been walking behind the maintenance shed, and he stood there grinning. At other times, when you'd expect to see some emotion, his face is flat, blunted. His expressions are incongruent, erratic."

"Yeah," O'Neil said.

"It's neurobiological. He has an inappropriate affect, emotional incontinence. It presents, literally, on his face. And now the enuresis."

O'Neil hit the siren and swung out of the school.

"Enuresis?" Patel said.

"Unintentional bed-wetting after the age of five. Remember, there's something wrong with psychopaths. They have a brain abnormality. That could lead to delayed speech, or delayed bladder control."

O'Neil ran a light.

"Psychopaths wet the bed?" Patel said.

"No, it's merely a predictor. If Scott Green is what we think he is, it's going to be a long list. Listen to how glib the man is, saying he'll call Bruce Dunlop. His son has killed their daughter, and he makes a joke."

O'Neil smashed his fist down on the console and swore through his teeth.

"He teaches science," the psychiatrist said. "We can assume he has some knowledge."

"Forensic sophistication." Patel turned. "There's something else," she said, "about Scott's involvement with Tom."

"Go on," Farquhar said.

"Remember we couldn't reconcile the timing? Marguerite was killed Wednesday, but Scott wasn't seen behind the maintenance shed until Friday?"

Farquhar nodded.

"The point was that if Scott was helping his son, checking on the plastic or cleaning up, why didn't he do it on Thursday, before we'd even arrived?" Patel said. "He'd had the time, and it would have been safer."

Farquhar swayed through a bend.

"It was because he wasn't helping his son," Patel said. "He knew nothing about Marguerite until the body was found on Thursday night. And then all he knows is what's in the news—that there's someone dead and wrapped in black plastic."

O'Neil recalled Scott Green at the scene, offering to ID the body.

"What does he do first thing Friday morning?" Patel said.

Farquhar didn't answer.

"He goes for a walk to check his plastic," Patel said.

O'Neil squealed onto Silverwater Road. He was doing 150 and remembering Riley at her desk that morning, hassling the lab for the chemical markers on the plastic.

◆ ◆ ◆

Riley stood with her Glock at face level in both hands and transferred weight through her hips to the door. It opened another inch, two, three, four, five, six. No sound. Leading with the gun, she swiveled into the room in a noiseless crouch, the weapon pointing up to the top right corner and then raking back across. No one. Two hulking water boilers. More shelving, packed with rope, chain, a folded sail, a face mask and snorkel, a wet vac, a wooden tiller, an anchor, boat paraphernalia. She sensed a void behind the boilers and shouldered up to one of the cylinders, edging around to look. There was space running into darkness—she didn't know how big.

The rusted water heater flaked in her hair as she turned her head. The desk was four meters away, the laptop open with something frozen on-screen. She couldn't make it out. Beside it, the old computer monitor was displaying a picture in black and white. She scanned the walls for a light switch for the area behind her. Nothing, just a single toggle by the door, already on. Her phone vibrated on silent. Her eyes, squinting, went back to the desk. The image on the bulky monitor—she'd recently seen something similar . . . the surveillance setup in Spratt's study. She was looking at a CCTV feed—it showed the main room of the rowing shed.

Spratt. He'd seen her come in on the monitor and retreated to the darkness. He'd know she'd come alone. Gladesville liked knives. Did he have a gun?

She had to get out—she couldn't hunt him blind in his burrow. Her phone was vibrating again.

There was a rhythmic drip from one of the boilers. Was there a back way out? Had he gone in the dark? No, she could sense him, evil in the room. They were down on the riverbed, and the door she'd come through was the only access. She edged along the second boiler toward the desk, shortening the distance to the exit. She was going to have to bolt, get up to the main room, cover the stairwell with her Glock, and call Tran.

The desk was two meters away now, and her eyes were drawn to the laptop. She sucked in a guttural sound, half groan, half growl. It was a video, paused on Lena Chatfield, gagged and alive, her terrible gaze pleading straight down the camera.

Riley knew the knife was there before she felt it, the cold steel point in her neck.

"Put your hands out."

He'd come from behind the boilers and spoke through closed teeth. "Move."

The blade pushed harder into her skin.

"Put the gun on the table."

She shuffled six steps and placed the gun beside the laptop.

"Hands behind your head. Step away." The knife steered her left. "You want to watch the video?"

Her phone was vibrating.

"No?" he said. "I was watching the video. Getting to the good bit."

His voice confused her. Completely altered but recognizable. The remnant of a lisp.

"You got my message that we'd play. You came alone." The knife pinched as he turned it. "We'll play the video."

"Craig," she said, "think about it. How did I get here?"

"*Craig?*" he hissed.

"The Water Police are on the dock," she said. "O'Neil's with them."

The pressure on her neck changed almost imperceptibly. He'd snuck a glance at the CCTV. She twisted fast, bringing her elbow into his

281

temple and pulling the long screwdriver from her belt with her right hand.

His mouth opened in surprise, and in a fluid arc, she rammed the shank in, using the momentum through her shoulder to drive the tip up hard into the soft palate and through the cavity behind the nose. She brought her other hand up to help grip the handle and pumped.

He gargled out a groan, and she kneed him in the groin. He crumpled and dropped the long blade. She felt the weight of him on the screwdriver.

Not Spratt, she registered. Scott Green. Blood ran from his mouth, under his mustache, down the shaft onto her hands. She pushed away hard and let go of the tool. He stumbled and went down.

He lay still, blood pooling, cheek to floor, eye open. Riley trod carefully to the table and picked up her Glock. Her phone was vibrating again, and she kept the gun on him as she dug in her pocket with a bloodied hand.

"Annie," she said.

"Rose, thank Christ." Tran was speaking fast. "Get out of there. It's Scott Green. He manages the boatshed."

She looked at the figure dying on the floor. "Not anymore," she said.

35

On the pontoon, Bowman breathed river air.

O'Neil had called and briefed him at the unit. "Start writing," the detective had said. "We want to get it out there."

Bowman had got in the car and phoned the story in to Alexander, dictating six paragraphs as he drove to Putney. The editor had typed it out and put it straight online. It named Scott Green, but the court orders around Tom prevented them from linking the father to the son. It said that Scott Green had been killed by police, but that was all. O'Neil had given Bowman no details.

At the boatshed, the roller doors were open, and O'Neil allowed Bowman to look inside but blocked his access to the scene downstairs.

There were five police boats tied along the dock, the uniformed crews milling. Emergency vehicles were clustered on the road.

"There's a metal trunk in the basement," O'Neil said. "Three padlocks and welded to the floor. But he had it open. He was packing up."

Bowman scribbled in his notebook.

"It's his treasure trove," O'Neil said. "Jill Sheridan's driving license, pictures of Lena Chatfield stolen from her house. Underwear, jewelry, several keys. Cable ties, gowns, gloves, masks, booties. Packs of wet wipes. A balaclava, a backpack, a digital camera, night goggles."

Farquhar came over.

"There's drums of bleach and ammonia on shelves," O'Neil said. "He wasn't going to stop. Here—talk to Wayne."

O'Neil walked away, leaving Bowman with the doctor. "He wasn't going to stop?" Bowman said.

"The opposite," Farquhar said. "He was accelerating. He'd broken into houses at North Rocks and Tennyson Point, probably others. With Gladesville, he'd escalated, broken the taboo of murder. But the fantasies he'd stored in his box would have become stale. He'd need to refresh them."

Bowman took it down. "I know I can't name Tom or even link him to Scott," he said. "But what . . . genetics?"

"No," Farquhar said. "Studies have been done on hereditary pathways—behavioral genetics—but there are lots of contradictions."

"So nature, nurture?"

"With Scott, it's nature. It's what he was. With Tom, I'd say it's nurture. Sarah says Scott was an absent father, but Tom still grew in his orbit, learned from him by watching, soaking things up. Learned things he didn't know he was learning—that's how it works with fathers and sons. Tom spent his childhood with a pathological liar, a combination of callous manipulation and neglect."

"You said it's nature with Scott. What was he?"

"Cunning, remorseless." Farquhar paused. "*Psychopath* is an overused term, but we have a diagnostic tool: the PCL-R, the Hare checklist. A classic, prototypical psychopath would score forty on it, but a score of thirty or above is enough for a diagnosis. You don't see many people who score thirty on the PCL-R."

"What would Scott have scored?"

"We'll never know." The doctor shrugged. "Forty is extremely rare. Ted Bundy scored thirty-nine, I believe."

"Rose said he was marking the victims?"

Farquhar looked in the open shed. "Come," he said.

Bowman followed him under a roller door to a line of runabouts hauled up inside. Farquhar walked around to the bow of one of the boats and pointed to a small, circular stainless-steel symbol mounted on a short pole, like a raised logo on the hood of a car.

"What is it?" Bowman said.

"An ornament, an emblem? I don't know. But he obviously spent a long time looking at it. He used the symbol as his signature—in the burglaries, and then to mark his victims."

Bowman snapped a photo with his phone. "Why?"

"The fetish burglaries weren't enough. The rituals built to binding and carving. Torture and death combined in intense sexual arousal and release."

Bowman closed an eye. He saw his initials carved in the wood of the desk that became Tom's. Nature, not nurtured, fathers and sons.

"If that's all, I'd better go," Farquhar said.

"Of course. Thanks. Um, I'll be in touch."

"Good. Take care. It's strange for you, your childhood home. And I heard about your brother. I've been reading your stories—they're broadly accurate. Keep going—there's consolation in work."

They shook hands, and the psychiatrist walked away. Bowman blew a heavy breath. "Broadly accurate" was actually high praise, the best a journalist could hope for.

He looked at his watch. He had to file. Farquhar was probably right: there was consolation in work—just not in the work Bowman did. There was no solace in leading Marguerite's father up the garden path. Should he get out now, while he was on top? Write the book on BMK and find a real job—mowing lawns, walking dogs, delivering the mail? Otherwise . . . He glimpsed his future—an old hack on Twitter, shoveling bile.

O'Neil came back with Patel.

"Where's Rose?" Bowman said.

Patel nodded down the dock, and Bowman turned. In the cockpit of the third police boat, two paramedics hovered over Riley.

"They've cleaned her up, but she might be in shock," O'Neil said.

Bowman stared. "Cleaned her up?"

O'Neil looked him in the eye. "She put a screwdriver through his brain."

Bowman stood with pen and pad. The tools of his trade.

"You can say hi," O'Neil said. "Then get out of here. We'll talk tomorrow." Bowman nodded, and Patel and O'Neil went back to the shed.

He walked along the jetty. In the police boat, the ambos had an emergency blanket around Riley.

"Permission to come aboard?" he said.

She smiled, and her eyes flickered green, channel markers in a storm. He'd never seen her smile. It looked like navigation—time to slip his moorings and move on.

She stared out over the bay, and he followed her gaze. The tide was getting low.

"You were right," she said. "The river."

ACKNOWLEDGMENTS

Several police officers and forensic medical specialists gave up their time to discuss aspects of their work with me. My thanks to Dr. Allan Cala, Dr. Anthony Samuels, Jenny Chrystal, Jim Migro, Dr. Isabel Brouwer, and Penelope Riley. The insights into their professions are theirs, and any mistakes in procedure are mine.

The escalating nature of BMK's offending, and the hunt for him, owe a debt to three superb works of nonfiction: Michelle McNamara's *I'll Be Gone in the Dark*; *Evil Has a Name* by Paul Holes, Jim Clemente, and Peter McDonnell; and the article "An Unbelievable Story of Rape" by Ken Armstrong and T. Christian Miller. The book Priya Patel refers to when she floats the idea of calling Philip Preston at 2:00 a.m. is *Mindhunter* by John Douglas and Mark Olshaker. In Adam Bowman's cottage, Rose Riley reads from *The River Capture* by Mary Costello. The "universal truth" cited in chapter 5 is from *The Letters of William James*. In chapter 12, the words *morally indefensible* are a reference to Janet Malcolm's famous first line to *The Journalist and the Murderer*. In chapter 22, Wayne Farquhar's Nietzsche quote is from *The Gay Science*. Bowman's "metaphysical" hangover is a tender nod to Kingsley Amis.

THANKS/LOVE

Meredith Rose.

Malcolm Knox.

Tom Gilliatt.

Gracie Doyle. Rachael Herbert. Sarah Shaw. Jarrod Taylor. Kellie Osborne. Lauren Whitticom. Jill Schoenhaut.

Angela Handley. Aziza Kuypers. Katri Hilden. Luke Causby.

Catherine Drayton.

Ben Ball.

Steve Waterson. Kate Mumford.

Rob Carlton.

Brenda Spencer. Scott Hedge.

Nitu Tran. Tosca Looby. Stephanie Smee.

Broughton Boydell. John Ferguson.

Colin and Christina Geeves.

"I'm Going Below" Bill Hammond, for his turn of phrase.

JDMB. PKF.

Sachin, Shivani, Sanjay: this book is not about you, but if you read between the lines, you're there in the best bits.

Ritu Gupta, without whom there would be no book.

In loving memory: PES.

About the Author

Photo © 2022 John Feder

Matthew Spencer was a newspaper journalist at *The Australian* for twenty years. He lives in Sydney with his wife and three children. *Black River* is his first novel. For more information, visit www.matthewspencer.com.au or follow him on Instagram (@matthewspencerauthor).